Dear Betty,
You have been
such a good friend for so
long for and I wanted you
to have this to express our
gladness to know you and
to say we appreciate you.
God Bless You
Amy 10/17/05
:)

THE
MIKOTA STORY
Days and Seasons

by
Andrew Nelson

authorHOUSE™

1663 Liberty Drive, Suite 200
Bloomington, Indiana 47403
(800) 839-8640
www.AuthorHouse.com

First published by AuthorHouse 07/06/05

ISBN: 1-4208-3922-5 (e)
ISBN: 1-4208-3921-7 (sc)

Printed in the United States of America
Bloomington, Indiana

This book is printed on acid-free paper.

DEDICATION

To the Lord for His constant care and keeping. To my wife for her continual encouragement. To my Son Greg for his ever available advice about mechanical things. To friends and relatives who have read my work and given valuable input. And to my Pastor, Captain Dan Leisher of the Salvation Army who does all he can to guide me and help me along.

Table of Contents

Chapter One

A BEAUTIFUL SUMMER MORNING

It had started out as a perfect day. The weather could not have been better. The sky was clear; the humidity moderate, the temperature in the middle of the summer activity comfort zone, and an unfailing breeze was there to cool those who overdid it. It was the kind of day that lifted a person's spirit and made him feel everything was going to go well.

John D. Knox had been up at first light and rekindled a small fire from the coals yet alive in his camp site fire ring. From the camp ground's hand pump he obtained water for his purposes. While a pan of water was coming to a boil, he used the last of his Tang for a cool drink. He used his last tea bag and then reconstituted a package of freeze-dried scrambled eggs. It was supposedly enough for two servings but without toast or sweet rolls, it was barely sufficient for the hungry man. He looked forward to a hearty lunch at the Santa Fe Café, a homey Mexican-American restaurant.

John was a tall fellow of medium build, plenty strong but not overly muscular in appearance. His ancestry was mixed but primarily Scottish and Mikotan Amerindian. His complexion was dark for a Scot, light for Mikota. His brow was heavy, his nose almost straight with a slight outward

1

curve. His face could be called angular. His eyes were dark and penetrating. His hair was an ebon frame to his strongly masculine handsomeness.

After eating, John pumped more water to clean his mess kit. Each primitive campground, of which there were several in the foot hills of the Bittersweet Range, had sources of pure water. Some of the camps were accessible by motor vehicles but this one and a few others could be legally approached only afoot or on horse back. Motor vehicles except official ones were banned access to them.

He had hiked in for a few days of solitude and to engage in rock climbing. There were not rock faces high or steep enough to challenge very proficient climbers, but he readily admitted these less arduous climbs were plenty for his amateurish efforts. He took down his small ultra-light dome tent and quickly stowed it and all his gear into his pack which was considerably lighter than when he had arrived for all his groceries were gone.

John had just graduated from the University of Michigan with a Master's degree in Business Administration. In September he was going to be installed in office as the Tribe's Business Manager, a position much like that of a City Manager. He would be much like a Deputy Governor and subject to all the rules of the Tribal Council, but would have great latitude in dealing with things that came up on a day to day basis.

His supervisor would be Esther Crowe who was General Manager. This position was derived from the old Mikotan concept of Chief. John could likely ascend to that position when Esther retired. She was beginning to feel the weight of her years. She was almost ready to admit she would rather tend to her grandchildren and great grandchildren rather than care for the whole tribe.

Women's suffrage had become a reality in the tribe in the first half of the 1800s. The title of Chief had ceased being hereditary and women had equal rights both to vote and hold office. But terms of office were rather vaguely defined. If an elected official wished to retire or resign, or the Council felt a person was doing too poor a job, an election could be called.

It was nearly a 20 mile hike to the café in Dundee in the Hidden Valley. The Foothills Loop, a scenic route, passed within a mile of John's camp site. He was planning on hiking north the ten miles to the Upper Bridge which crossed the Mikota River. Had he gone south it would have been about 12 miles to Bear Chopper Campground located next to the west bank of the river.

The full service campground, similar to a KOA, had over 200 sites and room for expansion as needed. From the north end of the campground ran the River Road which followed the water to the Upper Bridge where it merged with the Foothills Loop. Near the campground were a horse livery, a gas station, and a well-stocked campers' mini-mart.

The Foothills Loop crossed the Lower Bridge and there became the Chief's Highway. This ran north through Glasgow which was situated halfway between the Lower and Middle bridges. It continued north along the river until the water course curved toward the Hidden Valley, its source, and then followed the river west. At the Upper Bridge's north approach was a four way stop intersection. At this crossroads the Foothills Loop originated as did the Hidden Valley Spur which led to Dundee. The Chief's Highway turned right and went the 15 miles to the Mikota Territory entrance at the Interstate.

John knew he could make it to the intersection in plenty of time to hitch a ride on one of the Bluebird Tour buses which had capacities ranging from 25 to 60. The Tribe had a fleet of buses all of which had been converted from school buses for their use within their spacious Territory.

None of the buses had roofs. But each according to their size had a number of sturdy roll bars which replaced the normal metal tops. All passengers were required to use the safety harnesses for the often irregular terrain might cause unexpected bounces and lurches. But this was very acceptable for the open top gave an unsurpassed view which in mountainous country was often overhead. In rainy weather canvas tops were secured but fares were reduced because the view was restricted.

There were a number if different tours, most of which included a visit to Dundee in the Hidden Valley. The tour John expected to get a ride on would first have gone east through the Aberdeen Forest and then made a stop at the Mikota oil field. The big oil companies were very unhappy that the Tribal Council completely controlled drilling and output. There were only six current producing wells and Oil Company geologists insisted there ought to be 30. But Mikotans believed natural resources must be gently used.

Many vehicles passed John as he paced along in his steady and long-legged stride. To the uninitiated he seemed unhurried, almost leisurely. But his mile-eating pace would have left novices behind in a couple of miles. Several stopped to offer him a lift. Not too surprisingly, the offers came from cars containing alert single young women.

"Thanks, but no thanks. I appreciate your offer, but I really do need the exercise to stay in shape. But thanks again. Drive carefully. Bye bye." John was single and not immune to the lure of feminine charm and beauty, but a "harmless" fling or a sowing of wild oats went entirely against his moral fiber. Still, it was nice to be noticed.

When John arrived at the intersection he took a drink of lukewarm water from his canteen. He could have taken a drink from the river which was pure and nearly ice cold. He was quite warm from his exertion and preferred not to be drinking too cold things. He took off his back pack and

4

stretched out on the grass beside the road near the stop sign, using his pack as a pillow. He entered a half awake state remembering the past few weeks.

Uncle Lionel had come to his graduation and together they had visited the large McCormack family in Elmhurst, Illinois. John's aunt Maude was Lionel's baby sister, the youngest of Grandpa David's three children. John's father John had given him the middle name David after his Grandpa. Each generation of Knox's traditionally had three or four children so there were quite a few relatives scattered around the country. John and Lionel were the only two who had retained their Mikota citizenship.

Only citizens of the tribe could own property or businesses within the Territory, but non-Mikotans could have leases or franchises. The Knox Farm deep into the Hidden Valley was a permanent endowment conditioned only on citizens residing there.

Nephew and Uncle had returned there after their visit in Elmhurst. They engaged in what they called a 3F time of fixin', fishin', and feastin'. The latter only if their fishing was successful which it usually was. And then John had taken a week off for his little holiday.

As he rested, a truck rolled off the Interstate and up to the stop sign at the entrance gate to the Mikota Territory. A sign accented by a flashing neon arrow indicated all vehicles without Mikota license plates or visitor stickers must pull off at the information office. The driver pulled into a parking spot but before he could descend an attractive Indian girl came up to his door. Her flat-brimmed hat, neat tan uniform, and glossy black boots put him in mind of some state troopers he had seen in old movies.

His window was already down. The air conditioner did not work in the old truck. She greeted him with a big smile and said, "Sir, I'm Wanda Redfeather of the Mikota Public Safety Network. We assist, rescue and protect people, and also enforce laws. May I see your driver's license and vehicle registration?"

"Did I do something wrong?"

She smiled, knowing that even completely innocent people often feel nervous in the presence of a law officer. "Not that I know of, sir. But if you wish to enter you have to have a permit and I need those two documents and two dollars to issue one to you."

He got out what she asked and handed it over along with the money. In a minute or two she had entered the necessary information onto the pad on her clipboard and then reached in to place a removable sticker on the lower left corner of the windshield. She gave him a map of the Territory on the back of which was listed facilities and points of historic and scenic interest.

"Here you are, Mr. Bogardus. May I give you directions or answer any questions?"

"I'm supposed to make a delivery in Dundee and then I'm free to cruise on my Harley Davidson."

"Dundee's very easy to find. Go straight ahead 15 miles to the stop sign at the Upper Bridge intersection. Then right on the Valley Spur and there are no crossroads until you get there. But you mentioned your motorcycle and you'll also need a sticker on it if you use it in the Territory. It's also two bucks but they're both good until the end of the year."

He handed over the necessaries and within a few minutes they were at the back of the truck where she affixed the sticker to the bike's wind screen. She admired the ingenious rack that held the Harley. It was fastened to the rear bumper and could be cranked up or down for loading or unloading the machine. She asked, "Any questions, Mr. Bogardus?"

"Just one. I'm powerful thirsty. Do the restaurants serve beer or do I have to go in a bar to get it?" He squinted at her badge and continued, "Or do I have to get a special permit for booze, Officer Redfeather?"

"I'll have to disappoint you there. The Mikota people liked Prohibition so well we've stayed dry to this very day. There is no legal sale or consumption by Mikotans nor may they transport any in. But visitors are allowed to carry it in for private consumption. Public consumption or drunken behavior could result in fines, imprisonment, or both. And sales to our citizens could result in confiscation of vehicles and personal equipment plus stiff fines plus time in a cage. That's what I call a jail cell. Drugs may not be bought, sold, transported, or used by anyone. Offenders are turned over to the Federal DEA. We want you and all visitors to have a safe and sober time with us to enjoy to the fullest the beauty God has provided here."

He said, "You guys must be pretty strict on this reservation."

She replied, "This is a Territory, not a reservation. Most Federal laws apply here but we have exemption from income and estate taxes. In the deplorable past when dealing with my people of all tribes, government agencies cheated and robbed us of our land, reserved smaller areas of inferior land, and even forced us to move at gunpoint.

"The Mikota Tribe refused to be outwitted or cheated or robbed or evicted from our home land. We won militarily and also in the courts. Just remember, this is our Territory, not a Federal Reservation. But I understand your confusion. Should you like to look further into it we have free booklets which condense our history and also a major book of history about us written by Lionel Knox, one of our citizens."

His friends had told him a far different story but he was not dumb enough to argue with a brainwashed cop who packed a 9 MM automatic Glock pistol on her hip. He graciously thanked her and drove off. He felt very good about everything. He could not have had a better day to deliver the truck and prepare it for its intended use. He looked forward to riding the Hog again.

When Humphrey had agreed to help his friends, they had bought an old truck such as U-Haul rents out and converted it to be like a truck camper. There were crank out windows all around near the roof but these were darkened glass so it was not possible to see in. The overhang of the box above the cab could have comfortably held a double bed. The door was at the back right side and had a pull-down step beneath it. The overhead opening rear door had been welded shut. The truck had been given a tri-color camouflage paint job such as is sometimes seen on hunters' homemade campers.

Humphrey was enjoying himself. Everything was working well. He could hardly wait to cruise on the Hog. And perhaps he'd make new friends who would like to just sit and talk. Except for his special friends nobody ever wanted to be around him. And too many make jokes about his name, Humphrey Bogardus. He had heard hundreds of wise cracks about how he would have to lose about 200 pounds if he wanted to resemble Humphrey Bogart.

At the stop sign he saw a hiker stretched out on the grass. "Hi there, I'm going to Dundee. Need a lift?"

John got up and trotted across the road to say hi. Traffic was light yet. The 2000 tourist season was just getting under way. It was Wednesday, June 28th and the grand opening of the new Dundee Grand Hotel would be on Saturday, July 1st.

John declined the offer of a ride but said they'd probably bump into each other in town. The fat man declared he was nearly famished and John told him of several eateries ranging from fast food to rather exclusive gourmet, but recommended the Santa Fe Café.

Humphrey thanked him and was out of sight just as John heard a diesel clatter and snort just before it came into sight around the last bend. The bright blue Bluebird bus stopped at the corner. The driver levered open the door and called out, "Gutt morgan, mein herr."

John answered, "Aloha, kahuna." They both laughed for they had each used up their German and Hawaiian vocabularies."

The driver's name was Mitchell Knox. His bloodline included Kiowa on his father's side many generations back and an Arapaho on his mother's also many generations back. But they knew of no European ancestors. He had no provable relationship to John.

Around the turn of the century the tribe had adopted a legal system similar to that of the U.S.A. It had been felt that family names were needed for the new census rolls. Names such as Running Bear or Brave Eagle could certainly identify individuals in days of yore, but with the greatly expanded population, surnames became necessary. Many families had retained names with Indian characteristics such as Crowe or Redfeather. Others took famous names such as Washington, Jefferson, Lincoln, Calvin, Luther, and Knox. A number took common names such as Smith or Jones. Mitchell's ancestors tried to honor the first white man to come to them, he in whose bloodline was Lionel and John.

Mitchell had a flashback on first sight of his friend at the crossroad. He remembered the terrible event of a day when the two of them had been bare back riding. The two of them, barely teens, had been near the Upper Bridge on the Foothills Loop. They had been spouting off magnificent plans of what they would do when they didn't have to listen to their parents and could make all their own decisions. That had been in the summer of '87. They were both 25 now.

That day had been as perfect as this one. And then a Public Safety Patrol Jeep had come roaring up, lights flashing and siren screaming. They had hopped off their mounts as Uncle Lionel, solemn and ashen-faced, jumped out and ran over to them. He brought the awful word that John's mother and father, John Sr. and Clara, had died in a hotel fire. The man had been the Assistant Business Manager and he and Clara had gone as Mikota representatives to a sales convention. Clara had been nearly full blooded Mikotan.

At the funeral Esther Crowe in full Mikota regalia had delivered one of the eulogies. At one point she directly addressed the parentless son whose guardian now was Uncle Lionel. She had said, "Oh John, we all loved your mama and papa and we all weep with you. Do not be ashamed of tears. Do not hold them back. They wash away the hurt. Your father and mother both loved a song that said, 'Some through the waters, Some through the flood, Some through the fire, But all through the Blood.' Yes, they went through the fire, but they believed in Jesus and went through His blood. They are safely home now. And now, my Dear John, you must be very brave and follow in your father's footsteps."

Follow he had and was soon to be Business Manager. Mitchell had early on taken his friend's determination to heart and had followed in the footsteps of many of his ancestors who had been called witch doctors but were very wise in homeopathic medicines. For the past several years he had been guaranteed summer work and the Tribe had been subsidizing his education. In a few years he could serve his people as a full-fledged M.D.

"Shore is good to see yuh again, Jay Dee."

"You too. Hey Mitch, I got a stitch in my side and I itch for a ride, but I ain't rich so I can't pay so please don't pitch me out into a ditch on this fine day. Just give me a hitch."

Some of the passengers were chuckling over the interchange as Mitchell clicked on his mike. Rather than one or two speakers blaring loudly and often indistinctly, Bluebird buses had tiny speakers by each seat so all could hear.

"Folks, this dizzy clown is my good friend, John D. Knox, the next Business Manager of the Mikota Nation.

He's Scotch and wants a free ride but such perks don't come until he's sworn in. I know he drove buses last summer so I propose we make his earn his ride by driving. All in favor say I I I I I I."

The children and most of the adults let out sounds that seemed to be Hollywood versions of war cries; Mitchell vacated his seat and waved John into it. John put the bus in gear and they were off as Mitchell said, "For years the palefaces have taken advantage of us ignorant redskins. Today I turned the tables on one of them."

There were ten seats empty in the 30 passenger bus. Across the full width rear seat which could seat four adults and two children, were five adults, four women and a man. At the extreme right sat a cowboy or at least the man was dressed like one with a Stetson hat, hand tooled leather boots, faded Levis, a checkered red flannel shirt, a wide belt sporting a silver buckle with crossed Remington Rifles, and a fringed leather vest with silver buttons. At the beginning of the tour he had told them his name was Rafferty but they should call him Punch.

Next to him was Corinne O'Conner, a wealthy widow who was touring with her daughter Marian, aged 12. Both were green eyed, freckle-faced, and had flaming red tresses. They wore similar sundresses and had on matching straw sunbonnets and sunglasses. They were both normally reserved and quiet, but could easily become very animated and volatile.

Marian sat beside the window in front of Punch. Neither she nor her mother knew how long they had been stared at while in the Glasgow Inn swimming pool or while dining. In fact, Corinne had been very flattered at the sudden courteous attentions of the handsome stranger.

Seated next to Marian was Bernard Krause, aged 13. He was a serious, studious lad dubbed "book worm" or "Encyclopedia Bernardica" by his class mates. Following

Bar Mitzvah part of his gift had been this trip to the west. Stopovers were conditioned on there being first class accommodations for them. The Glasgow Inn had a three star rating and the soon opening Dundee Grand Hotel was expected to be even higher rated. Herman would be joining his wife and son there after the opening and then be traveling with them.

Analysis of the black hair and facial features of son and mother could have linked them, but she was short and plump and he thin and tall, already eye to eye with Mama and likely could be taller than his father. Maxine had hit the big five oh a few years before but would only admit to being in her forties. Bernie, the child of her old age would always be her baby. His three sisters were already married and she loved them dearly but her little "Quiz Kid" would always be her favorite. And she was pleased at the rapt attention Marian was paying to his every word about dinosaur remains which had been found in the Bittersweet Range. Maxine amply occupied the middle rear seat.

Seated at Maxine's left was her niece Jolene, aged 17. The girl's father Harold, Herman's younger brother, had married into money and a cushy job that called upon him to spend more time over seas than at home. Jolene had severe Down's syndrome and had Mongolian features. Her parents were ashamed to be seen with her. Aunt Maxine and her family had literally raised the sweet girl who time after time had been dropped off for a few days that always seemed to stretch out into a few months. The girl was cheerful most of the time and always quick to do those things within her limited capabilities, especially if she was rewarded with peppermints or other candy.

So it was not a totally unforeseen possibility when she was brought home drunk by police who had found her lost and hurt and crying because she didn't know what would happen to her for losing the picture books she had been bringing back to the library. At the time Jolene was 13 and could only tell how nice some older boys had been to her telling her how pretty she was and then giving her sweet strong things to drink. She could not remember anything else until waking up in an alley.

The truth soon came out how she had been used for tests showed she was pregnant. Her violators were never caught. Her parents were outraged at how carelessly she had been protected. While on a short stateside trip from their new home in London, England they took away their daughter and placed her in a private care facility for feeble minded unwed mothers and paid the bills but never visited her.

About six months before this trip, Herman had finally found out where his niece was and took legal steps to get custody of her and her baby. This was the first time Herman and Maxine saw their grandnephew. Jolene had named him Jojo; the birth certificate named him Joseph Krause.

He was three now and after having lived in the Krause home for five months had disproved the diagnosis of the institution's overworked staff psychologist that the little tyke was sub normal. A more expert medical friend of Herman had declared that development is hampered when there is a lack of stimulus. Jojo was most severely behind in vocabulary skills but in the very talkative Krause household had been charging into better vocal skills and was racing ahead in all normal three-year-old activities.

Jolene had been very lethargic and non-responsive most of the time and might have lived out the rest of her life that way in the care facility, but being in a normal active home with alert responsive people around her had been rapidly improving even to the point of showing initiative in tending to many of her son's needs. Still there were times when she would stare vacantly into space perhaps not thinking at all. Such was the case when Maxine gently shook the girl's arm coincidental with the bus stopping for a road crew patching the tarmac. "Jolene, honey. Jolene!"

"Huh? Oh! Auntie Max? What?"

The aunt leaned close to whisper in the girl's ear so the others would not hear. "Honey, you had your mouth open and you were drooling a little. We must keep our mouths closed when we have gum in them. You must chew it without opening your mouth. Otherwise you'd look like a little girl and you know we are both grown women."

"Okay, Auntie Max. I'm sorry. I'll chew closed. I promise. I love you."

Just then an audacious saucy Blue Jay flew to the parked bus and landed on the middle of the roll bar just ahead of the children. Jolene's face lit up as she saw it and her mouth gaped as the Jay began scolding. "Look! I see a pretty bird. See the pretty bird, Auntie? See the pretty bird, Jojo? What a pretty bird. So pretty pretty pretty."

As soon as his mother mentioned the Jay the boy saw it and exclaimed excitedly, "Jojo sees the pretty bird. See the pretty bird, Julie? What a pretty bird. A real pretty bird, Mama." His sudden outburst along with his big gestures had no doubt startled the Jay for it fled its perch and flew away still scolding.

As the bird flew away Jolene realized her mouth was wide open. She quickly shut it, covered it with her hands, and ducked down with a hankie so no one would see her wipe her mouth. She then clasped her hands on her lap and sat up with a sly smile and chewed carefully.

The four women had happened to come together the previous morning around the pool at the Glasgow Inn. It had been the children's doing. Jojo and Juliet had been the only little kids in the shallow end of the pool and had been throwing an inflated beach ball back and forth. Marian was not much of a swimmer and had been in waist deep water and had been holding onto the edge of the pool to practice kicking. The boy had accidentally bopped her on the head. Unhurt but startled she had lost her finger hold and went under. She had bobbed up sputtering as Bernard, a good swimmer, raced to her rescue. He apologized for his cousin's poor toss and soon was showing the girl how to swim better.

The four women had already spent their time in the pool and had been lounging and sipping frosted beverages. Jolene had thought the beach ball incident hilarious and had laughed and clapped. Aunt Maxine mildly chided the boy and cautioned him to be more careful but knew it was not likely. The three older ladies had begun chatting about the antics of children and soon were getting better acquainted. Before you knew it, the eight tourists were having their meals together and were forming an impromptu group.

At breakfast before the Bluebird tour, Jojo had let loose with a loud child's impersonation of the big-handed chef on the Muppet Show, re-runs of which were on one of the satellite channels. He had splayed his fingers and waved his arms around and said, "Birduh Birduh Birduh. Birduh Birduh Birduh." Julie joined in to the amusement of fellow diners, but when Jolene stood up and added her efforts, a now embarrassed Aunt Maxine stepped in to shush all three. From across the room the cowboy, from behind dark sunglasses, observed the group, paying particular attention to Corinne and Marian.

Bernice Eberhard at the window was the quietest of the three oldest mothers on the bus. She was treasuring this time with her 4 year old, Juliet. In spite of it having been her husband's philanderings which had destroyed her marriage and brought about the trial separation, his family had the necessary finances to retain high-powered attorneys who very likely could cause her to lose custody. It just wasn't right.

Bernice and Juliet were both blondes but their basic behavior patterns were as different as night and day. Juliet

15

was more like her maternal aunts who had been tom girls joining in the athletic activities of their father and male cousins. Bernice had been her mother's "little lady" and the most genteel. But she was glad Juliet and Jojo had hit it off so well. They were a pre-school dynamic duo.

She very much appreciated the friendliness of the other women. Her heart went out to Maxine and she ached for the niece although she wondered if being unaware of troubles might be a good state to be in. And Maxine's automatic leadership was a boon as was her constant running commentary on all that happened. Oh, she never failed to listen to others' comments, even the wee ones, but there was never a lull in the conversation with her around.

One of the hopes attached to vacations, beyond recreation and contented idleness, is to leave behind for a while the troubles and cares of everyday life. It should be an up-building time. Over the centuries religious retreats have served a similar purpose regarding spiritual well-being.

The type of activities most of the above mentioned people were engaging in and the beauty of their surroundings should certainly have a positive effect. But to most of the above mentioned people and one not yet mentioned, the beautiful weather and surroundings would become the back drop for a tragic event which would drastically change their lives.

Chapter Two

A PLEASANT SUMMER MID-DAY

Above the east end of Dundee cliffs rose up over 250 feet. The Narrows, a zigzag passage through them, carried the Mikota River which bisected the town. In the Narrows the water violently cascaded down 70 feet before reaching the lower level and then meandered eastward between the foothills until swinging south at the Upper Bridge. The Narrows' twisting rapids were popularly named the Corkscrew but had the official name of Knox Rush.

The Hidden Valley Spur followed the river until nearing Knox Rush. A long ramp approach such as might be seen at the Mackinac Bridge allowed an easy grade. But at the top a most unusual suspension bridge made an S curve through the Narrows. It was unusual in that the suspending cables were anchored at the top to the cliffs rather than to steel towers. It resembled a giant unfinished spider web. Vast amounts of accumulated oil field earnings had gone into making the valley accessible for two-way vehicular traffic.

When the original John Knox had arrived, the only access had been a treacherous foot path barely wide enough for laden pack animals. It followed alongside the Corkscrew and was often drenched by capricious surges of water. The Mikotans had devised hand holds and rope railings in the most dangerous spots. In the 1800's when railroad lines were being blasted into mountainsides, judicious blasting in the gorge had enlarged the foot path to accept wagons and later on motor vehicles on a single narrow lane.

Dundee was built on a gradual slope. The west end of town where the Dundee Grand Hotel was due to open was a full 30 feet higher than where Knox Rush started. Continuing west to the far end of the valley 20 miles distant entailed an 800 foot climb. It was about a mile and a half wide at midpoint and tapered down to both ends.

Ribbon Lake at the far end, just a couple of miles past the Knox Farm, was roughly triangular in shape. Literally dozens of small falls cascaded into it on both sides from the eternal ice fields in the high country. Ribbon Lake was the source of most of the water in the Mikota River but numerous springs and mountain rivulets all along the river were also major contributors.

At the upper end of the Canyon around Ribbon Lake the surrounding mountains were steep but could have been climbed even by novice mountaineers. Once past the valley walls there was so much rugged terrain that only well equipped and trained alpine climbers could negotiate it. It was not impossible to go through the Bittersweet Range, just unreasonably risky to try it. And the shortest escapes were to the west where desert sand ruled.

As the rock fence around the valley narrowed at the eastern end, it also steepened. Surrounding Dundee on two sides were vertical cliffs. These came together in a shallow vee with its vertex at the Narrows. The south wall here was quite regular with only minor ins and outs to its outline. But the north wall immediately inside the Narrows had a semi-circular dent nearly big enough to hold a football field. Just east of this was a large outgrowth of rock which jutted toward the river leaving a pinch point where there was only room for the two traffic lanes and a sidewalk.

What was remarkable about this outcropping of stone was a column which originated near the river and climbed skyward until its top was even with the sloping mesa of the cliffs. The monolith was free standing and about one sixth as wide as tall. It stood immovable on a stratum of bedrock and its separation from the cliff began about 50 feet up.

Various fanciful names such as chimney or tower are often applied to such weathered rock formations but it had been early discovered that when the sun was just right, the shadow cast was that of a giant man. The Mikota Tribal Council, though definitely not superstitious, had in their publicity named it the Sentinel and hinted that he guarded Dundee from calamities.

The rock from which the Sentinel arose had been discovered to have a labyrinth of small passages and a number of large chambers. There were also numerous vents in which tiny creatures could find refuge. Coincidental with the growth of Dundee as a tourist haven, the chambers were made into a small museum and rest rooms. The small passages connecting with these rooms had been sealed off and the vents securely screened to prevent animal incursion.

The Sentinel Museum's entrance was about 30 feet back from the street on the side of the rock facing west toward town. About 10 feet in front of the entrance stood a huge round boulder which had been in the way during the road construction. It had been moved to its present location and the rough corners had been chipped off. A brass plate affixed to it declared it to be the Sentinel's Cannon Ball.

Humphrey Bogardus arrived in town at noon. He turned right at the first drive which led into the big dent afore mentioned. Snug along the east wall was a booth for the attendant of the self-service Red Arrow gas station. In front of it was an island with four pumps which could be activated by credit cards. Against the rock wall and next to the booth were four above ground storage tanks which supplied three grades of gas and also diesel fuel. These tanks were enclosed by shoulder high concrete retaining walls capped by a wooden lattice fence which partly hid the tanks and beautified the area.

The balance of the flat area was used as one of the free municipal parking lots. Larger vehicles could park diagonally all around the rocky perimeter of the lot. Ordinary vehicles could park within the lines in the middle. A diagonal spot was open next to the fourth tank which contained the premium fuel.

Humphrey pulled in and was sandwiched between the tank and a delivery truck bigger than his. The business name on it said Mikota Hauling. The driver had brought it and left it. It was locked and full of fireworks for the grand opening on Saturday and also for Independence Day celebrations in both Dundee and Glasgow.

Humphrey put on his new black Stetson and reflecting sun glasses. He was dressed all in black save for red suspenders. He wore untooled leather boots. He double checked that all was locked and then strode across the almost empty parking lot. He checked the map Officer Redfeather had given him. On the back of the Territorial map were street maps of Dundee and Glasgow as well as listings of attractions.

"Hm. That tall rock must be the Sentinel and right beyond it is the Santa Fe Café. Good. Here I come, Pilgrims." He stepped forth purposely the way John Wayne would going to a shootout. But he looked like a fat goose waddling.

The café had only a few patrons. Stella glanced around to see where she might seat the very obese man coming up the steps onto the porch. As soon as they neared each other inside, she thought quickly and then asked him if he might prefer a very special table on the patio in back.

"There's an awning to shade you and usually a little breeze and fresh air is healthier than air conditioning.

Besides, there's a little park back there and you can watch if children play."

He agreed it sounded very nice and she was so friendly he felt his Bogardus charm was bringing him special treatment. She was indeed, but on behalf of those within for she had immediately noticed that he emitted vile body odors. He seemed to be constantly flatulent for he had erupted after entering, a loud passage of sewer gas and he had not seemed to be aware he had done it. His diet caused him to be constantly gassy. In two words, he stunk.

His tiny cottage at the private college in the Deep South had a compact tub but no shower. He worked there as a grounds keeper and a stable boy and was used to working with manure and compost. So since the dirt didn't bother him and since he couldn't fit in the tub anyway, he was accustomed to just washing his face and hands almost every day. So there was always dirt behind his ears and under his cuffs and everywhere you could not see. He needed no hair tonic for the grease and dirt in his hair were enough to slick it down. Underarm deodorants were useless when there were so many yards of flesh which would be missed by it. As for clean clothing, he did wear clean outer garments when needing to be presentable, but what reason was there to change underwear more than two or three times a month? Do you suppose this explains why no one wanted to be near him and does it not tend to make the attentions of his special friends seem suspicious?

On his odorous passage through the dining room the short and wide man had scanned the pictorial menu behind the counter and also checked out the pastry display case. "I'd like two chicken pot pies and a large chocolate malt right away and a cherry malt to go when I leave."

"Sir, the pot pies require 20 minutes of baking and many couples split them because they are quite large."

"Oh. I see. Well I'm awful hungry so I still want two but I need food right away so bring me a bowl of pea soup and a three bean salad while the pies are baking. And please hurry."

He was eating for nearly an hour. By the time his pies arrived, his malt was gone and he ordered black coffee. "Without sugar or cream. I'm trying to cut back." To complete his meal he had dawdled over pieces of apple and cherry pie, both ala mode. He also ordered pastries to go with his second malt. "Two strawberry Bismarcks, two chocolate glazed nutty donuts, and two pecan Danishes. I'm gonna pour the malt into my thermoist bottle for later when I have my afternoon snack with those pastries. It'll all go in the saddlebags of my Hog."

Stella's full name was Estellita Juarez. Her mother, Isabella Jefferson and her younger sister Bonita were Mikotan on their father's side and Latin-American on their mother's. Both had been Mikotan citizens but Isabella had married an outsider, Miguel Juarez, a second generation U.S. citizen. They had moved to Des Moines and had forsaken her birthright. Stella had been born in Des Moines but by virtue of her bloodline could claim her Mikotan citizenship at age 21 if she chose so. Bonita had married Raymond DuPres, an immigrant from New Orleans who had claimed naturalization after seven years by virtue of residence and marriage.

Ray and Bonnie had four children, Maria 16, Rosita 18, Charles 20, and Frank 22. All worked their shifts at the café which was the family business. Frank was destined to become manager if his father ever retired.

Stella had just completed High School in Des Moines. She had worked for Aunt Bonnie and Uncle Ray the previous two summers and had jumped at the chance when offered full time employment which besides salary and tips included room and board in the spacious family apartment above the restaurant. She was 18 and the oldest of nine Juarez children. She was sending half her salary home to help tide the family over until her twin brothers graduated the following year and could get full-time employment and pay board. Next summer her father would be 65 and eligible for his Social Security plus a generous factory pension. At that time the meager family finances would be greatly improved.

She was an attractive young woman, dark complected and with sleek black straight hair. She was not svelte but her stocky peasant build was well proportioned and not a bit overweight. She was graceful and light on her feet, quite strong but ever gentle. She tended to be a bit flirty with men she knew to be single but it was all in fun. Had anyone made unwanted advances she would have emphatically and perhaps painfully halted them. Had such advances continued her uncle and cousins would have been even more emphatic. She always wore a chain and small crucifix on her neck and was determined never to bring reproach on the Virgin or her Son.

Shortly after Stella brought the first installment to the fat man, she noticed a Bluebird Bus let off passengers before proceeding to its reserved parking place next to the Village Hall and Post Office two blocks west. Punch and the party of eight exited followed by John who waved on seeing Maria and Stella inside. He detoured to the men's room under the Sentinel to shave and spruce up a bit. In the anteroom were located coin operated lockers in one of which John stashed his pack until later. He might even leave it overnight and get it on Thursday.

Cousins Charles and Maria efficiently moved some tables together for the party of nine. The group had decided beforehand to have a quick lunch to allow them time for shopping. They had until 2:00 p.m. before the bus would pick them up for a loop through the Hidden Valley. Right across the river were the Moc Shop and the Bead House and then a whole string of quaint places. There was a foot bridge in front of the Café and three others at intervals as well as two vehicular bridges in town, one at the Knox Farm, another half way there, and a third just west of town by the campground.

Jojo loudly announced, "Wanna peambuddah Jell-O samwich." Juliet concurred and Jolene said, "Me too." Bernard wanted an all-beef hot dog and Marian copied him. The others settled for tuna or chicken salads.

John came in as Maria was hustling the group's order to them. Stella was working behind the counter by the coffee urn. He sat on a swivel stool nearby. She saw him in the big mirror and smiled broadly and said, "Howdy, stranger. What can I do you for?"

"Waal, how's about iced tea, a big bowl of chili with plenty of shredded cheddar and a couple slabs of that fresh baked bread I smell. And hey, gal, you must be new in town. I know all the good lookin' ones and I declare I'd never fergit a gal as purty as you. You're a sight to heal sore eyes."

"Thank you, handsome. I shore hope you take it in mind to stick around these parts." And then she couldn't keep from laughing and could not maintain their charade. He and his uncle had been frequent visitors and in little chats they had been coming up with a dialogue of sorts to amuse tourists.

"It really is nice to see you again, John. And Aunt Bonnie told me that you would be our new Business Manager after Labor Day. Please let me congratulate you."

"Thanks, Stella, it's nice to see you, too. And by the way, will my new job mean I get a discount here?"

With a failed attempt at derision she snorted, "Scotsmen!" and flounced away to get his order.

As he ate he overheard Punch telling of his horseback riding abilities. Corinne and Marian admitted they knew nothing about it and Punch gallantly offered to teach them the following day. Corinne was definitely not into athletics or outdoor activities and declined. The man seemed crestfallen. She said, "Perhaps if Marian would like to learn you could teach her." Behind the man's sunglasses his eyes flashed in anticipation. Silent and sullen Bernard stared at the man from across the table, not liking or trusting him one bit.

By 12:30 the four children were done eating and the little tykes were itching to get to the playground. John had been just ready to order pie when he heard Bernard say, "But Mama, I'd be very happy to take Joseph and Juliet to the playground and be their sitter. And perhaps Miss O'Connor could assist me."

Mrs. Krause replied, "Absolutely not son. I insist an adult must be with you. Jolene and I will do it."

Punch interjected, "Let me. You've all been wanting to get into a few shops. I'd be delighted to tend the children."

Bernard snapped, "Skip it then. We'll all go shopping." Maxine was about to reprimand her son when John stepped over to the tables.

"I beg your pardon. Stores don't interest me now. I've been in all of them here. I'd be very content to sit out there by that picnic table and eat my dessert and also watch the children. And I'd enjoy talking to this young man who seems so well informed and also to this girl who asks such intelligent questions. I bet she could stump both of us. Let's see, it's Bernard and Marian, isn't it?"

"I'd like it if you called me Bernie."

"Done! And would everybody call me John?"

Maxine had trusted John almost from first sight. She agreed saying to him, "Honey, you'll make a good mayor. We'll be back here about 1:40 for coffee before Mr. Mitch brings the bus back at 2:00 to show us the valley. We'll see you then. Oh. I'm inviting you for coffee too. It's going to be Punch's treat."

As Stella readied John's pie to go she murmured to him, "That was really nice. Even if you were just doing it to promote tourism, it's still a good thing."

As the tall man led the children out the back way they had to go past Humphrey. He did not even notice them. As he stuffed himself he was intent on his daydreams of the other Hog. Juliet crinkled up her nose, pinched it with her fingers and made gagging noises. Jojo rather loudly said, "Poo poo."

All had a delightful time in the little park. Juliet leaped with abandon around the monkey bars. Jojo managed to keep up to her but moved more cautiously. The older children became fast friends of the man as he related legends of ghosts in the valley.

"Actually it's never been real ghosts. I've never seen solid proof that there are such things. But there have been hermits who lived just behind the first row of mountains who had secret paths into the valley from the Bittersweet Range. They would come in to harvest wild berries or fruit and fish and hunt for game. They always traveled at night during full moons and sometimes the smoke of their little campfires would be noticed. But if someone went to investigate, they would always be gone without a trace. During a real bad winter when no one could travel they might hole up in an abandoned cabin and sometimes their smoke might be spotted. But no real ghosts. Just stories to keep strangers and kids from wandering off into danger."

At about 1:30 a Public Safety Jeep stopped in front of the Santa Fe Café. Burly Sheriff Claude Talon stepped in and inquired whether a pretend cowboy had been there. Bonnie had known Claude all her life and figured it had to be serious matter for the head of the force to come. He assured her he expected no trouble but some questions had to be asked and then proper action taken. She pointed the way and Claude and a well dressed stranger crossed the foot bridge. A Deputy remained at the Jeep.

The ladies and Punch were just entering the bridge to cross back when the Lawman reached them. The Sheriff introduced himself but not the elderly gentleman with him. "Are you Mr. Rafferty?"

"Uh. Well yes. Do I know either of you?"

The stranger said, "No, but you knew my sister Lorna and here is a picture she took of you." He showed it to the man and the officer. "I don't know what your real name is but I know you've called yourself Peter Randolph, Paul Rickover, Phil Ransom, and who knows what else. But whatever your name you robbed my sister of $25,000 and I've been tracking you down ever since."

"That was a loan. She'll get it back. Being late paying back a loan is no crime."

"What about the other six women I know about from whom you disappeared after getting their money. And how many others we don't know about, always wealthy widows hoping for companionship?"

"They'll all get their money. I've got some business deals cooking that'll net me a million or more."

Claude said, "Even if borrowing without planning to pay is legal outside this Territory, don't even think of trying it here. We get very riled up by people who try to cheat us and our court will pass sentence and our jail doesn't mollycoddle folks who come in to hurt us. Ever hear of hard labor?"

Punch was sweating more than the temperature warranted as he replied, "Well, I've no intention of doing any business here so you can just be on your way, Sheriff."

Claude said, "Not exactly. There's the matter of a warrant issued for you in Newark because you jumped bail. The name is different but fingerprints we got from your breakfast dishes are a perfect match."

"I can explain everything."

"I'm sure you can to the Judge in Newark. Extradition papers are being prepared and an officer is on his way to get you. In the meanwhile you are going to be my guest."

"Sheriff, I can save you a lot of trouble and go back voluntarily. I give you my solemn word I will. I'll swear on a Bible."

The law officer's answer was to handcuff the man. The ladies were incredulous. Maxine asked, "Since when do people get treated like criminals for bad debts? People have done that to my husband. Herman sued them."

The stranger said, "If only it was just that but he's a pedophile. The bail he jumped was for a criminal case with several counts of molesting children and one of statutory rape involving a pre-teen girl. Wherever he went conning widows, his eyes were open for available children. This thing before us, whatever his name, had been pretty slippery except on one occasion when he was careless and adult witnesses could identify him with his victim."

Jolene was fascinated at seeing a man being arrested. The other three were horrified and angry. There were almost as angry at themselves for having been taken in by such a predator. As Corinne thought of her daughter and what might have happened she came to a rapid boil. Words she had often heard but never used came to her lips in a vehement withering curse, the force of which caused the fake cowboy to cringe. And then she dashed at him. She swung her arm in a wide arc and connected with his face in a resounding slap that spun his chin around and knocked his hat and glasses into the river. It knocked him off balance and only the officer's tight grip on his arm kept him from following his hat over the railing.

After a stunned moment of silence Punch protested. "I was assaulted. She had no right doing that. I know my rights. I want her arrested."

Claude said very softly into the man's ear, "If you make too much of a commotion, I'll consider it as part of resisting arrest and I'll use my own discretion at how much force to use and some might be reprimanding me for not using enough. We consider all life sacred and anyone who in any way abuses women or children will find no mercy in our court system. Crimes against children in particular deserve the most painful punishment. We can become savages again so you'd better shut up and march."

As the trio went back to the police car, Maxine put her arms around Corinne and said to them all, "Ladies, not a word of this to the children. If they ask just say he was called east on urgent business. And as for Marian, we can all thank God that absolutely nothing evil happened to her. Just smile and think of good things that have happened. Even clear skies can have a dark cloud pass over. Oh, one other thing, the coffee is my treat."

Before the arrest, at about 1:15, Humphrey had paid his considerable tab and left an impressive tip out of the generous expense money given to him. As Stella received the money at the table he said, "I need the toilet bad. Where is it?"

"Sir, our men's room is very tiny with hardly room to turn around. But a beautiful modern and spacious lounge under the Sentinel is there for you and if you're interested there's a small museum of Mikotan artifacts on display."

From Triangle Park behind the Santa Fe Café a narrow walkway went between it and the base rock of the Sentinel. Stella pointed and said, "Take the short cut. It saves having to climb up the half flight back here and then having to go down the front steps."

The Café was first in a long row of side by side buildings, mostly retailers and eateries. In back, Triangle Park was the tip of a wedge of flat ground which widened a couple of blocks down to where there was room for a back street

29

with a bed and breakfast, a couple of boarding houses for summer help, and a few private summer residences. All of the buildings within a hundred feet of the cliff wall were made of reinforced concrete poured to resemble adobe and every roof was also reinforced for at times in winter snow or ice might tumble down bringing with it any loose stone. At the beginning of the back street a cross street traveled over an auto bridge. From here west all streets were laid out in checkerboard pattern.

Uncle Ray patted Stella on the back and praised her for diverting the stench bearer to the public facility which had a good venting system and strong deodorizers in each stall. She said, "I feel sorry for a person in that condition and I didn't want to offend him, but I wasn't about to offend everybody in here."

Humphrey left the Sentinel facilities at 1:35. He trudged very slowly back to the truck and didn't look well. Gabriel Elkhorn was manager of the gas station and was overdue for his quitting time. His brother Jed had phoned in pleading car trouble and promised to be there by 2:15 at the latest. Since business had been light, Gabe was shutting down save the credit card pump activation. A chalk on blackboard sign inside the now locked booth asked cash customers to return after 2:15.

When the gasman saw the fat man approaching so slowly and holding his free hand against his chest, he called out, "Mister, are you okay?" He feared the onset of a heart attack.

"Yeah, I think so. Just heartburn. Got Pepto Bismol in the truck." He stood still and let loose a barrage of loud belches, then smiled and said, "There, I feel better already."

Gabe followed him to his camper, just in case. He did hold the bag for him as the Harley was cranked down. But on getting a whiff of his fetid over-ripeness eased away to get breathing room. The man took a less than clean Thermos bottle out of one saddle bag and said as he poured his malt into it, "See, my Thermoist bottle will keep this nice and cold for hours until I have my afternoon snack. And I really am okay, but thanks for checking."

Mr. Elkhorn took a series of deep breaths as he moved toward the Café. He and Maria were developing a great fondness for one another and had been meeting frequently. He remembered her saying that she and Stella had the afternoon off and he expected to have lunch with Miss DuPres. He was also wondering if she might know what the Sheriff's stop had been about.

Maria had been expecting to see Gabe. She and Stella had rushed upstairs after their shift and while changing into dungarees and sweatshirts had teased each other about their romantic possibilities. They were glad to get into more casual garb and out of their Mexican appearing full skirts and frilly senorita blouses.

The DuPres apartment had outside entrances onto the front porch and back patio. The stairways were inside. Maria came out the front door just as the Sheriff's Jeep buzzed away. She stepped into the street to watch him go and saw her heart's interest talking to the fat man. She ducked out of sight behind the Cannon Ball.

Stella used the back entrance intending to walk through the park to head to the Post Office to send her folks a letter and she would not mind if she happened to see the tall Scotsman. Just as she came out, the playground group was moving toward the patio following their escort.

Jojo had suddenly rushed over to his cousin Bernard, tugged on his wrist, and announced, "Gotta go potty." Juliet had followed him over to the older children and said shyly to Marian, "Me too." As all of them arrived at the back door of the Café the agitated mothers came in the front door. They scurried to the back to check on their loved ones, the so very precious children. Stella followed them in so she could assist if needed.

Bernie spoke first, "Mama, I know there are rest rooms but I was hoping we could go into the Sentinel and check out the museum stuff. Mr. Knox said he'd go with us."

Maxine objected to the idea. "But there's Juliet. I'm sure Mrs. Eberhard wants a grownup woman to go in the Ladies' Room with the girls. It would be improper for a gentleman to go in there with them. One of us, or maybe all, should go along."

Jolene whined, "I don't wanna go there. I'm thirsty and I wanna root beer. Auntie Max, you promised."

Stella offered her services. "I'd be glad to take the girls over there. Then you could all relax here until the bus comes."

John added, "Stella is the oldest child of a big family. She knows all that's needful about tending little ones. You couldn't do better."

The three older mothers glanced back and forth at each other and nodded. Spokeswoman Maxine said, "So go. Shoo! We don't want the little ones to have an accident." She waved them on. Stella took the hands of Jojo and Juliet and John followed her with Bernie and Marian. Maxine called to Rosita, "So do you have Cappuccino?"

The sextet met Maria and her beau by the Cannon Ball. Stella asked, "Hey cuz, would you take this to the Post Office for me after you eat? Hungry, Gabe? Pass on the chili. She made it."

John bent over in mock pain, held his belly with both hands and groaned out, "Oh no! I'm poisoned."

Gabe laughed and said, "Cut it out, you clowns." The couple joined hands and walked away in unspoken agreement to go to the Post Office first.

Massive twin doors guarded the entrance of the Sentinel facilities. In spite of their extreme weight they opened very easily and their closers shut them effortlessly. They were made of four inch thick vertical oak planks held together by stout wrought iron bands inside and out. Strong carriage bolts through all bound iron to wood to iron. Massive hinges joined the doors to their iron frames fastened to the rock. The doors shut not against each other but against a stout steel center post.

In keeping with the fortress idea there were small knee high openings in each door and on display inside were two small mortars encarriaged so their muzzles were just the right height to fire through the doors. In olden days a charge by besiegers wielding a battering ram could have been stopped by the firing of shot at legs. There were also a couple of loop holes higher up on each door through which muskets could be fired. All openings were sealed with thick safety glass. Nearby display cases showed typical muskets and shot canisters.

A couple of honeymooners were leaving as our six entered and they then were the only occupants. After necessary uses and washing of hands the three males met the three females in the inner display room. The little boy and girl were getting tired and ready to start being cranky and cross. The two were expected to zonk out once riding the open air bus and then get needed naps. John kept close tabs on the time so they'd be back in the Café before the bus came for its pickup.

Humphrey, after Gabe left him, stashed away his "Thermoist" bottle and sweets and made sure other personal things were ready to go. He then entered the supposed camper for the final time. It had a greatly beefed up suspension with eight ply tires and it was heavily laden with tanks used for industrial gases and stout metal containers the contents of which the fat man could not have understood or explained. He could almost remember word for word the little farewell speech Reginald S. VanderMaas III had said to him before he had departed on his errand.

"You're a very special guy, Hump. You're brave like pioneers and war heroes in undertaking this. That's why the League of Purity and Justice is rewarding you with that motorcycle to drive home. We know you stand 100% with us in believing the white race was chosen by the Almighty to rule. It is superior. Black and red and any other non-whites are inferior and look how they cheat us. The blacks do half a day's work and want a full day's pay. The red men cheat us in their gambling casinos and flaunt game and fish laws. So in a non-violent peaceful way we are going to send them a message about how the situation stinks.

"You know how to set all the switches. Then be sure to put in your ear plugs before you set the master switch. In a minute the sound will start. The outside panels of the truck are made to vibrate and are actually giant loudspeakers. Everyone for a mile around will hear our message. You must have the Harley idling before you do this so you don't hurt your ear drums. We certainly don't want to see our special friend harmed. No sir.

"Then five minutes after that the big stink starts. By then you should be a couple miles away and just keep going. You know what a stink bomb is. The whole truck is a gigantic stink bomb. By the time that spray starts coming out of there by the hundreds of pounds, people will start making tracks out of there. It's ten times as bad as a skunk and last ten times as long. River water will stink for weeks, not poisonous, just nauseating. And where the spray hits solid objects it sticks like Super Glue. It won't die away for months. Those stinking Mikotans won't make any tourist money this summer.

"So go with our blessing, dear friend. Years from now the history books of the New Order will brag up your contribution. You might even get medals and have a monument raised to you. All the snobs who think they're too good to spend time with our good buddy Hump had better decide which side they're on before it's too late or they'll be sorry."

While thinking over what Reggie had said, he had needed to rest from his multiple exertions. First had been the long walk back. Second had been the cranking down of the bike and getting it loaded for his tour. It looked very good but was old and nearly worn-out. His third and greatest exertion had been in getting it started. He sat on the step and ate two Hershey bars before going in. In elaborate day dreams he gloried in visions of himself receiving praise and adulation.

When he finally entered it was seven minutes to two. He set all the controls at the indicated positions and inserted his ear plugs. He marveled at how quickly the bass thrumming of the Hog died to a whisper. He hesitated before flipping the master switch to once again check all settings. Better safe than sorry.

By then Gabe and Maria were back from their leisurely walk to the Post Office and were turning in to climb the steps to the Café porch. They had seen Mitch sitting in the Bluebird driver seat reading a magazine. Most of the other passengers were already aboard awaiting the momentary resumption of their excursion. Gabe happened to see that the Harley was running for he saw smoky exhaust but river noise masked any exhaust sound.

Inside the Sentinel, just after John had called to the children to return to their mothers, Stella approached him to apologize. "I'm so sorry, John, but I forgot to tell you your Uncle Lionel stopped for coffee this morning and asked me to tell you he'd be gone until late Friday. Something about a galley proof and some art work. I'm really sorry."

"No problemo, Senorita Estellita. I had thought of phoning him for a ride but he's outside more than in when you call. It's simpler just taking the bus. It's too great a day to sweat the small stuff."

Yes, except for the little shadow cast by Punch it had been a great day all around. And then Humphrey threw the switch.

Chapter Three

A DISASTROUS SUMMER AFTERNOON

The children were just gathering to move toward the doors when a shock wave vibrated the rock surrounding them and then a deep rumbling was felt as much as heard. Perhaps no other sensory stimulus can so rapidly invoke instant fear and disorientation to most people as what they perceive to be an earthquake. This tremor was not enough to knock things down or even move them in the Sentinel rooms. Had there been stalactites they would have been undisturbed for this was a rock stratum with fault lines much like that found in the very stable Mammoth Cave. It was a relatively short manifestation which hardly lasted a minute and had begun a few seconds after 1:55.

Jojo was startled for a few seconds and then must have got the idea people had done it for fun because it tickled his feet. He clapped his hands and said, "More." Juliet imitated him, but Bernie stepped aside to John and asked, "Don't you think we ought to get out of here fast?"

John replied so the bigger ones heard him, "If this is a seismic shock from an earthquake somewhere, there may be some after shocks. We're probably much safer hear than out in the open under the cliffs. Things might fall. We'd best wait a few minutes in here. Mitch and your mothers would never leave without you."

Hardly had he spoken when at 1:58 there was a tiny tremor followed a minute later by more rumbling and then a sound as of battering rams beating on the door. The thickness of the doors as well as the tight seal of their closure prevented most outside noise from being heard within so this sudden invasion of sound was very alarming.

But what followed next was even more alarming, even frightening, for the lights flickered and went out. The familiar humming of the ventilation fans also began to die. But after a couple of seconds a relay clicked and the muted emergency lighting came on. Eight different low voltage floods came on as well as three exit lights.

On seeing a scale drawing of the floor plan of the Sentinel rooms, an imaginative person might say its outline resembled that of a sitting goose. The entry chamber, holding its mortars and cases, could have been a head. The size dwindled down to adequate but narrow passage which curved to the left approximating the neck of a goose before leading into the large inner chamber whose outline was a goosey profile.

Partitions laid out like an F separated off the rest rooms, the women's closest to the street. The space outside the rest rooms made a comfortable waiting room. The balance of the space beyond the rest rooms was the display area. This area was lit only by lights within the various cases which gave it an aura of mystery and adventure.

In the waiting room was a bottle fed water cooler, two overstuffed leather sofas, a guest register, a couple of lightly padded ladder back chairs, a pay phone, and the lockers. One of the lockers had ventilation slots and housed a deep draw battery which powered all the emergency lights. This battery was kept charged by a trickle charger which was supposed to run as long as there was 110 volt current. But

John knew the charger had been malfunctioning and was scheduled to be replaced. He was also the only one who realized the lights were much dimmer than they should be yet adequate for safe movement.

Two of the now battery powered exit lights were above the doors on the insides of the rest rooms and each had companion floodlights as did the exit light above the only outside entrance. There was also a light in the museum room and another in the waiting room. The ninth light was at the juncture of the entry passageway and shined toward the exit.

John said to Stella in a joking tone, "Looks like someone forgot to pay the light bill." The young woman was as apprehensive as he was but smiled back at him and said, "It was sent in by mail. You know how slow the stage coaches can be out here in the wilderness." Both were intent on keeping the children from thinking there was a serious problem until it was known for sure.

John had them all use the sofas until he could check. Jojo and Juliet thought it was a blast to bounce their rumps on the cushions. Bernie had a solemn look on his face but managed a weak smile for Marian. They sat side by side and the girl smiled back but there was fear in her eyes. She had taken hold of the boy's hand during the rumbling and now they self-consciously let go. Stella began to sing tra-la-la to a cheerful Spanish air.

John went to the door and was soon back. "The push bars are jammed and with the light shining down in my eyes but not on the doors, I couldn't tell what the matter was. I'm going to get my flashlight out of my back pack."

He fished the key out of his pocket, opened the locker, and set his pack where light shone into it. He located his miniature light which used AA cells and was handier at night camping than having to light his candle lantern for just a few minutes of illumination. It had a tiny but bright beam and could be clipped onto his shirt pocket. "Would you please come with me Bernie? We men should check this out."

Bernie got up and moved with alacrity. After Bar Mitzvah he knew he was spiritually counted with the men in the congregation, but he was not conceited enough to think he was one physically. Yet it was surely nice that this important man was treating him like one.

He immediately noticed and pointed out fan-shaped layers of sandy grit close to the door which had not been there when they had entered. John had patted him on the back and said, "You've got eyes like a hawk, young man. You don't miss anything. This has to mean there was a fierce blast of wind to force all this past the weather strip on the bottom."

All four pieces of loophole safety glass were intact but the penlight revealed that gravelly dirt was jammed against all of them. The two larger pieces of safety glass on the bottom were likewise jammed against but badly cracked and curved inward yet the now mosaic was still held in place by the criss-cross wire in the glass. The steel center post also seemed to be slightly bowed in.

"Well, Bernie, it looks like the tremors made the Sentinel's cap slide off and there may have been other slides but your mother and the rest were inside under reinforced roofs and I'm very sure they are safe."

The two reported this to the rest and Jojo served as spokesman saying, "Me wanna see." So all went to take a look. The little boy announced, "Jojo open it." He grabbed one of the push bars and grunted and lunged. It was quite comical and evoked some laughs but Juliet was impressed and said, "Let's help him." She pushed alongside him and the rest pushed to humor them.

Back in the waiting room Marian asked, "Isn't there a back door?"

Stella replied, "I don't think so. Is there a service access. John?" When he shook his head no she asked, "What are we supposed to do then?"

"I guess all we can do is wait."

"How long, sir?" asked Bernie.

"Probably several hours. People outside know we're blocked in and I'm sure work will start immediately to get us out. But we are in no danger so we can just relax. I think there will be wisdom in turning off all the exit lights and any emergency lights we don't need. They seem kind of dim. They look like the battery might not have too good of a charge. Bernie, will you help me? I'll get my Swiss Army knife out of my pack. It'll do most any handy man work."

Together the two undertook the task. John showed the lad how to open the fixtures and remove the bulbs. He could have done it more quickly alone but assisted by moving a chair into place and then holding Bernie steady. They stopped when only the light in the waiting room and the one shining down the hall were lit. These were considerably brighter now but left vast dark areas which seemed very spooky to the little ones.

They pressed up tight against Stella and the little girl began to whimper, "I'm cold and I want my Mama." Big tears formed in her eyes and began to course down her cheeks. The boy followed suit. "Mama. Auntie Max. Come get Jojo." Stella said, "Pretty soon your Mamas will come. Let me give you big hugs for them."

She put an arm around each of them and drew them even tighter to her. "It's okay. Men will come with bulldozers and big big trucks to take the dirt away from the door."

Jojo echoed, "Big BIG truck. SEMI truck. Vroom vroom." His sudden shift of attention showed that the momentary distraction had been helpful and he and the little girl stayed safe within the sheltering arms.

John had caught Juliet's remark about being cold and he became aware of the chilliness of the cave rooms. They never froze in winter but in summer they averaged 10 to 15 degrees less than the average outside temperatures. The ventilation was normally on all day as were the lights so that during the tourist season warmer outside air was constantly being drawn in and stale bath room air removed. Thus with the fans running it would only be a bit cooler than outside but when they stopped, the cooler rock temperature would begin reasserting itself. The air was never damp but cool enough to chill summer-clothed visitors who stayed in an undue amount of time.

John went to his pack and unwadded a lined windbreaker, a heavy parka, and two T shirts. He then unstrapped his bed roll and cut one of his heavy wool blankets into two squares. Rolled into the blankets was a flat rubber item.

He beckoned to the little ones to come close to him and said, "Know what this is? It's a pillow." He handed it to Stella and said, "Let's see if she can huff and puff like the big bad wolf and blow it up." As she did, the little ones puffed out their cheeks and blew too.

'"Thank you, windy lady. Children, I'll put this in the middle of the sofa so you can see how it works. Both put your feet on different ends of the sofa and your heads together in the middle. Now let's see if my special camping blanket is nice and warm."

Stella and John tucked them both in and then she gave them each a kiss on the cheek and said, "That's from your Mothers and Aunt Maxine."

John said, "Now watch what we do. Marian doesn't look very warm in that sundress with bare arms and shoulders. Would you put on my parka? You can roll the sleeves up because they're way too long for your arms."

Marian gratefully accepted it. She handed her straw sunbonnet to Stella. The girl slid the parka over her head and worked her hands through the sleeves so she could shut the short zipper at the throat. The hood hung in back.

Stella clowned with the hat. It was too small for her so she tried to balance it on her head. It kept sliding off one way or another, on purpose of course. The little one giggled in amusement but they were both yawning and their eyelids were drooping. Within just a couple of minutes they were both soundly asleep.

While the waitress had been amusing her little charges, John was asking Marian, "Do you mind messing your pretty hair? You'll be a lot warmer if you put the hood up and tighten that drawstring."

The girl did so and said, "Thank you so much Mr. Knox. This is much nicer." Because of drooping over her much narrower shoulders and also because of their height difference, the waist hung near her knees. And there was a warm muff-like pocket at the belly where she could put chilled hands if she elected to keep the cuffs rolled up.

John turned to Bernard, who like the two youngest had limbs covered by trousers and sleeves. John also noticed that except for Marian's open sandals and his hiking boots, all wore canvas shoes with rubber soles. He handed his wrinkled jacket to him and said, "Here, slip this on, Buddy. It'll keep the chill off you."

"Thank you, Sir, but what about you and Miss Juarez?"

"I was getting around to us. Stella, do you mind using this campfire smoke perfumed T shirt under your sweat shirt? I'll keep the sweaty one."

Neither of the adults were uncomfortable yet but an extra layer would be welcome later. She slipped into the ladies' room and left the door a bit ajar for light, but stood out of the line of sight. The man did the same in the other room so as not to embarrass her. Then the three alert ones sat on the second sofa and John pulled up a chair and sat facing them.

43

In subdued tones so as not to disturb the sleepers, he talked about old Mikota customs and what life must have been like in 1804 when his ancestor John Knox had arrived. It was interesting but under the circumstances hard to concentrate. At about 2:30 there came an awkward lull.

Marian asked, "If people are working outside, shouldn't we hear something?"

John answered, "The thinnest rock wall between us and the outside is at least six feet thick so no sound will get through until they're right by the doors."

Bernie said, "So we're sealed in? Could we smother?"

"No way. Did you notice the suspended acoustical ceiling above us? There is a high dome roof which has many small openings to the outside. They're all closed off with fine mesh screen to keep out bats and insects but through them you could say this cavern breathes."

Stella said, "I don't know why I didn't think of it until now but there's a pay phone over there. I'll call the Café and see what's happening." She fished coins out of her purse and tried to make a call. "It's dead."

Bernard ventured, "I'll bet the phone line and power lines come in together. Maybe a rock slide severed them both."

John agreed, "We'll just have to wait patiently. There's nothing else we can do. No, that's not so. I'm wrong. We can all pray that everyone is okay outside and that help comes quickly."

At 1:55 as Gabe and Maria each had a foot on the bottom step of the porch; a blinding light had come from the parking lot. They were in the shade of the protecting Sentinel but luminance reflecting off the opposite canyon wall made everything look like a bleached out extremely over-exposed black and white photo. Along with the extraordinary light was a sudden sensation of intense heat, enough thermal energy to blister skin and ignite fires way up the street had it persisted.

This was followed by an ear-numbing shock wave of sound which had immeasurable decibels of volume. Instantly on the tail of the noise came a blast of air expanding down the street at tornadic speeds. Windows and doors across the narrow river were devastated, broken glass flying, doors torn off their hinges and flung tumbling. In the lee of the Sentinel the Café suffered a caved in front plate glass window and smashed street facing upstairs panes. No building within two blocks escaped damage but the structural concrete mainly suffered a scarring of the painted facades.

Both Gabe and Maria were knocked face down onto the steps and he instinctively covered her with his body and threw his right arm over her head. Then he placed his face against that arm and covered the back of his head with his left. Though his vision was dazzled and blurred from the blinding light, he could make out as if in slow motion a black on white silhouette of the Harley gyrating through the air and crashing against the other river bank.

Almost simultaneously he saw a car tumble end for end over the guard rail into the river followed by two others. One slid on its roof spinning like a giant top and the other rolling over on its side, but both remained on the road. And then there were several lesser blasts and a great outpouring of fire, the flames of which belched up cliff high.

He'd scrambled to his feet yanking Maria up with him and they'd bounded up the steps into the Café yelling, "Get away from the side windows. Get down behind the counter."

The ladies were the only patrons at that off hour. They were at a table near the counter. The entire on-duty staff happened to be in the kitchen behind the counter. The sudden noise and the urgency of the warning gave impetus to Maxine's group to move quickly as told. They all ducked down in back of the counter. But in the long mirror behind

45

them they saw a sudden rain of dirt and stone and then billiard table size slabs of dirt come down blocking the entrance to the Sentinel rooms. Some falling stones bounced against the side windows of the Café and shattered them but no one was hurt by flying glass. The only minor injuries sustained had been when the young couple had fallen on the steps.

But others were not so lucky, particularly those in the shops across the river. That side had no protection from the Sentinel. One man was blown off the bridge near the Post Office. Fortunately he was a good swimmer but the current was too strong for him to get to the bank. But the bridge where the Sheriff had done his job had cables stretched across in the water to prevent foolish boaters from being swept to their death in Knox Rush. The man in the water was able to use the cables to get to shore. The only damage to him was a few scratches and damaged clothing. Many others had worse injuries but none were life threatening. Flying glass had cut several and some had bruises from being knocked down.

A tourist by the name of Clarence Henderson was on the middle bridge about a half mile from the site using a video camera with a good telephoto lens to capture the river, the shops along it, the cliffs, the Narrows, and the spider web of cable which held the S curve span. It was an imposing sight.

Clarence had his fifteen minutes in the spotlight. He had been looking at the video screen and had not been blinded by the awesome light. He had recorded continuously for over fifteen minutes and from the video and his eye-witness account the authorities later were able to establish the exact sequence of events. Excerpts of his tape appeared on CNN and the major networks that evening.

The most awful part of the disaster happened several minutes after the initial blast. The prelude to the worst was when harmonic vibrations and shock waves caused what

46

John had called the Sentinel to loose his cap and come tumbling down. A slanting fault line near the top of the monolith had been secure for centuries but the chain of unnatural stresses had made the top shift, slide, and fall. There had been so much erosion that the crack which had always been there had never been seen.

But this tip-top tipped layer also occurred about fifty feet below the top of the Narrows. Again erosion had hidden the fact. The geologist who had checked the area with small charges of explosives and seismometers or whatever they call their sophisticated equipment had missed the tiny problem. Thus it was an event deemed totally impossible when a semi trailer sized slab of rock face on the north side of the Narrows broke loose and twanged cables before falling on the structure of the bridge.

Two cars were entering the S curve as it happened. Through his open sun roof the lead driver happened to see it break loose and floored the throttle to get out from under. As he left the bridge he had to make two squealing turns to avoid the two burning cars on the street. Then a momentary wall of flame shot in front of him and in swerving to meet it he slammed into the end of the railing of the foot bridge. The car stalled and the man, his wife, and two teens bailed out and ran away from the fire with all their might.

The trailing car's driver skidded to a stop about fifty feet onto the steel span after seeing what was happening and burned rubber in reverse until he was well down the ramp. He slid the car to a stop, did a 180 degree turn creasing his car against the guard rail in the process, and drove as fast as he could to flee the Territory. Even as he was backing up, more rock was breaking loose. Small avalanches began cascading down from both sides.

As the weight on the steel bridge rose to double and triple its maximum design capacity riveted plates began popping free and cables broke away, some from the ironwork and some from above. As the load on the remaining cables went vastly beyond design limits, they began to snap like guitar strings. The stress on the rest caused their anchors to the top to begin cracking the rock and shifting it along the fault line. The deluge of granite accelerated as the S span broke into pieces and fell into the Corkscrew.

Only minutes were required for the total demolition of the bridge. When all was over the faces of the Narrows would be unrecognizable. Worse than that, the rapids were sealed by a monstrous pile of intermingled structural iron, cables, earth, gravel, rocks, boulders, and slabs of rock. A dam had been built which would hold back a lake about 35 feet deep at the Narrows and reach all the way back to the Dundee Grand Hotel. Much of the village would be flooded in varying amounts. The waters would eventually cut channels between slabs of stone, but it might be decades before the work was accomplished. And what would be found out later might render the assistance of engineers with their blasting powder out of the question.

As soon as it seemed to the people huddled in the Café that the rock fall was over, they got up in a daze and hurried to the windows to look out. The Cannonball was completely buried. It took a few seconds for the implications of this to sink in to the adults. Jolene just looked puzzled.

"Mein Gott in Himmel, the children!! My baby's in there and Jojo. Hurry. We have to dig them out." No one could have said or done anything to stay Maxine, nor did they try. She rushed to the pile and got down on her hands and knees to attack it. She quickly ruined her shoes and hose and bloodied her knees and hands. She wailed out, "Help me. Please help me. My baby."

She clawed away loose dirt at the bottom of the heap and threw rocks behind her. The other two weeping mothers threw themselves down on each side of her and added their efforts. The pile was so big that had it all been sand and had the three been experts with shovels and wheelbarrows, it might have taken more than a week. But the pile was not sand. There was only a little dirt filling the cracks between tangled rocks and boulders and slabs many of which were wedged behind the buried Cannonball.

Minimal understanding but elemental fear motivated Jolene. Her baby needed her. She picked up stones and staggered with them to the guard rail to splash them into the water. The mothers were pouring heart and soul into an exercise in futility but at this point in time no amount of reason or persuasion could stop the operation of mother love.

Gabe heard the noise at the Narrows and stared at it with the DuPres family members. It was like a modern movie's computer generation which looked real but could not possibly be happening. He said to the rest around him, "Try to stop the ladies from hurting themselves. I'll try to bring help."

He took off running toward the Post Office. Other municipal offices there surely should have people who could radio out for help and perhaps call in the little Caterpillar which had been used to level the grounds around the new hotel. He did not think there was any more danger from slides.

A greater danger came from other sources. All the fuel tanks had blown off their tops throwing tons of liquid fire onto the cliff walls behind them, into the river, and all over the parking lot and adjacent street. Perhaps half of the fuel had been retained by the concrete walls and could burn sootily all through that day and most of the next. The heat was no danger to anyone not in the immediate vicinity.

What was actually worse was the increasing deterioration of the air. A cloud of fog-like dust was moving up the canyon from the various avalanches. It could be very irritating and the least effect would be to cause coughing spells. To people with asthma or emphysema it could be life-threatening.

But a greater danger was the mixture of sulfur and other oxides from the fireworks truck which had gone up in an instant, coupled with smoke and fumes from the petroleum conflagration. A diesel mist added its noxiousness to the other fumes. And if anyone would check they would also find very dangerous level of carbon monoxide.

To these there must be added one long-life enemy. The dust from the initial explosion had spread in all directions finding lodging on any horizontal surfaces not shielded by the Sentinel. But much of it had gone straight up and there would be fall-out for several miles around.

Mitch had fired up the diesel just as the explosion took place and then declined to drive toward the trouble with his passengers. The noise had instantly initiated action by the two Public Safety Officers assigned to the Hidden Valley. Sergeant Howard Smith and Patrolman Clyde Clearskies were in their Jeep and racing back from the Dundee Grand Hotel before Mitch had decided to take his empty bus to the Knox Rush end of town to get his passengers and any others who wanted a ride.

Gabe heard the police siren and flashing light before he was halfway to the Bluebird bus. He flagged them down and tersely gave his report. Officer Clearskies got on the radio and a fortunate signal bounce off the Sentinel and through the now wider Narrows was received by a patrol approaching on the Hidden Valley Spur and then relayed to headquarters in Glasgow. Then a call was made to locate the Caterpillar operator.

Howard was top ranking Mikotan official on the scene and as such responsible for the immediate response. He saw the dust rolling over them and smelled the abrasive air and came to a quick conclusion, that of evacuating everyone and moving them to the hotel. With the help of Ray DuPres and his sons Charles and Frank, the mothers were forced to their feet and forbidden to continue. Bonnie threw her arms around Jolene trying to calm her as the distraught girl kept bawling out, "Jojo, Jojo, Jojo."

The Sergeant said sternly but kindly, "You can't stay here. We all have to leave."

Maxine sniffled as she said, "But we can't leave our babies. They're under there. We have to get them out."

"Please look around, will you? Where's the bridge now? Knox Rush is dammed. The water is blocked. It'll back up to where we are and more. And look at the size of the pile blocking the entrance."

Corinne's eyes flashed as she yelled, "That's why we can't stop. We have to get them out before it's too late."

"Ladies, my partner is right now calling for a bulldozer. And the way the air is fouling, he'll have to wear a gas mask. He'll do the job, but you can't be here in his way. All of you have to leave."

Quiet and tractable Bernice vehemently protested. "No! We won't go without our children."

"If you won't listen and come with me voluntarily, I'll arrest all of you and call it protective custody. But you will come. You've no choice."

The same steel was in his voice that had been in the Sheriff's. If they were thrown in jail how could they do anything? But what was more convincing were the tears welling up in his eyes and how tenderly he said, "I know how you feel. I have three kids of my own. I love all children. It tears me apart when any child is hurt or threatened. You have my solemn promise everything possible will be done to return your children safely to your arms.

At 3:00 P.M. Esther Crowe, armed with high powered Bushnell binoculars, scanned the Narrows from a safe altitude in MAF 1. Glasgow had an air strip for small planes and had a control shack but no control tower. It was primarily for official or emergency use. It was not intended for tourists but if the need arose they could use it. The Territory owned one beautifully maintained Piper Cub for search missions and fire patrols. It was proudly named Mikota Air Force One.

The Hidden Valley had no air strip. First of all, planes are too noisy and intrude on the tranquil serenity for both humans and wild animals. Secondly, too much beautiful forest land would have to be cleared and the meadows were full of rock formations which would have to be leveled. Thirdly, the rapidly shifting winds off and between the mountains brought turbulence and down drafts that the amateur pilot might be able to safely cope with.

Esther's grandson, Sidney Crowe, was piloting the Cub. He was one of three authorized to fly it. As soon as she'd heard of the disaster she'd convened the Tribal Council via conference lines to make an immediate decision and set up a meeting later in the day. She'd also ordered her staff to call for Federal assistance as well as to inform the Salvation Army and the Red Cross.

A smoggy layer now blanketed the village most of the way to the Dundee Grand Hotel. Visibility was down to less than fifty yards in the inversion layer, but it was only thirty feet thick. She could see quite clearly looking right down into it.

A crew of six men wearing construction hardhats and gas masks were at the Sentinel. One drove the bulldozer, vainly trying to clear a way to the doors. The five other men wielded picks and shovels attempting to clear enough space behind some of the slabs of rock so they could slip cables behind them and tug them free from their wedged in places.

Esther saw how the river already had flooded the parking lot which was the lowest point in town. She knew that the entrance to the Sentinel was a few feet higher that the lot and that the inner passage sloped up so the floor was about on level with the porch of the Café. Two questions plagued her. Had the ceiling of the restrooms collapsed and could the opening be cleared before the water rose too high?

She knew John well and also his uncle whom she had learned was out of town. Her people were right then making an effort to reach him. She prayed she'd not have to speak at the young man's funeral as she had done at his parents'. She had so much looked forward to grooming him to take over her job. And there was the waitress, such a pretty girl, so polite and helpful when Esther had dropped in for lunch a few days earlier. "Oh Lord, there are four children, too. Please help us get them all out safely."

She saw a few tourists using their cars to bring the others to the hotel. Far behind them, moving at snail's pace, was good Mitchell Knox in the Bluebird getting stragglers. Behind the bus was the Jeep, loudspeaker ordering folks to higher ground. Bus and Jeep were moving slowly enough to stay even with a group of volunteer adults and teens who were successively searching buildings to make sure no one was left behind in the evacuation process,

By 3:30 the village was empty save for the six struggling workers who strained desperately in their futile task. Even if they had been making inroads on the pile, they could never have beaten the rising water which kept inching upward.

There were more than 400 gathered in and around the hotel. The town power was off but the emergency generator of the hotel was effectively meeting the needs there. Snacks and beverages were freely offered to all and anyone could have had free supper and lodging. The bruised and cut were being tended by the village nurse ably assisted by an LPN on vacation and a former G.I. Medic.

At 3:55 a number of large twin rotor military choppers set down on the impressive lawn in front of the hotel. A contingent of troops all wearing protective white suits with what looked like space helmets disembarked. They could either breathe through filtration canisters or switch to a self contained oxygen system on their backs.

Eight of the soldiers carried equipment to test the air for biological or chemical threats and also had Geiger counters to determine radiation levels. These men only carried pistols. Six soldiers were unarmed and carried cases of first aid and necessary medical equipment. The rest were fully armed, combat ready.

No vehicles had to be commandeered for civilians were glad to volunteer their cars or vans for ground transport for the troops. Six of the eight environment testing men went toward the Corkscrew, or what had been it. The other two checked around the hotel and declared it safe. The civilians were herded into the grand dining room which could easily handle a banquet for over 400. There was a stage at the focal point of the big room.

A precisely moving husky man with silver hair cropped close marched in and stepped up onto the stage followed by another person. He took off the space helmet and the female officer with him did the same. She sat on a chair behind him as he took the microphone.

"I am Major Harold Russell and this is my aide Captain Jennifer Harding. I wish to apologize for any scares we may have given when we arrived in these protective garments and also for any seeming rudeness when we ordered you all in here. Like my men you probably think me pretty bossy but I was acting on behalf of your personal safety.

"You see, we came in with inadequate intelligence of the situation and had to be prepared for the worst. There have been times we have been called in and then been fired upon by rioters or looters. You have all been well behaved, cooperative, and helping one another. That makes me very proud of you. But we couldn't know that for sure until we got here.

"Then there is the matter of these suits over our uniforms. This could have involved chemical or biological terrorism with an explosion to start off the trouble. We came prepared. We just didn't know. We did receive word that a truckload of fireworks had gone up, so even a bad accident was not out of the question. But as we flew over we could see there was much more damage than could have been triggered by pyrotechnic devices. We're not absolutely certain yet.

"Relax if you can. As soon as we know for sure we'll inform you. I for one will appreciate a few minutes to take a break. I was up all night at the hospital with my daughter and my son-in-law. They had a baby boy. I'm a grandpa now."

He was applauded as he went down to a table where two of his men flanked him to give him room from the crowd. But Maxine and the three others approached him looking distressed and he motioned his body guards to back off and beckoned to the ladies to sit down with him. They had been cleaned up and scratches and bruises attended to. They had been given mild sedatives and were much calmer. Maxine told him of the six trapped in the Sentinel rooms.

The man who had momentarily relaxed now tensed up and called his aide over to him. "Captain Harding, find out if any of our men can drive a bulldozer. Then as soon as we have an all clear from our sniffers send him and a half dozen volunteers to help those rescue workers and give them a break. We must speed up that work. Let the volunteers know there are children at risk."

"God bless you," and "How can we ever thank you?" came from three ladies as they all grabbed for the Major's hands and squeezed them. Jolene dimly realized the man in a funny white pair of pajamas was going to try to bring her son back to her. She came up beside him and gave him a tight hug and a sloppy kiss on the cheek and said, "Thank you, Rabbi." The officer was a bit embarrassed and puzzled until Maxine said, "Rabbi is the most respectful thing she knows to call someone."

The group waited for what seemed hours but was actually only 20 minutes before the Major wearily mounted to the stage. He had just had a private conference with the men he had called sniffers and had issued a recall to all to join them at the hotel. He took the mike, sighed, and came to attention.

"I deeply regret having to inform you that all is not well. The smog is toxic but any by-products of combustion such as is taking place would be. If that was our only problem, we'd hang out here tonight. My latest meteorological report is for a heavy rain tonight and that could wash most of the pollutants out of the air. With just that problem we would continue trying to open up the Sentinel until the water got too high.

"But as my men moved toward the fallen bridge they encountered a spotty pattern of radioactivity. The spots were closest together across the river from the Sentinel and very hot there. But radiation levels increased dangerously as the now flooded parking lot was approached and my men backed off as they are supposed to. The lot was obviously ground zero. At the Post office the levels were acceptable for short visits.

"The standing water behind the dam was very murky and had a dangerous level but what was in it will probably settle to the bottom so that when the river reaches the overflow point the water will most likely be safe down stream but will require monitoring. There is also a small amount of suspended dust but there is a light breeze from the west which should keep it away from us until the rain settles it.

"It's my guess a small nuclear device was set off. My men have taken samples of dust and water. These are in lead enclosed bottles and will be analyzed tomorrow by experts who should be able to determine the type of device used.

"But we are all leaving the valley. We will all be checked with Geiger counters and necessary decontamination attended to. Those without any traces will be taken out first but we will not separate families. Shoes will be most likely to be contaminated for any of us who have walked on dust. We will provide sandals but radiated shoes will stay behind.

"Should you have any readings on your person besides on your shoes you will be required to thoroughly shower and dispose of any suspicious clothing and underwear, coveralls, and jackets will be provided as well as the sandals. But nothing radiated comes out and we cannot bring luggage or other personally items along.

"You will be flown to Glasgow and every person will receive individual post trauma stress and medical checkups. Medications such as insulin or for your heart will be provided should you not have it on your person now. Also I've been informed the Mikota Nation intends to give you market value on vehicles abandoned and replacement cost on anything else.

"By 1700, that's 5:00 P.M., a tent city will be going up to house those who were lodging in the valley. Employees who work in the valley but live outside will be provided transportation to their homes after their medical check up.

"We can thank God for the Salvation Army and the Red Cross. Disaster units from each are already near Glasgow. The Salvation Army has come with clothing and food primarily, and the Red Cross is engaged in setting up the tent city. The important plus of the Salvation Army is they have brought in many salvationist Officers who will be holding small services, praying for folks, and counseling people on an individual basis as needed, in general encouraging folks. So you'll all be well cared for."

Corinne O'Connor yelled out, "But what about our children behind the rock pile?"

There had been a lot of murmuring and whispering in the dining hall until this question rang out. Now there came total silence. The Major cleared his throat and paused before answering.

"This is one of those times I hate my job and what I have to do. No officer likes it when he has to make decisions as to whether others live or die. I would to God there was another course open to me. But I absolutely cannot allow any of you to have their lives or health jeopardized. And the valiant six civilians who tried so hard are forbidden to go back."

By 1730 no known living souls were left to be airlifted out. Plastic signs that said, "Danger! No trespassing! RADIATION!" and had on them the distinctive symbol had been affixed to all doors of all buildings as far west as the Post Office. At this point all intersections of the cross streets were blocked by overturned vehicles. The Bluebird lay on its side blocking the Valley Spur to the Narrows.

At 7:00 P.M. Esther Crowe and the eight members of the Tribal Council appeared live on CNN from the Council Hall. All wore traditional beaded buckskin and feathered headdresses. All carried ceremonial lances, symbols of their authority. The other networks would be rebroadcasting later.

Esther exuded an aura of strength and control. Her sure smooth movements, her keen eyes and determined expression, the way she tossed her vertical lance from hand to hand without looking or letting either end of it contact a thing; all this caused one cameraman to whisper to one of his helpers before air time, "They say she's 80. I sure wouldn't go up against that old broad in a dark alley."

When she spoke it was with a strong clear voice. "A terrible thing happened today. A gift of God to my people was despoiled by a stranger. It was an act of hate. We have no idea why. We are a religious people, a Christian Nation of many denominations. We all believe there exists a most evil one opposed to God and goodness who rebelled ages ago and considers himself the god of this world. He blinded the eyes of a young man to do a dastardly deed. This person was Mr. Humphrey Bogardus. We are certain he died in the very blast he set off while obeying Satan.

"We do not rejoice in the death of a wicked sinner. We hope that he like the thief on the cross repented and believed in time but we think it is highly unlikely. We are sad that Mr. Bogardus threw away his life for an evil cause.

"We are even sadder that six others, two with Mikota blood in their veins, and four we had welcomed as visitors also were victims. We have chosen Friday as a day of mourning over them for all our people and we shall be having a memorial service. But right now we are not mentioning their names until all their relatives have been notified.

"We are also regretful that vacationers who were enjoying the Hidden Valley suddenly faced an awful time and some were hurt. We thank the Lord that none of them suffered serious harm.

"We also wish to extend our sincere thanks to the Federal Government for its rapid response to our request for help. Particularly we wish to say thank you to Major Russell and his soldiers for their thoughtful and wise actions. And we have great gratitude to the Salvation Army and Red Cross whose joint efforts have been helping evacuees make a transition back toward normal.

"Finally I come to the real reason for this air time. We have been told there is a possibility a miniature nuclear device may have been the instrument of destruction. The village of Dundee has areas of radiation which will be there for many years to come. The lake forming behind the dam also has lethal leftovers from the event. We have named it Blast Lake.

"By plane I personally inspected the eastern end of the valley before the troops arrived. I convened a meeting of the Council as soon as I got back. We had to make some very difficult decisions. The report to us by Major Russell regarding the radiation confirmed the necessity for our decisions.

"God gave us the valley. He let us discover and use it centuries ago. We have been blessed by it for hundreds of years. On this day we abdicate any and all use of it. We return it to our Maker for the use of His wild creation. We include any mountain men or hermits in our permission to use it for they never harm it and just wish to live as wild creatures do alone and undisturbed.

"In the light of what has happened, we therefore forbid anyone from entering the Hidden Valley. We forbid aircraft from flying over it or landing in it. It is to be set aside for God's use with our profound thanks to Him for our past use of it. We apologize to Him that we were not wise enough to prevent what happened.

"We speak for the Mikota Nation. We are the elected representatives of our people. We are their voice. We decree the Hidden Valley exists no more. It is now the Forbidden Valley. How say the Council?"

In order from eldest to youngest the Tribal dignitaries responded first in Mikotan and then in English, "So be it!" As soon as they had spoken each person accented his words by sharply rapping the unpointed end of his lance on the floor three times.

When each had responded, Esther declared, "The people have spoken through their Council. The decree is binding on all who dwell in or enter the Mikota Territory. So be it!"

She loudly rapped three times with her lance making the act final. With great dignity the members left, again the eldest first followed by the youngest. Esther remained to be interviewed by CNN and to answer all their questions.

Thus the now Forbidden Valley was doubly cut off from the rest of the world. It was cut off by Mikotan Law. The people themselves and their police patrols would vigilantly keep intruders out. But should some be foolish enough to evade the guardians and somehow scale the Narrows, the invisible guards of radiation could get them.

Chapter Four

AN OMINOUS SUMMER EVENING

At about the time the helicopters arrived, the little ones were soundly asleep and the older children playing Othello. John had taken a pocket set along camping lest he have to kill time in the tent on a rainy day. Stella was on the sofa watching the game.

John had moved one of the ladder back chairs away from the wall and had tilted it back and rested with his heels on the second chair in front of him. His head was cradled by his fingers interlaced behind it, his knuckles against the wall.

He appeared to be dozing for his eyes were shut and his breathing regular and shallow through his open mouth. Stella smirked as she noticed this for she thought he would soon be snoring. But he was just fully relaxed yet alert. He had been pondering their circumstances and had begun to pray silently.

"Father, I haven't spent much time with you lately. Been getting careless. Even forgot my Bible when I went camping. And now here I am needing to lead others a while and how can I do that right if I'm not following you close? I'm so sorry. I haven't gone astray in my treatment of others and I haven't ignored human needs or offended anyone I know of. But I have ignored you and that's worse than if I'd hurt anyone else.

"I do intend to build my prayer altar in my heart again. I got so busy being too busy in those last few weeks of school I chose the wrong path. I put you, if not last, third or fourth. Please, my Father, forgive me for slighting you and neglecting your Word. I want to correct all those things.

"I humbly repent and seek to make changes and go back where I ought to be, and since you know my thoughts and intents, and since you love me and gave your Son to redeem me from sin, and since you promised to mend everything between us, and since I have confessed my sin, I claim Your promise to forgive me and cleanse me through the power of Jesus' blood.

"And Lord, you know I am perplexed by our situation. I have no idea what is happening outside or how our rescue is coming along. I am stymied as to what I should be doing or if I should be doing anything. I haven't a clue. Please give me wisdom. And if you would see fit to send a sign or two to direct me, let me be conscious of your leading.

"And no matter what happens to me, please protect the children and Stella. And all this I bring to you, Father, in the name of your Son, My Lord and Savior, Jesus Christ, Amen."

Having been an outdoorsy person all his life, and having early learned to be aware of sights and sounds and smells, college days had been difficult for him for his environment was constantly polluted by smells and noises. Things there had never been anything like the serene purity of his Hidden Valley home in the Bittersweet Range. It had taken a couple of weeks after his return to get back to normal. The 3F time and the camping had restored his senses.

The man suddenly got up being careful not to make too much noise which might rouse the little ones. He stepped back and forth with his head tipped up sniffing the air. Stella asked quietly, "What's wrong, John?"

63

"Do you smell anything out of the ordinary like smoke or sulfur or diesel?"

"No, I don't think so. Do you, children?" Marian and Bernie both looked up, took whiffs, and shook their heads no.

John stepped up close to the players and said, "Probably my imagination. I must be getting old. How's the tournament going?"

Marian said a little smugly, "Pretty good. Two to one in my favor. He beat the first one and thought he was pretty smart so I took him down a peg." But they were both enjoying the other's company so much that neither really cared about wins and losses.

John returned to his chair and beckoned to Stella to sit near him so they could quietly converse. "When Jojo and Juliet wake up, they'll each want their mothers and probably be hungry, too. As to the first, do you think you could keep them distracted and amused until rescue or bed time, whichever comes first?"

"Oh yes, John, I'd be glad to. I've had tons of experience." Bernie chimed in, "I'll help too. I know lots of little things he likes." Marian added, "I'll do whatever I can, too."

John smiled and said, "You are all godsends. Bless you. But we have a different problem, food. My Uncle Lionel told me a snack machine was on order but not due until Friday. It would vend candy and cookies and such. But it's tough to get what's not here yet. However, when I got the clothes out of my pack I discovered some munchies there. I hadn't put them there so it must have been my uncle to surprise me. So we've got two snack packs of raisins and two of M&M's."

Bernie offered, "That should be plenty for the little guys with a big drink of water. As for me I would very much like to practice self-discipline and go on a fast until breakfast."

Marian replied, "If a mere boy can do it, it ought to be easy for a girl. Count me in."

John told them he knew their motives were to help the sleepers and such actions were the kind that made God smile. They returned to their game. Then the waitress and manager-to-be had a nice chat telling about home life. Stella told a humorous tale of how a pipe had sprung a leak in the basement and how her brothers' repair attempt had made it twice as bad flooding the basement.

Marian heard this and looked up ready to ask a question just as John stood again and said, "There it is again. Diesel and sulfur. Am I hallucinating smells?"

Stella wrinkled her nose and said, "If you are, it makes two of us."

Marian said, "Three!"

Bernie added, "Four! But where's it coming from?"

They all paced around sampling the air until they agreed it was strongest in the very dark museum room. John offered an explanation, "Those air passages I mentioned in the rock admit air on the windward side and wind going around the Sentinel will draw air out on the opposite side. Remember I said it breathes? So if there was a bad accident involving a diesel and it was burning close to the tower we'd smell it. I just hope the Bluebird Bus wasn't involved. But we'll solve the mystery as soon as we get out."

The Othello was resumed and John said to Stella, "Now tell me the conclusion to your water-logged tale."

But before she could continue, Marian said, "Excuse me please, but I have a question and I hate it if I don't get answers to questions."

"Go ahead, Honey."

"Okay. I saw that all the pipes go into the floor. If they have a leak do they have to tear up tile and floor and everything to fix it?"

"Good question. The answer's no. There's a crawl space under the bathrooms and this room. The true profile of this part of the cave is like a slightly flattened garden hose. If you look close you'll see chrome rings around all pipes where they enter the floor. The holes the pipes go through are considerably bigger than the pipes and the rings cover the gaps."

The girl asked, "So is there a hidden trap door to get to the crawl space and did they have to drill real long holes to get the pipes in and where do the pipes come from?"

"Whoa, Marian. First there is no trapdoor. Second they didn't drill for the pipes, but they did do a bit of blasting. Well they had to do some drilling to blast for they needed holes for the charges, But the pipes and drain come in and go out through a storm sewer such as big cities use to drain streets."

Bernie said, "The more you said, the more confused I got."

"I'll try to unconfuse you. It was necessary to put a sub floor down first and steel trusses and planks were used. Three or four inches of concrete were poured over wire mesh which prevents cracking. No wood was used because it could rot. Drain and pipe holes were pre-cut into the steel and mesh before pouring. All repairs could be made by a pair of men with walkie-talkies, one above, one below. This floor right under us and the bathroom floors have that crawl space which varies from three to four feet in height."

Stella asked, "So there's no crawl space under the museum room? And there's a storm sewer I never heard of? And how do the workmen get to the crawl space?"

The man replied, "If you'd been in here before the work was done, you'd understand. The floor of the display room was very flat to start with and had cement poured over it to rid of bumps and cracks. It was about three or four feet above the crawl space, something like a split level, a half flight up. But beneath it, opening onto the lower level was a passage which went way back and came out at the back corner of Triangle Park. Before I go on maybe my buddy Bernie will tell us about that concrete building in that corner."

At this point his contemporaries at school would have dubbed him a walking guide book for he had pored over one the night before at the Glasgow Inn. But he was very pleased to be asked by John who seemed to know everything about Dundee.

"The construction people blasted a big hole in the corner lower than the opening to that passage. They built a big sunken tank to hold sewage from the Sentinel and all the houses up to the Post Office. There's another building there. They're both pump houses. All the sewage is automatically pumped to the sewage treatment plant at the other end of town, the high end. We heard the pump running once when we were in the Park."

Enlightenment showed on the boy's face and he said, "I get it now. The drains and pipes go through the passage to connect this place with the pump house."

John patted him on the back. "You've got it. The original passage was enlarged to put the storm sewer pipes through which are big enough to carry all the pipes and also allow room for a worker to scoot through to work underneath. But there's no way to get in it from here. It's concrete and steel under us. Oh. Let me show you something."

He led the three into the dark room and by penlight showed then what looked like a floor drain. "The storm sewer is flush with the rock here and both are covered by concrete. But this is an air vent, not a drain. The ventilation fan system has an exhaust tube which pulls air from under the ladies' room. Thus air is sucked into the crawlspace continually when the fans are running and it never gets damp or stale."

Somewhat past 4:30, about when the air lift was starting, a big yawning noise came out of the wide open mouth of the little blondie. "Ahhh. Mama?" She began to rub her knuckles against her eyes and repeated the yawn and call.

67

Before Juliet could even sit up and begin to cry, Stella had picked her up blanket and all said, "Hi, Sweetheart. Shh. Jojo is still asleep. We mustn't wake him. After he gets up you can play together until Mama comes." Stella's back was to the others and they all smiled and waved back as the wee one peeked over her protector's shoulder and waved. Then she whispered something into Stella's ear.

The young woman said, "John, may I borrow your flash light? We ladies need to be excused. You too, Marian?"

As the three were absent, Bernie asked, "If the power is off, how come we have water pressure?"

"It's gravity feed. Just beyond the hotel and several stories higher is one of those towers that resemble a golf ball on a tee. It has a smiley face on it."

As the ladies' room was vacated, another country was heard from, the little boy loudly asking for his Mama and Auntie Max. Bernie jumped over to him and did as Stella had done. "They'll come later. I'll take care of you." Juliet came over to peek-a-boo her new friend and they were soon playing on their sofa and wrestling for the pillow.

Marian asked, "Is it getting darker in here?"

Indeed it was. The gradual depletion of the battery during the two hours of nap time had caused such a slow dimming of the bulbs that moment by moment it was imperceptible, but once attention and memory were focused, it was obvious it was many degrees darker. John was sure there'd be no more light within an hour. He thought quickly and then announced, "Time for lantern light and after a while we'll have a candle light picnic. Won't that be a lot of fun?"

John had a digital readout sportsman's watch whose battery was nearly dead and at times the LCD numerals were hard to make out, especially in the dim light. He had noticed Bernie's beautiful new Bulova which had been a Bar Mitzvah gift along with CDs of the bank not music type. The lad told him, "It's 4:39. I checked it against the time reading on the Weather Channel this morning in our rooms at the Glasgow Inn."

John fished his candle lantern out of his pack and put his Bic lighter and an almost empty box of Rosebud matches in his shirt pocket. He was well aware of how long the small candles burned and estimated it could give light until about 8:00. After lighting it he showed it around. It was about the size of a coffee mug.

"Stella, isn't this about the size of the votive candles you burn at St. Peter's Chapel?" She agreed. "You wouldn't happen to have a few in you purse, would you?" They both laughed.

John disconnected the hot wire from the battery in the special locker and then he and Bernie disconnected the two bulbs in the waiting room. Next he reconnected one of the bulbs in the display room which could shine down toward the air vent. The man explained that letting the battery lie dormant a few hours might help it build up a bit for later.

Many of the display cases were like those in candy shops or bakeries. They were glass on three sides and with plate glass tops which could serve as counters. The back glasses of most cases were mirrors to show the backs of artifacts and also to better diffuse the light of the fluorescent fixtures in them. The mirror on the wall behind the case nearest the floor vent had been intended for a taller case and extended a couple of feet above the case. John placed the lantern on this case's counter.

The four older ones now dragged the sofas into the museum room and arranged them in a shallow vee facing the candle, the vent midway between sofas and case. The little ones pounced on their sofa and played as before, once in a while peeking over the back at the visible but very dimly lit room behind them.

Stella and the older kids chatted about their backgrounds. Bernie mentioned his home town of Evanston, Illinois and his father's tax consultation and accounting firm with twenty employees. He mentioned the museums and zoos he loved in the Chicago area. Marian's home was Elmhurst and she liked the same places he did. They had a lot of geography in common.

John pled the need to stretch his legs and began pacing in the dark, always with the candle as a star to guide him. He thought of many things that had been directing his thinking. The yet present smell in the air, though not irritating could be a warning. A sign? And if the smell kept coming, must that not mean a fire was still burning? And if it was still burning, why was it? The big fire trucks from Glasgow would have come to help the village volunteers and foam should have snuffed out any blaze. So if it was still burning, either it was too big a blaze for the departments to put out or they had not come or both. And if the blaze was near the Cannonball, that could prevent rescuers from clearing a passage inside. Where did all this leave them without an exit?

He remembered an incident during construction of these unique rooms a number of years back when he had helped on the job during his summer vacation while in High School. At lunch time one of the workers had lagged behind to finish a few more minutes of nailing as the rest went out for lunch. They had barred the big doors so he couldn't get out to eat. One of the crew had ducked into the Santa Fe Café and got a couple of tacos and a can of pop and had then crawled through the sewer pipe, lifted the grate, and deposited the food on the floor and then closed the vent.

He had then called in spooky tones, "I am the ghost of Christmas to come. If you are a good boy I might let you out on Christmas Eve." Upon being freed a while later the prisoner had announced, "Shucks, if you keep feeding me like that I might not want to come out."

The chain of references to trap doors and drilling pipes and the crawl space and plumbing had jogged his memory as to the prank. He had been one of the instigators. He began to wonder if the smell and memory were subtle signs to lead him.

He pondered more and realized that if a hole had to be broken through later to put in a trap door, the vent was in the ideal location. It would be too hard to go through the floor over the crawl space. There was reinforcing mesh in the concrete and steel under it. It would require acetylene torch work and then welding to return strength to the structure of the floor above the crawl space.

But the cement poured in the museum had no reinforcing. There were three inches or less above the center of the storm drains and to put in a trap door or manhole cover would only require going through a maximum of eight inches. Of course the storm drains were of cast cement and would probably have some mesh in them. Once he and the children were rescued, he would make this project one of high priority on his new job.

At 5:00 cups of water from the cooler were brought over to the counter by the candle for all of them. Next John set the candle by the vent and put his other blanket on the floor near it. He used his knife to make three slits in the middle of the children's half blankets. He helped them slip their heads through the middle slit and their arms through the other two

Stella said, "Now you have ponchos." Jojo stamped his feet and marched around the sofas raising and lowering his arms so the poncho flapped. Juliet copied her hero's actions. Marian giggled and said, "You are Poncho Jojo. You are Poncho Juliet. Now all we need is Poncho Villa."

The corners of the ponchos dusted the floor but not low enough to trip them. It took quite a bit of doing to get the irrepressible pair to settle down on their picnic blanket in front of their "campfire." They guzzled the water given them and asked for more. Bernie and Marian fetched it.

Stella opened the little boxes of raisins and told them it was their picnic food. Jojo remembered how his mother always gave him part of any goodies she had and said to him, "We share." He held the box up and said, "Jojo share." Each of the four dipped thumb and forefinger into his box and pretended to take a raisin out and then made a show of chewing and swallowing and rubbing their tummies. Juliet did the same as the boy and said, "I share too."

When the raisins were gone John got two Dixie cups from the cooler's dispenser and Stella dumped M&M's into them. Once again the tots held up their cups to share but the boy did stuff a couple into his mouth first. As soon as the picnic was over, the two returned to their padded leather play area, apparently satisfied regarding hunger for the time being.

The man put the candle back in front of the mirror and the room was better illuminated. Stella was about to fold up the picnic blanket but John motioned toward Marian and the girl was able to cover her bare legs with the blanket.

John opened up a conversation about his plan to initiate work on an escape hatch right where the floor vent was as soon as he was the Business Manager. They laughed over the account he told of the silly prank he had been involved in. He used a spooky voice to quote what had been said through the small vent opening.

Marian asked, "Mr. Knox, is that a secret tunnel?"

"Oh no, most of the people that work or live here are aware of it and many of the town's maintenance and repair people have been in it at one time or another."

The girl pondered briefly and then asked, "So if there are rescue workers trying to get us out, don't you suppose they'd have tried to phone us and when the phone was dead wouldn't someone have thought of getting in touch with us through the tunnel?"

Her questions caused a solemn moment but Bernie lightened it by quipping, "Yeah, the Santa Fe Café ought to have a Tunnel Takeout Service." There was a forced laugh. "I'd order another hot dog."

The boy became less flippant and asked, "Do you think if we took the vent grate off and yelled in the pipe the sound might be heard by someone playing in the Park?"

They tried but only heard a faint echo in reply. However the pump house was quite sound tight. And they concluded the outside power must also be off for none of them could remember hearing sounds of the pump since they had been trapped.

At 5:30 John had a powerful feeling that he ought to be doing something; he just wasn't sure what. He did not mind hard tasks; he reveled in them. The hardest thing for him was waiting and doing nothing. Stella's apprehension was great, her nerves frazzled, but she kept control because John had an untroubled appearance and always seemed to know the right thing to do or say. The older children were somewhat bothered but were looking at the whole thing like an adventure which they could share with friends back home. They tried to keep things carefree and comical for the little ones' sake.

John announced, "I'm sure we'll be getting out of here but it might take as many as eight to ten hours to clear away the debris. That could take us until way past our light burns out and I don't think any us would like to be sitting in the dark. I'm going to see what I can find in the custodian's closet or under the sink counters. Sometimes plumbers use wide candles to see under sinks. I'll hurry. My penlight is getting weak after all the use it had camping."

John entered the Ladies' room briefly and left it empty handed. But it took him longer in the Men's room and soon they heard him begin to whistle. The whistling stopped just before he came out for he held his light in his teeth. He carried a container of floor sealer and a fire extinguisher.

He set the things down, handed the light to Bernie and said, "C'mon along, Compadre. You'll be my light bearer."

When they came back out, Bernie had the light in one hand and a wringer-bucket half filled with water and a mop in the other. In one hand the man carried a second container of sealer and in the other a metal pot full of sand mounted on tripod legs. It was about two feet high and a sign had informed patrons that if they had to smoke, the butts belonged in the sand, not the urinal. Under his arms he also carried rolls of paper towel.

Stella asked, "What in the world is all that for?"

He replied, I thought a camp fire would be nice. Just kidding. Only a tiny fire to give us light. What does this label say on the can of sealer?"

Stella read out loud what he pointed at. "Danger! Flammable! Use only in well ventilated areas and avoid using in proximity to sparks or flames."

John said, "We've a full gallon can and one about half full. The idea came to me that if we shove a roll of towel down into the sand with just a couple of inches sticking up and then soak the towel and sand with thinner, it ought to burn for hours. But if it burns too fast we can extinguish it. If it throws any sparks, we can douse them with the wet mop. Of course there's not much in here that can burn. It's probably mainly the solvent that can burn but it's worth a try"

They prepared the torch pot as said. They moved the two sofas to the two sides of the display case on which the candle sat. They swung them out so they were facing each other at an angle with the case the base of a flat bottomed shallow Vee. The vent was between the ends of the sofas. John placed the contraption a couple of feet beyond the vent.

At 6:15 he cautiously lit it. It poofed once from accumulated fumes and then a yellow flame worked its way around the circular end of the towel roll. The flame increased until it was about two inches tall. It burned with a lot of smoke and some odor. John used the mop handle to pop up one of the two by four foot acoustical tiles and shifted it to the side above the torch. He opened another air circulation hole in the opposite corner of the room and then blew out the candle.

They all basked in the abundance of light. The odor of the resin mixed with some diesel smell and sulfur was noticeable but not obnoxious or irritating. Any little odor was endurable in exchange for the room being lit six-fold better.

They had a chance then to take a good look at the displays, but had to squint to read the labels. There were many Stone Age tools, not necessarily of Mikotan derivation. Mostly of flint were knives, axes, arrowheads, lance points, and also various tools for such tasks as scraping hides. Also displayed were purely Mikotan clothing with beads and feathers.

There was no jewelry or worked metal since the Mikotans had never found or tried to mine copper, silver, or gold such as some tribes had found and used. There were also on display besides the aforementioned military items, quite a collection of paleface metal work such as utensils, sabers, knives, and firearms used by Federal Troops during the Indian wars period.

But by 6:30 the bright mood induced by brighter light was fading away. They'd been there over four and one half hours with not one indication of rescue work. Stella and Bernie had taken seats by the little ones and were trying to keep them occupied and pacified. John and Marian were seated side by side on the other sofa. Marian was first to air her fears. Everything was weighing on her mind and her hunger pangs did not help.

"I know you don't want us to be scared, but I am. I know you keep telling us help will come and we'll see our mothers. And I'm sure you always try to tell the truth, but you're wrong. Help isn't coming. We won't see our mothers. You fixed us a bright light to keep us hopeful, but after it's gone and after the candle and flashlight are used up and the other battery is dead, it'll be pitch dark. And….And…. And…."

She was beginning to lose control. John held open his arm and she scooted up against him so he could circle her shoulders with his arm. She snuggled against him shivering, but not from cold. The others had not heard their words for they were singing silly nursery rhymes. He whispered, "And what, Honey?"

She sniffled, "And…And…And we'll all die in the dark and I'll never see my mother or the light again. I'm too scared to die in the dark."

He replied, "No! Absolutely not! I'm completely certain we won't die in the dark. You must keep hoping and praying. God is watching over us. I asked Him to."

She took a few raggedly deep breaths as she absorbed this, and then straightened up from leaning so hard against him. He asked, "Do you want me to take my arm away?"

"No. It feels strong like my father's arm used to when I'd be sad or scared and you even said words like he used to say about hoping and asking God." She nearly sobbed as she moaned out, "I miss him so much it hurts like crazy."

John said, "I wish I could have known him. Could you tell me about him?"

"I'll try. He died two years ago. An accident. My uncle and him owned a construction company. A cable broke on a crane and a big load of iron fell on him. He was trapped like us but crushed."

She spoke almost mechanically as from a memorized speech she had given over and over. Her mother Corinne had always insisted she speak out and not lock things in.

"If he was alive he'd tell a man to run a jackhammer and knock a hole to get us out. That's what he'd do. When

76

I was real little he took me to see his men working and one was using one and I got scared and cried but he held me and made he see everything was okay. Mr. Knox, can't you knock a hole for my daddy and get us out?"

She suddenly swiveled toward him and flung herself on his lap and threw her arms around his neck and asked plaintively, "Please get us out. Won't you do that for my daddy? There isn't anyone else who can. Please, please, I'm so scared."

He held her tight for a few minutes to lend whatever comfort a hug can. He whispered, "I don't have a jackhammer but I do have a rock chipping hammer and a hatchet. I don't know what I can do but I'll try as hard as I can. And you must be brave."

As she shifted back off his lap onto the cushion, he gave her a hankie to dry her eyes and cheeks. He smiled at her and said, "I'm getting an idea." He stood and announced to all, "I'm gonna try to knock a hole in the floor right there."

Bernie queried, "Have you got a drill or chisel?"

"Nope. Pitons. About a half dozen of them. They can be hammered into rock for climbing. Well what is concrete if not man-made rock?"

Putting a silly grin on his face he asked Stella, "Do you have a lipstick and a mirror in your purse? May I please use them?"

Wondering what kind of prank he had in mind, she fished them out and handed them over. "Thanks, Stella, I'll replace your Maddening Orange Gloss later. Or do you have a felt tip pen in there I could use instead to mark with?" She didn't.

He drew a rectangular figure on the floor after removing the vent grate. The figure was not a true rectangle for the corners were well rounded. It was roughly one by two feet in size and the vent opening was against a short end. The length of the figure followed the length of the sewer. From the vent hole the figure went towards the pump house. Had he gone across the pipe with what he hoped to use as a cutting guide line, he would have to cut through thicker cement.

He put on his sunglasses and explained, "I always wear these when I climb or want to chip away at a rock sample. Chips do fly up with force. Always protect your eyes. These are clear now but in direct sun light they turn a dark amber."

He moved the converted ash tray next to the display case and its mirror could thus give him maximum illumination. He put on a tight pair of cotton work gloves he often used while monkeying with firewood, brought his tools over to the reddish outline, and began to sing, "Hi ho, hi ho, it's off to work I go."

It was about 7:00 when he began to pound. He first attacked the short ceramic tile into which the grate fit. The bell end was of course up and flush. A few sharp raps with the flat reverse end of his hatchet head badly cracked it. A few rougher blows shattered it and the broken shards fell. Once it was out of the way, he used the mirror to reflect light down to see inside the sewer.

He announced, "It's big enough for Jojo and Juliet to walk in if they duck their heads. Us big guys will have to crawl. Didn't I tell you we had a crawl space?"

As he began to work in earnest he had an overpowering sensation that he was doing exactly what God wanted him to do. He was certain the Holy Spirit had somehow triggered thoughts and words of all to aim his thinking. Smells and crawl space and spooky words and pipes and vents, a young girl's fear and tears and jackhammer had sequentially worked to steer him.

He would let the theologians argue over just what constituted a sign. He knew he had been led. His knowledge was hindsight but he was convinced. He had followed the clues as surely as a good hunter follows signs of game to a successful conclusion of a hunt. As he worked he thanked God for leading him. His confidence showed so much through his smile and actions that the rest all had their hope increased.

Chapter Five

A LONG HARROWING SUMMER NIGHT

The pitons were effective but slow. He would start four or five of them to make a half circle at the edge of the existing opening. Then he would rap them successively deeper until a piece broke free. The first to break off had caused him to chuckle for it looked like the outline a person with teeth missing would make when taking a bit bite in a slice of bread.

And then another and another following the line he'd drawn. Progress was slow but he did make progress. Often the sharp end of his rock chipping hammer enabled him to break away pieces particularly as he got into thicker cement of which the bottom of the hole did not clean out easily. And then he began to encounter wire reinforcing in the sewer and his efforts were briefly thwarted.

He mentioned the problem. Bernie came to the rescue. "John, there were some horseshoes and nails used by the cavalry blacksmith in a case over there. I think I saw some files in there."

John checked and said, "God bless you, Hawkeye. Don't anyone get nervous. I'll pay for the damage later." He rapped the glass to break in and pulled out a hoof rasp and a file. "They used these to give a horse a manicure. I think I'll manicure those wires."

By the time 8:30 came around, the little ones were asleep. They had become hungry and cranky and close to impossible to mollify. John commented as they made an uproar, "Thank God they have such strong and healthy lungs." When the Knox clan had gathered in the Hidden Valley for yearly reunions, there had always been scads of very noisy little ones under foot and John had learned the line from so often hearing it from his Uncle Lionel. But John was relieved when the two had worn themselves out fussing and crying.

Jojo the dark haired dynamo was again sharing the inflated pillow with his golden haired friend. At her feet was seated Marian, at the boy's Bernie. The older ones made sure the sometimes tossing and turning did not uncover the little ones or roll them off the sofa.

Stella at first sat on the opposite sofa, ready to lend assistance by taking a turn now and again to relieve John's cramped limbs and tiring hands. They had both been pleasantly surprised at how Marian had sung the children to sleep. She had sung quietly to them but the man knew from playground yells that she had a strong voice. She had quite a repertoire of children's sung such as Puff, Rudolph, Peter Cottontail, and the like.

At 9:00 as he worked he realized he had only pounded a slot about a third of the way around. He prayed, "Lord, I'm not growing weary of well doing; I'm just getting weary. Help me to wisely ration my strength and let it be more than equal to my task. Thank you."

The thought immediately came to him that neither he nor Stella had shoulders or hips that were two feet across. A hole twelve by eighteen inches would be big enough for them to get through. That way he'd save six inches of chopping on each side.

As he paused to mark the new boundary, he heard a distinct dripping noise emanating from the vent hole. He put his ear to the hole but had not any sure idea from whence the sound. He beckoned to Stella who had just been adjusting the torch. As the paper toweling had charred away it was necessary to adjust the "wick." The point of John's knife worked fine for this task and they did have to keep adding sealer. When she listened, she was as puzzled as he was. They wondered if the quake had loosened some plumbing joint and vibration from his hammering may have also contributed.

By 9:30 Bernie and Marian had dozed off. John took the blanket off the girl's lap and cut it into two squares. Stella tucked the halves around each of the older children's legs being careful to wrap around the girl's bare legs. It was noticeably chillier and she put one of the ladder-back chairs over next to the torch and insisted she was comfortably warm near their "camp fire." The man of course was warm from his continual exertions.

When Stella spelled him at 10:00, they both noticed the sound of trickling water. The opening now resembled a flattened letter C but most of it was a narrow slot. The original opening was still the only place wide enough to see in with torch light reflected off the tiny mirror.

John looked in and exclaimed, "Oh oh. We might have a problem. There's about an inch of water in the pipe."

"Where's it coming from?"

"Beats me. It can't be on account of any leakage in the crawl space. The floor of the crawl space is several inches lower than the drain pipe. The water is just laying in there. Hardly any flow. But the tunnel is pretty level. The drains from here enter it high and go out low on the other end. It's over 80 feet from here to the pump house."

"Then it's coming in from the pump house end?"

"Has to be. There must be a leak there. Maybe the quake's vibrations caused leakage in the main water supply and it's oozing into the tunnel. At any rate we'd better get chipping, huh?"

John and Stella were puzzled but not dismayed. Had they any inkling of what was going on outside it might have a different story. Had John not felt led to begin his chipping, had he done nothing until water began seeping in under the front door; nothing would have been the perfect word to describe what his efforts would then have availed.

If there had been no rain, it would have taken the Mikota River about a week to fill the Blast Lake basin to its maximum and then overflow. In the meanwhile the lower river emptied itself almost dry near what had been Knox Rush. Glasgow's water plant would still be able with rationing to meet the minimum needs of the town for there were a number of rivulets and springs which fed the river between the former Corkscrew and the town.

In the Forbidden Valley the water level rose rapidly at first, several feet in the first few hours but the rate of rise lessened as more and more area was flooded over. At full lake height the Santa Fe Café would be completely submerged as would the shops across the river from it for they were at the lowest part of the village. At the west end of town the Dundee Grand Hotel was on high enough ground that only the street east of it would have shallow standing water on it. Many stores and homes up there would be surrounded by water and have flooded cellars, but have little or no water on the first floor. This flooding might have taken a week had not the predicted rain come.

John was growing apprehensive but said nothing to reveal it, yet Stella knew. They began working as a team, the man doing the more difficult pounding, and the woman the filing. He picked up the pace disregarding fatigue and the blistering to his hands. A bit after 11:00 the center chunk began settling down held only by a few wires. As the oval finally fell, he said, "Praise the Lord. That's it. Waken the kids."

As she did this the man hammered at any protruding wire or sharp protrusions of concrete so no one would be cut or skinned going through. Then he slid his feet in, rested on his forearms, and kicked the rubble into the crawl space. There were now about two inches of water slowly flowing through and beginning to accumulate on the floor below. He knew something had to be very wrong.

It was very difficult to rouse the little ones and they both awoke very cross and mewly. Bernie and Marian awoke and big smiles came over their faces as they saw that the hole was cut. The wee ones cheered up immediately when they knew they were going out to see their mothers. They were quite interested in how the woman, under John's directions, had cut off the angling corners of their ponchos so they would not drag in the water.

John said, "We'll need all the light we can get in the tunnel. I'm going to put our torch on the floor of the crawl space right next to the tunnel and it'll shine right in. While I do, would you reconnect that battery wire for us, Bernie and Stella can hand the torch to me."

He again went in feet first and had to almost sit in the water to duck his head in. He went onto his hands and knees and backed toward the pump house to be clear of the opening. As soon as the dim emergency flood came on she handed the torch down to him. He placed the stand on the floor and then added the rest of the sealer and set the wick higher for maximum light. Then he twisted and wiggled back up.

In their Exodus they were led by a Jew like the Children of Israel. Bernie went first with the flashlight. Marian followed close behind her new friend. The two of them had to crouch and duck walk although this is a very tedious method of propulsion, quick to cause back and leg strain. But they'd only be doing it a few minutes.

John used a spare shoe lace to hang the lit lantern around his neck. He'd left behind his pack with camping equipment but had taken from the Janitor's closet in the men's room a small Vice-grip and a small adjustable wrench. Of course he did not abandon his Swiss Army knife. Then he entered the tunnel and began to crawl backwards after the little ones had been handed down by the woman. The candle hanging down from his neck shed light for those to follow him.

Juliet and Jojo squealed as the cold water soaked their canvas shoes and their socks. It could have been very scary to them, but with John's smile and light in front of them and Stella crawling in the water behind them, it wasn't so bad. They walked together holding hands and hardly had to duck their heads. In fact after the initial unfamiliarity of the situation, they made a game of stamping their feet splashing the man and woman.

The tunnel went straight back for about two thirds of the distance and then veered to the left at about a 45 degree turn. After they rounded the bend the torch light no longer reached them at all. The failing flashlight and flickering candle were barely able to dispel the darkness. It seemed to be an extremely long time before Bernie gave them a report.

"I'm entering the Pump House. Hey! The water is twice as deep in here."

On the outside concrete wall was a work bench next to the door. There were no windows. Bernie helped Marian up onto the bench so she'd be able to sit with her almost bare feet out of the water. He made the gallant but futile effort of using his recently purchased bandanna to dry her toes and ankles. It did not help much, but the girl was appreciative of his thoughtful attention.

After John backed in and straightened up he set the candle on the bench next to the door. He lifted the two little ones and sat them on the bench next to the door and motioned to Stella to join them. He signaled the lad to douse the electric torch he carried and then addressed the group.

Huddle close together, gang. It's getting pretty chilly and awfully damp. I bet it's under 50 degrees. Shh. Listen a sec. Hear raindrops splashing outside? But we're safe."

"He asked, "Don't you think we ought to thank God He heard our prayers and helped us get this far?" He put his palms together and bowed his head as an example for the wee ones. As he shut his eyes he said, "Okay now. All eyes shut. We're gonna say a prayer to the Lord."

"Dear Father in Heaven, thank you for letting us get out of there. Now we are locked in behind a pad-locked door and we need to get out. Please help us get out, find food, find the Mamas, and have a nice warm dry bed.. Thank you very much. Amen."

Bernie noticed that this Presbyterian man (whom he knew was a believer like other Presbyterians and other Christian denominations that Jesus was God) had not closed his prayer using Jesus' name as he'd often heard Christians do. Perhaps John did not wish to offend Jewish believers in God. Well, he, Bernard Krause had been taught by his Rabbi that there were some big mysteries surrounding Jesus and how he died and supposedly rose again. And it did seem like a lot of prophecies may have come true in the Carpenter. His Rabbi had said, "We're pretty sure of the truth of our ancient faith, but it couldn't hurt to keep an open mind."

The door had a solid wooden core with thin stamped enameled galvanneal faces laminated to it. The door swung out to open. It had pulls and push buttons inside and out to operate the latch, but there was no cylinder lock. Rather, a large Master Lock secured it and was always hung on a special hook inside to prevent even the slightest chance of a worker being locked in accidentally. The door swung on hinges fastened to the door by bolts through the door which were secured by lock nuts.

John said to his assistant who held up the candle so they could inspect the door, "Look here, Hawkeye. Plated bolts. No rust to hinder us. But it would be easiest to get the nuts loose if you took the Vise-grip outside and kept the bolts from turning while I use the wrench on the lock nuts."

The Jewish lad looked at him in puzzlement for a few seconds and then burst out laughing. John joined in and then said to the group, "Let's all be happy. Marian Dear, would you sing Puff for us and follow it with a lot of happy songs?"

The actual procedure was to hold the end of each bolt of which there were 15 (5 through each of the stout hinges) and turn the nut out far enough so the Vise-grip could lock on under the nut and then complete the removal of the nut with the wrench. John used the wrench as Bernie held the candle after locking onto the bolt. While they worked they noticed water dribbling over the sill which was several inches above the floor.

The first few nuts to be removed took the longest as they established a good working procedure. The average time was about two minutes and they used up a half hour before John could tap the remaining bolts out with the flat of the wrench. But some hung in and the man had to repeatedly put his shoulder to the door until it broke free and was knocked akimbo, held only by the hasp and padlock. It was 11:50 when the way was clear.

All those inside could see that the outside was brighter lit than the museum room had been. The illumination was flickery, but considerably more than would have come from a full moon in a clear sky. Overhead it was all black clouds. A continuous pattern of rain varying from drizzle to deluge was taking place repeatedly.

John stepped out briefly into a six inch puddle. Fortunately for our six, there was a grade down from the foot of the cliffs to the river bank even as there was a grade from the hotel down to the former bridge. The water was beginning to lap onto the front porch of the café and also onto the patio. But there were two feet of water in back as against four feet in front.

"It's flooding. The tallest of us will have to wade and carry the others. Bernie, could you carry your cousin? Stella, Juliet? And Marian, since you have bare legs, I don't want you wading and I'll carry you. It's only about 40 yards to the patio steps."

Jojo and Juliet rode horsy back clinging to the necks of their noble steeds. The redheaded singer put her arm around John's neck as he carried her in his two arms. At this moment there was a brief lull in the rain so none were wet above the waist when they went under the patio awning. Shortly after they reached shelter, the downpour began again.

Stella had her purse and from it by John's dying flash light found her key ring. The purse had long adjustable shoulder straps and she'd snugged it up and used it as a belly pack before leaving the cave to enter the tunnel. The restaurant had never been locked when she'd been out and she'd never used any of the keys so she didn't know which was which. The DuPres winter home in Glasgow had keys on the ring also so it was trial and error to find the right one.

As she was fumbling, John pointed out the huge pile fallen over the Cannon Ball and the entrance. He said, "There must have been other slides which blocked Knox Rush and started the flooding. And since the streetlights are out and no other lights lit, the power in town must have gone off when ours did. The power lines into town come through the Narrows. So it must be that folks in danger of flooding must have been ordered to higher ground. With that much water there could not be a bulldozer operating.

There's a good chance the whole town is having free room and board at the hotel."

Once they were inside, Stella borrowed John's matches to light a few candle bowls which graced each table. She had to come back for his Bic for the matches were too wet. She seated the children at a table which unknown to them had been occupied by the ladies when the rocks started falling. She told them she'd try to heat some soup or cocoa for them because the stoves and ovens used LP gas which was piped in to the buildings from a huge tank near the hotel.

John inquired about some regular lanterns or full size flashlights. She answered, "I think Uncle Ray kept some in a cabinet next to the freezer. I'll take a candle and go check."

As she did this Marian asked, "Mr. Knox, is there a big fire making all that light?"

He went to the front door avoiding broken glass near the outer wall. He saw fire on the river down stream. "The fuel tanks must have been burst by falling rock and caught fire. The fuel must be leaking into the river."

He was very correct about spillage into the river. As the water level had gone up, it had reached the top of the fuel dump's retaining wall and had spilled over it. Since petroleum fuels are lighter than water, the water went to the bottom and began lifting the multiplied tons of fuel until they rose above the retaining wall and flowed outward much like pancake batter does when poured onto a griddle. Once the flow started it would not cease until all was on the water spreading flame and smoke. The flaming oil slick was rapidly fanning out and within a few minutes would reach the porch.

As quickly as he perceived what was happening he called out to Stella, "Didjuh find some lights? Skip lanterns if you got a couple flash lights. We gotta scram. There's fire coming this way."

The lights were quickly given to the older children for later use as needed. Stella scooped up the two little ones and handed the boy to John as they exited. Bernie and Marian began trotting on the porch toward the hotel end of the village; the burdened older pair was right on their heels.

Up to the Post Office each business establishment had a porch. These were level but each successive one was a step or two higher than the last so they were no longer splashing along after they got to the second porch. They were in no danger of being trapped by the rising water or threatened by the fire it carried. But as they went along the oldest four noticed the government radiation warning signs. Without consciously doing so they all increased their paces.

By the time they had begun to move along the second porch, the rain started up again and rapidly increased to a soaking chilling downpour. They could have slowed down after going past the overturned vehicles which designated the boundary of the danger zone for they were all soaked through and couldn't get any wetter, but sauntering along would have kept them from shelter longer.

They breathlessly kept going to the Red Arrow Mini Mall. The hotel's main entrance was off the Valley Spur which ran next to the Mikota River for another couple of miles to a scenic turn-around and ceased. From there on two improved tracks went on to the Knox Farm. The Mall was the street one over from the back parking lot and rear entrance of the hotel.

At this point it was necessary to begin using flashlights for away from the Valley Spur they had moved into the shadows. The best part of the strip mall was that of a covered walkway which joined all the side by side shops. The tired tots were put down to walk once under the shelter of the canopy.

John gave a running commentary as they moved from one end to the other. He had seen no light at the hotel which he knew had its own generator. He had no choice but to assume the town had been evacuated for west of the hotel up the valley there would be no more lodging than for a few dozen people. His commentary was to delay the inevitable, "Where's my Mama?"

"This first shop is The Paper Place. They sell books, periodicals, and board games…..This is Top To Bottom, a leisure wear shop…..This is The Pill Mill. It's a drug store for prescriptions, patent medicines, and natural remedies and aids…..This is Fixit's. It's a place for a handyman to find tools and supplies, you know, hardware…..This bigger store is The Food House. It's not exactly a super market but it does have good meat, produce, dairy products, baked goods, etcetera. But we have to get dry before we worry about food.

"Ah, here's the one I want, Paradise Outdoors, the last shop. Ever hear of Murphy's Law? Like why does the other checkout lane move so much faster than yours? Or why does the store you want the most always have to be the last one? This place caters to campers, hikers and fishermen but not hunters for only Mikotans may hunt in the Hidden Valley and there are only a few permits given by the Tribal Council."

At the last, John was using the blade of his knife to slip the latch of the simple lock on the door. The first thing when they entered was to find and light four battery lanterns which had fluorescent bulbs. They placed them on several cases and the small shop was quite well lit, indeed it was the best lighting they'd had since the power went off.

The very next step was to attempt to dry up as much as possible using the big decorated beach towels sunbathers love to sprawl on. The little ones were the first to be worked on after removing their ponchos. As Stella and the bigger children blotted and rubbed them, John sought out the parka and windbreaker displays. There was a wide range of sizes and after the little ones were as dry as could be under the circumstances the man ordered them into parkas covered by jackets.

Jojo sleepily protested, "Want my poncho. Mine."

Stella answered, "Well of course it's yours. Mr. Knox gave it to you. But it has to dry first. Then you can wear it. For now we'll put it in a plastic shopping bag and keep all our wet stuff together. Juliet's too."

The older children followed the example of the younger in donning double layers. In addition the man found some "one size fits all" knee high woolen sox and ordered Marian to don them. Then he himself put on a disposable plastic rain coat with hood.

"I'm going to get us transportation and take us to the Knox Farm. There are a number of regular passenger cars and some sport cars over in the hotel lot but it's risky trying them. They're too low and the puddles over the farm road might be too deep. We'd bog down in the mud. The Bluebird Bus has high enough clearance but even if it hadn't been turned on its side, we'd have had to put the canvas top on.

"There are sample packs of trail mix and dried fruit on that counter. Help yourselves while I'm gone. And there's some Gatorade on that shelf. Then find raincoats like this one for each of you and plenty of blankets or sleeping bags to cover with when we drive. A car I find might not have a working heater."

He took Stella aside and suggested she get rid of the wet sweat shirt and tee shirt and replace with dry layers.

"There are three reasons we must not stay here. Flood, fire, and radiation. I hope to God we haven't been seriously exposed, but it could only have been after we left the pump house. We had all that stone protecting us the rest of the time. And be sure you eat, too. I'm certain there would be no radiation problem with those sealed packs of food this far from the radiation danger zone."

"What about you? You have to eat, too. And I don't want you to get too cold and maybe get sick."

"Stella, you're one very sweet girl, always concerned about others more than yourself. But you should know about Indians and Scots. We can run around in blizzards in loin cloths or kilts and be worried about getting heat stroke. I'll be just fine but I can take some trail mix along to nibble on."

As she handed him a few packs she noticed that he kept his knuckles up to hide sight of his palms and the inner sides of his fingers. After he pocketed the food she suddenly grabbed his wrists and twisted his palms up. His cotton work gloves were very dirty but also soaked with blood."

"Oh John, what have you done to yourself?"

"Shh! Just a little blistering. We have salve at the farm. Don't mention this. It's no big deal."

It was slightly after 1:00 when the young woman saw a vehicle with six bright lights pull into the lot. In addition to the normal headlights, there were four floodlights mounted on a bar above the roof. The horn was tooting even as the car entered the lot. The man bounced the vehicle right over the curb to stop under the canopy so his charges would not be dampened getting in.

Bernie dashed out and gave a report. "Jojo and Juliet started yawning as soon as they drank some Gatorade and she climbed right up of Stella's lap. When I held my arms out to him he ignored me and got up on Marian's lap. I guess girls' laps are softer to sit on. After you left we set up some folding camp chairs with canvas seats and backs and arm rests. Hey, what kind of car is this? It's strange."

"It's a Subaru Outback. All Subarus have all wheel drive. My friend, Tommy Thunderhawk owns it. But the passenger window won't close. He put extra lights on top and had the frame jacked up and put on over-size wheels for cross country runs at night where there are no roads. There it was in his carport by their summer cottage, waiting for us to use it."

"Could we have stayed in his house and slept on the floor?"

"They were all gone. Everyone is gone. We may be the only left in the Hidden Valley. That radiation. Something very bad has happened. We'll check it all out later. Now let's get the kids and our wet stuff in. You sit with me with your rain hood up. There will be water coming in that window. The lap kids can sit on the same laps."

It took several minutes to load all in and also the wet gear behind the cargo space behind the rear seat of the wagon. As John circled the Red Arrow Mini Mall to get back to the Valley Spur, a dog's barking could be heard in spite of the hiss of rain into puddles and the car noises.

Juliet began to whine. "I wanna pet the doggie. I can't pet my Ginger. She's in a canal. I want my Ginger and I want my Mama." Stella's loving hugs and kisses calmed her after she started a tantrum and she yawned mightily still protesting, "Wanna pet doggie."

Her uproar roused Jojo to similar thoughts. "Want Mama. Mama! Mama! Auntie Max!"

Bernie ordered, "Cool it, cousin. It's too dark to find our mothers. Maybe tomorrow when it's light and maybe John will let us look for the dog. Anyhow John and Stella and Marian and I will take good care of both of you. Okay?"

With drooping eyelids the little lad looked around at all his protectors and must have felt safe for he murmured, "Okay," and promptly fell back asleep.

It took about 45 minutes to drive to the farm, twice as long as usual for the already great downpour had muddied the road. In the lower places were puddles in the ruts but the worst hazards were the numerous spots where tiny mountain waterfalls traveled under the road in culverts. Heavy rains caused a small torrent of water to overflow culverts and made finding the road a tricky proposition. But John had traveled the road all his life and knew each trick and trap.

John and Stella were the only two awake and she barely, when they arrived. The two lap children had lasted only a couple of minutes after leaving the Mall. Marian had hung on for about 15 minutes and Bernie about 20. While the two older children had been alert, John had told them about the farm.

"We don't have electric power lines running out there. Nearest transformer is about 10 miles from us. But Uncle Lionel has a big generator, about 50 amps I think, but it's really just for running machines in the shop. So that line you see (Aren't these floodlights great?) is a phone line strung from tree to tree about 10 feet off the ground. It's forest most of the way so they only had to put in a few dozen poles.

"We are somewhat primitive and like it that way. Oil lamps and candles. Wood heat. Nothing much electronic. But the wind mill fills a high storage tank so we have running water and flush toilets, just like back in civilization. And we have propane for cooking and our water heater and refrigeration. Got a full-sized box in the Lodge and a compact one in the Honeymoon Cottage. Mostly we cook on the wood ranges. The wood is free. Propane gas isn't. Remember the Knox clan is part Scottish.

"And we have a smokehouse and drying shed for produce, fish and meat, and a jerky maker. We do a lot of canning and drying of foods and even have a grinder for our own home grown wheat, Lots of gardening and we have berry patches and some fruit trees. We lack nothing…..
Stel, did Marian drift off? Relax, Bernie. That rain coming in on you isn't making you too cold, is it? Heater's on high. Close your eyes. We'll be there in a jiffy."

It seemed to Bernie if he had just closed his eyes when John called out, "Up and at 'em, Hawkeye. We're at the cottage. Be ready to help Stella bring the little ones in as quick as I have lights on inside." The man left the Subaru engine running but turned off the roof lights before making the several yard dash onto the porch.

Now would be a good time to tell about the Honeymoon Cottage. It was an extremely strong and durable dwelling, built of large logs, rough-hewn beams, and native stone. Its roof was now of modern shingles over heavy plywood but originally had been of cedar shakes made in the valley.

All the doors had been crafted before the Great War in the trenches of Europe. All the doors were solid, no hollow cores or veneers. The hardware was all solid brass, hinges well oiled and all the doors shut smoothly and quietly. Except for the bathroom door which had jewel cut glass knobs, all doors had solid brass knobs which screwed onto square rods with threaded corners which operated latches. The outside doors had old style locks which required skeleton keys. These hung high on hooks on the inner door trim, but never in John's life could he remember locked doors on the farm and doubted the mechanisms would even work any more.

All foundations were of stone as was the massive fireplace in the living room. The front porch ran full length and had wicker furniture and a rocker on it. Its roof protected the entry and the front windows from the weather. The back porch was centered on and about twice as wide as the rear door but it too was roofed and sheltered the entrance.

The front door was about a third of the way from the east end of the house. The porch faced south and paralleled the road. A single window, open top and bottom, was for the bedroom to the east of the door. The trio of living room windows west of the door was also open.

All windows of the cottage were very old and had cords, pulleys, and within the framework balancing sash weights. Depending on size each of the sashes had from nine to sixteen panes apiece each individually puttied into the checker board of mullions and crosspieces. Some of the panes were so old there were detectable variations of color and some panes were apt to distort the view due to their irregular surfaces.

The layout inside was simple. Two bedrooms on the east end. On the north wall next to the rear bedroom was the bathroom. The kitchen occupied the rest of the rear half of the house, the living room the entire south half save the bedroom area. The fireplace occupied most of the east wall of the living room. On the west end of the kitchen was a wood range and along the partition were adequate cupboards, the L.P. range and refrigerator, and counter space. The sink was on the wall next to the bathroom.

In the kitchen were two hanging pull-down lamps with reflective shades. Two lamps graced the stone slab mantel of the fireplace and two wall lamps plus two candle sconces could beautifully illuminate the living room. Two wall lamps in the bathroom, one on each side of the mirror above the sink, were ready to do their job. In addition there were wall lamps above the heads of both double beds and also miniature lamps on the dressers should dim night lights be desired.

The cottage had pegged plank floors, partitions were paneled with tongue and groove Knotty pine, the ceilings were beamed and had in later years been heavily insulated, and all was beautifully varnished and kept up. Mikota made braided and woven rugs adorned the floors in strategic locations.

It was furnished with mostly home made in the style often called rustic. Branches, poles and, rough hewn wood were used. Arm rests were of poles split down the middle. Back rests were of woven branches. But all pieces were comfortably padded. One anachronism was Lionel's new leather Barca-Lounger. Wardrobes, dressers, and cupboards were far from crude, having been machined in the farm's workshop over a period of years.

It was definitely bachelor quarters as evidenced by the lack of trim a woman would provide in matters of upgrading curtains and such things. But unlike many bachelor quarters, it was clean and orderly, not a pig pen. After all they had been through and seen, it seemed like heaven.

John quickly lit the porch lantern which hung on a bracket beside the front door, then scurried in to light the two mantel lamps. Stella had given him back his Bic lighter while driving and this he used although there were cast iron match dispensers at both the fireplace and wood range. With light in the house he dashed out to welcome all to the Knox Farm.

Bernie carried in Jojo, Stella Juliet, and Marian brought in the wet clothes. John seated the four children on the sofa and then deposited the wet things in the bath tub. Stella asked what she could do and then shut the windows and went from room to room lighting lamps as the man got a fire going.

The sofa and Barca-Lounger were comfortably close to the fireplace and faced it. It was Knox practice to always have kindling and starter pieces in stoves or on andirons when they were not in use and also to keep wood boxes and cord hoops full.

As soon as the fire was going well, John added bigger pieces and excused himself. He went out to move the Subaru Wagon under a nearby lean-to meant to shelter horses of which the farm had not had any for years even though there was a wild herd in the valley. He could not leave a friend's car with a broken window exposed to the elements. He doused the porch lantern before he entered.

Stella handed him a note she'd found on the kitchen table addressed to "Junior." He said, "Now you know my secret. Uncle Lionel has always called me that in private.

My father was John Sr. and he's the one to first call me that. But Uncle never uses it when others can hear it."

She asked, "And what do you call him in private?"

"Only Uncle Lionel or Mr. Knox. Honest. No fooling." But there was an impish grin on his face as he said it. "He says there's a kettle of stew in the fridge and cookies in the jar. He made them both. If you could help the girls get dry, particularly their hair, and get them into dry night clothes, I'll rustle up some grub for us. There's an extra chest of drawers in the back bedroom, that's mine, and in it are about a dozen various sizes of warm flannel night shirts. Some are faded pink and have a bit of lace on them for girls and some are faded blue and just plain for boys. And you can show Bernie and he can help his cousin. Oh. I almost forgot. There should be assorted slippers and robes and toys such as stuffed toys. Like a Teddy bear for the guy and maybe a huckleberry hound for the girl.'

Although the chill was leaving the house as the children gathered at the table, John had lit the oven of the gas stove and left the door open to add warmth to the kitchen.

The tots managed to eat a couple of peanut butter cookies and glasses of warm milk before succumbing. Jojo was assigned to John's bed and his cousin would join him shortly. The little guy slept with both arms hugging his bear. As Juliet was tucked in she likewise clutched Huck, sure Ginger would be a good friend to the stuffed toy. Marian would join her.

After bowls of stew and warm milk and cookies all around, the older children joined their bedmates. Neither objected to being given hugs and being tucked in by both John and Stella. It was approaching 2:30 when the bedroom wall lamps were extinguished and the tiny night lights lit.

The man gave Stella a flannel nightgown suitable for a grown woman along with his uncle's quilted robe and slippers. "Get into the bathroom, get out of all your wet clothes and dry your skin and hair properly and then put these on. I'll take a towel along and change in my room into my PJ's and robe. Then we'll put all the wet things on that collapsible drying rack I set up near the hearth. Then there are a couple of things we should talk about before bed. And I get the Barca-Lounger. Seniority, you know. You get the couch."

They were soon sitting in the kitchen sipping chamomile tea. He was first to speak. "I don't know how to thank you enough for your constant help with the kids and everything. I don't think I could have done it without you. I really appreciate you."

She replied, "I feel just the same about you. The kids and I have you to thank for keeping us alive. You saved our lives. I try not to think about it but we could have ended up drowning in the dark. And John, we still might die from radiation."

"Well Stel, uh, do you mind if I call you that Senorita Estellita?"

"I like it. No one else calls me that. It's like a special name only a special friend would use."

He grinned and said, "Just for that you can call me Junior. But only when no one else can hear it. I don't like it or allow it except from very special people like you, my special friend." He gestured as he spoke and she caught sight of his raw palms and fingers. She was stricken and began to sniffle.

"Where's the medicine cabinet, Junior?" She said it flippantly, keeping things light to keep her pent up feelings from breaking loose. He pointed toward the bathroom and told her the cabinet was above the sink. She brought back the needed things and bade him stand by the sink so she could bathe his hands in lukewarm water. She cleaned them with peroxide, wincing when he did. She then gently dried them and applied an herbal salve supplied to the Pill Mill and its counterpart in Glasgow by Mitchell Knox's grandfather from an old remedy used by witch doctors. She wrapped gauze around his hands and taped it, then used Band-aids on his fingers.

When Stella finished she put things away and returned to the kitchen but stood with her back to him. She put her hands on her face and began to take small gasping breaths but tried not to cry aloud. He softly placed his hands on her shoulders and turned her around. "Can you tell me what's wrong?"

"We're going to die. The radiation. It takes time to kill. I'm so scared. I don't know what to think or do. And where would we be if anything happens to you? I've never been so scared."

The tears began streaming down her cheeks and his own eyes were beginning to mist over. He moved close and put his arms around her and pulled her against him. She pressed against him and clung to him with her face buried against his chest.

"I don't get credit for saving us. It was God working through us. God used four of us so all six of us would get to safety. You needn't be afraid. God never sends evil. He loves all of us. And as for radiation, I'm certain we could not have taken a lethal dose or even health-threatening ones. But my Uncle Lionel has a Geiger counter he used to check for Uranium deposits one time. We'll use it tomorrow to check things out.

"And it is very important we be realistic and understand we might be stuck here a few weeks until people come back. I tried to get some kind of radio reception in the Subaru but all that came was static, probably an after-effect of radiation. So we will shop for clothes, non-perishable foods, and anything we think we might need.

"So don't be scared. God wants us to trust Him. Okay now? At least we're not alone and trapped in the dark in a hole in the ground…..Say, maybe you better rinse your face and then just leave one lamp on low in the bathroom. And aren't we lucky like the kids? We both had a good hug to make us feel better."

When she came out, it was darker in the house for he had left just one lamp in the kitchen turned down low and one lit on the mantel he'd soon get to. She said, "I feel positively ugly in this old-fashioned night gown. You don't think I look too bad, do You?"

"Missy, you're the most beautiful woman in the house, although it might help if I had a few others for comparison."

She whipped her pillow at him for his impudence and retrieved it before removing the robe and slipping under her covers. She smiled and bid him good night. His words and actions had gone a long way toward restoring her normal exuberance. She trusted the man and felt quite safe. She wasn't sure she trusted the Lord like he did but felt that being around him could make greater trust in the Lord attainable.

By the flickering fire light he long gazed at her until sleep claimed him well after 3:00. His last conscious thoughts were of gratitude to God, a sense of serenity and safety, and a bit of amazement at how their paths had all crossed and joined.

Chapter Six

SEGMENTS OF EARLY SUMMER

Lionel

The afternoon before the explosion, on Tuesday, June 27th, Lionel had been called by his literary agent. He had been writing a series of Christian fiction books for children which told of adventures of Mikota youngsters in the early 1800's. He entitled the series "Tales of the Red Arrow." The artist who'd illustrated the first three books had finally given in to the ravages of arthritis and was retiring to the tropics. It was time to make a decision as to who should succeed the elderly gent.

Lionel had said, "No! You can't fax me samples of their work. You know I don't have one of those infernal contraptions. I want to meet the artists and maybe have them spend a few days out here to meet the people and see the country. Tell you what. I'll drive to your town tomorrow and stay at the Ramada Inn. I want you to have them there at 7:00 sharp for a breakfast meeting to get acquainted and then spend the day with them. Then I can head home on Friday and my nephew and I can attend the grand opening of the Dundee Grand Hotel. You can set it up? Okay. And I believe it's your turn to pick up the meal tab. Fine. See you there."

The man had spoken using the extension in the Honeymoon Cottage. The main line went to the Lodge. He hung up and returned to his work in the kitchen. He had been mixing up a batch of peanut butter cookies. A large pot of stew was simmering on the wood range for his supper and a couple of meals for John whom he expected to return the next day. Being a bachelor had necessitated him becoming a Jack-of-all-trades. It was learn or lower the standard of living he'd enjoyed as a child. He'd chosen to learn because his natural inclination was never to spend money paying others to do things you could figure out how to do for yourself.

But his frugality did not extend toward his one extravagance which was his '37 Plymouth Coupe. He'd first seen it when Junior was 5 or 6. He had felt an immediate kinship with it. His first glimpse of it had been in an elderly widow's barn. It belonged to an earlier age and that was what he felt about himself.

The owner was having an auction of all furnishings and farm equipment. She was selling the homestead and moving into an assisted living facility. The old hulk was not even on the auction block. It had been destined to be hauled away to be compressed into a cube smelters could melt into useful metal.

All the tires were flat and rotting away. The plugs and ignition were gone, the pistons rusted into place. Half of the glass was broken. The upholstery and cushions were crumbling away. The ceiling fabric was hanging down in fragile ribbons. The rear bumper was caved in against the body. Hardly any chrome was left. The rubber on the running boards was checked and fell off in rock hard pieces. The paint was faded to where even most of the primer was gone, but there was a surprising lack of rust, no holes through, only surface oxidation.

It had taken Lionel fifteen years to restore it for use. The total money spent could have bought him one of the pricier models of Mercedes. Younger folks were never disrespectful in his presence, but away from him they snickered and made fun of his folly. The gray hairs, those who were in possession of some wisdom, applauded him as a restorer, one who builds up and does not tear down, one who engages in a labor of love even if the object of that love did not seem worthy. They knew the world was a better place when folks built up through love rather than tear down through hate.

Restore it he had, but to modern specs. Oh, the appearance was original; mechanically it was up to date for modern road use. It had radial tires and disc brakes, an air shock suspension, a turbo-charged EFI Dodge engine, automatic transmission, custom leather upholstery and carpet, a multi-speaker AM-FM cassette radio (He still rejected CD's) and a beautiful gray metallic finish with air-brushed red arrows below the sills of both doors. It was not a hot rod but could scoot pretty well and also was vastly better for MPG than the original.

On Wednesday morning he loaded a small suit case, his manual Adler portable typewriter, and two stuffed briefcases into his car. He filled the tank at the Red Arrow station in Dundee and parked on the lot. He intended to saunter down to the Post Office as soon as it was open and see if the confirmation of a purchase order of stocks he had placed with his broker had come to his box. He had time to stop in the Santa Fe Café for coffee and a Danish and to ask the girls, should John drop in, if they would tell him he had gone away for a couple of days.

Dour dowager Linda Crowe, ten year younger sister-in-law of Esther, was Post Mistress of the Dundee Post Office. As was his custom with people. Lionel greeted her with a smile, "Good morning, Linda."

With her typical scowl she had shot back, "What's good about it? It's gonna be a bad day. I can feel it in my bones when it's gonna be a bad day and my bones tell me this is gonna be a bad day. But I had a bad dream too."

Knowing she'd tell him whether or not he asked, he politely inquired, "Wanna tell me about it?"

"I can't. Forgot it when I woke up. But I know it was bad. Mark my words; something awful is gonna happen today. You be extra careful you don't get hurt in it."

"Thank you. I will. And may I please have my mail?"

He walked back to the Plymouth with it, smiling as he went about the old prophet of doom and gloom's prediction. Every day she made the same prediction. A forgotten dream was a nice added touch. And on any given day she could pick up a newspaper and find some bad news and say she'd told you so. He knew that anyone who keeps looking for trouble is bound to find it. But he got sick of only being told bad news when there was so much Good News that ought to be shared instead.

The state capital where he was headed was a 400 mile drive away. He had filled his tank, checked in at the Ramada, called his agent and then walked to a nearby restaurant for supper. He was back to his room before 7:00 and had planned to pound out a few more pages of his book-in-progress.

He first clicked on CNN for any news updates. He was shocked to see the Mikota Tribal Council and horrified by Esther's talk. He wondered if it was some kind of hoax but had his mind changed when excerpts of Clarence Henderson's video record were shone. He felt as if a steel vise was tightening on his chest and had a hard time catching his breath. He dropped to his knees by his bed and prayed more intensely than he had in a long time but none of his prayers were for himself. Just after he got up from his knees his agent told him he ought to head home, the appointments with the artists had been cancelled.

He tried to call Esther or some of his council crones but all lines were besieged with calls. At 8:00 he checked out, glad his tank was full. It was raining now and the drive was nightmarish. At midnight he was halfway home and exhausted too much to even consider going on.

He stopped at a cheap motel and slept for a few hours in his clothes. He fell asleep with questions chasing themselves around in his mind. Was John okay? Had Linda had a real vision of a disaster? Had he had a real coronary and dare he risk delaying seeing a doctor? Were the DuPres's okay? Why in the world had Bogardus killed himself that way? What must he do now?

He arrived in Glasgow about 8:30 Thursday. He immediately sought out Esther who hugged him fiercely and wept with him after telling of John and the others drowned in the Sentinel Rooms. She ordered him to stay with her family for a few days. Her son Frank who was the same build gave him a suit and clean shirt for the two hour memorial service which would start at 3:00 on Friday.

The afternoon sky was clear, the temperature balmy. The service was held outdoors about a mile from the Narrows. A platform had been set up on the Spur Road with seating on the road and shoulders. Besides vast numbers of floral baskets and arrangements there were so many fresh wildflowers gathered by citizens that it was like a sea of flowers in front of the stage and the back drop to it all was the row of ancient cliffs.

The entire service was taped by CNN and the major networks for edited release later. Present and taking part were emissaries of the President, the Governor, U.S. Senator Michael Montana and U.S. Representative Harold Hawke, two Mikotan politicians, and of course Esther Crowe and the Tribal Council. Stella's Priest from Glasgow, the Rabbi of the Krauses, a Bishop from the Diocese where the O'Connors lived, and John's Presbyterian Pastor, were all present. All the above brought words of sympathy and condolence along with prayers and words of comfort.

Herman Krause had arrived with his three daughters and their entire families to join Maxine and Jolene. But when Harold, the father of Jolene, arrived with his wife, they were turned away by the Sheriff's men on instructions from the rest of the Krause family. The family's attitude was that since they had not wanted or needed their daughter when it counted the most, now she did not need or want them. Herman knew there could be a law suit but he was more than willing to face his brother in court and expose him for what he was.

Juliet Eberhard's father and his family never showed up. Bernice had lost all that was dear to her and the revenge of the Eberhards was now complete. The DuPres and Juarez families were also there in force.

The Tribal Council furnished the funeral supper and ate with all the relatives in the Glasgow Inn's dining room. In the lobby was set up a continually replenished table of finger foods and beverages for any and all mourners other than family who might wish to sign a big register to show support and sympathy.

When dessert choices were brought to the tables, Jolene looked at the piece of chocolate cake she had ordered and began to cry. She still did not have any clear idea as to what had happened. She suddenly jumped out of her chair and began to chase the waiter. She tugged on his sleeve from behind to get his attention and stop him.

"More cake. Chocolate. Please, for my Jojo." She began to bawl and call out, "I want my baby. Make him come to supper right now."

She was behind Lionel when she said this and he rose to put his arms around her before Herman could get there. "Hush Dear. Jojo can't come."

"Why not? I want him. I'm his Mama."

"Hush, Sweetheart. I know. But angels came and took him to heaven where he can have chocolate cake and nobody ever hurts children. No bad boys there. Everybody loves him and the angels will take care of him until you get there."

On Saturday morning before leaving the Territory, Lionel met with the Tribal Council regarding the Knox Farm. He was told that since his circumstances were so extraordinary, a chopper would be provided to take him in so he could haul out any possessions he desired.

"Thank you, but no. The rules have to apply to all and I fully agree with your decision to make it the Forbidden Valley. I have my car, my typewriter, outlines of stories to come, and a head full of memories. I'm thinking of following a dream I've had for a long time, that of visiting Scotland where some of my ancestors came from and seeing the true Dundee and Aberdeen and Glasgow. I've all the money I could ever spend. It would have gone to John. If you ever need me you can get in touch through my agent. Oh. One more thing. The live stock. The cow and calf. The chickens. The miniature hogs. They're all free to forage at will and they have shelter if they want it. That's it I guess. Maybe in a year or two I'll take you up on that offer of a parcel of land in the Aberdeen Forest and build a cottage. Well, anyhow, may the Lord watch over all of us until we meet again."

Executive Order

Saturday evening two old friends of the President were admitted to the Oval Office. All three went way back and had lent mutual support to each other in many election campaigns. Senator Michael Montana and Representative Harold Hawke had never asked the man in the White House for favors so their request for an appointment had received immediate attention and a quick invitation to come.

The President warmly greeted them with firm handshakes and slaps on their backs. "Harry, Mike, long time no see. Refreshments? Wine? Bourbon? A cocktail? Just name what you'd like."

Mike responded, "Orange juice would be great. You know us redskins might go on the war path if we drink firewater." Harry concurred. The three men were almost teetotalers and the offering of drinks whenever they met was a traditional opening gambit.

The President commiserated with them about the awful act of terrorism and assured them some of the best investigators were looking into it and had good leads but no definite answers yet. "We're keeping a tight lid on what we've learned. You'll be among the first to know. But that's not why you're here. I assume it's a tribal matter and you gentlemen are serving as spokesmen for the Mikotans."

Sen. Montana spoke. "Yes, Sir, it is Mr. President. The Tribal Council is invoking a strict enforcement of the terms of the Treaty of 1850. To the best of our knowledge, it has been adhered to more closely by both sides than any other Indian Treaty. Our side and yours have scrupulously followed its terms, and we have a number of court cases in which the decisions have verified our interpretations.

"Mr. President, the Treaty is still alive and well today. Both sides agreed in writing it would be good as long as the sun shines and the rains fall and the grasses grow. We can't deny these terms exist so it must still be in force. Is this your thinking, Sir?"

"Absolutely, friends. As soon as I got word of the disaster I had someone do my homework for me and yes, the Treaty is valid. I also know the Tribe retained title to the land, everything that grows on it, all creatures that live on it, and also anything of value under the land as far as men can dig or reach.

"And that gave you undisputed petroleum and natural gas ownership. You've been models of wise stewardship and preservation of the environment. Conservationists hold you up as leaders in these areas. With this having been said, what is it you're after? Disaster aid?"

Harry interjected, "I think we're in better condition to give it than to take it."

A bit impatiently after glancing at his watch the Chief said, "Yes, yes, so what is it you do want?"

Mike continued, "Sir, when the treaty was signed a year before the original John Knox died, he had been reading about balloons and how they had a use militarily. So when speaking about ownership and the right to use and control our resources, we included wording that says the airspace above us is also our property as high as a balloon may rise or an eagle fly. Several legal experts we have consulted all agree this means we have sovereignty over our air space as any nation does."

The tired President acted as if this got his back up. So you want the right to shoot down planes that intrude? What about unintentional over flights due to mechanical or instrument failure, or accidents?"

Harry eased what seemed like tension saying, "If us braves are out on a hunting party and a plane buzzes us, we just might take 'em down with our bows and arrows. And if they swoop too low over our tepees, our squaws might throw rolling pins at 'em....But seriously, Sir, you know we'd give aid like we always have. However, if fliers defy orders to avoid our airspace and land unnecessarily, we might confiscate their planes and perhaps take other legal action besides."

Mike took it up, "Whether or not an actual nuclear device was used, we want to eliminate the possibility of someone flying over and dropping one in the Forbidden Valley or any where else on our land. We also do not want any media people flying over taking pictures or videos. If any person wants to see our land they can come in on a tour bus or drive in if they have a permit."

"I understand. What precisely is your request?"

"Mr. President, we humbly submit that in accord with our Treaty, our airspace must be restricted and all over flights must be authorized by the Tribal Council. No commercial airlines fly over and that must not change. Private planes must not intrude. Military training flights or air maneuver exercises must not take place over the Territory without our permission. But ultra level spy plane flights or flight required because of national emergency are naturally exempt. We believed all this could be done by an Executive Order and a few strokes of your pen."

The President replied, "Five times you said must. Are you telling me the United States is compelled to comply?"

"Sir, our Treaty demands it. Duly authorized representatives on both sides signed and you agreed the Treaty is valid today. We only ask the Government to keep its promise, and we believe you agree with us."

The President smiled and gave each man a copy of a document out of a folder on his desk. "Does this say it satisfactorily? Sorry I strung you along. I knew what you wanted before you came. A little birdie told me. I had already decided to do it. As of 12:01 Sunday morning, it goes in effect. Your airspace is restricted and the Air Force is hereby ordered to enforce that restriction."

No Chance

Norman Orville Chance, whose widow sister Lorna Dickinson had been cheated by "Punch" Rafferty AKA Peter Randolf etcetera, was a highly respected and paid private investigator who did much work for various branches of government. During his vacation he had tracked down his sister's swindler. He chanced to be on hand immediately after the disaster and he was put to work to back track into Humphrey Bogardus' part.

He was a tall trim man, quite fit for a person soon to be 70. Thanks to Grecian Formula he looked much younger, but his trade did require changes of appearance. He liked to say regarding possible physical conflict associated with his line of work, "I'm neither a fighter nor a lover. I'm a thinker."

In High School he'd been considerably thinner than now. He had tried out for various sports and always seemed to end up on the bottom of the list of team members, so much so his physique and results combined to give him the nickname of "Slim Chance." In college he did manage to get on a wrestling team but after losing every match his nickname was changed to "No Chance" and it was appropriate that his initials were N and O.

He didn't care. He excelled academically, top of the list there. What Hercule Poirot called use of the gray cells was his forte. He was relentless in ferreting out bits of seemingly unrelated information and by proper interpretation arrive at the truth. It was wrong doers he was after who had "No Chance."

Maryvale College, a private liberal arts school deep in the heart of Dixie-land, had never conceded its view on white supremacy after the Civil War. Wednesday, July 5th, a week after the blast, it had two seemingly unrelated but significant visits. Both visits were to the fraternity house in which dwelt student members of the League of Purity and Justice. Only members of the league were welcomed as residents. Reginald S. VanderMaas III had a sumptuous suite on the top floor which also housed the offices of the league. The vast basement rec. room was where meetings were held in complete privacy.

R. S. VanderMaas II was on the board of regents. Sheriff Hayes, a like-minded friend of Reggie's dad and the other men on the board, came regretfully at 10:00 A.M. accompanied by a DEA officer and two state troopers. He said apologetically to his friend's son, "Been someone complaining that underage students who came to your open house Sunday drank some beer and maybe hard liquor here. Some who were questioned said you guys had marijuana and illegal pills they could use when they were here. I've been ordered from higher up to cooperate with these officers. It's not my idea."

Reggie replied, "I'll admit we had a wash tub full of ice and beer cans, but no hard liquor. We didn't check ID's at the start, but later when we discovered under-age drinkers, they were ordered out and escorted back to their dorms. As for drugs, well, some of the outsiders may have had them along but we pride ourselves on in keeping our blood pure genetically and also in avoiding chemical pollutants. I assure you we allow no illegal controlled substances here."

Up to this point the conversation had been taking place on the veranda. The impatient DEA officer snatched the warrant from the sheriff's hand and presented it to Reggie. "Enough stalling. This is a legal search warrant. Are you trying to block us from searching the premises?"

Reggie swung the big door wide, stepped aside, and waved them in. "I wouldn't dream of hindering due process. Come in. Look everywhere. And when you get to the office, help yourself to our free literature."

He maintained an expression of pleasant willingness but was seething inside when he saw Judge Aaron Knox's signature on the warrant. Aaron, like his cousin Lionel, deeply believed in Civil Rights and equality for all regardless of race, religion, or gender. He was a thorn in the side of radicals or bigots. Reggie was further infuriated when he saw State Police cars parked so that all sides of the dorm were under surveillance.

The search was thorough but not messy. When it was all over the unwilling Sheriff told Reggie nothing wrong had been found. But unknown to either of them, several electronic devices had been unobtrusively placed. Aaron Knox had authorized phone taps.

That afternoon an agent of World Wide Life Assurance came to see Reggie. The agent was a temporary employee better know to us as Norman Chance. He already knew the League had led Humphrey to get money from his 401K to purchase the van and Harley. With their help he had gotten a loan from his retirement fund and had been paying it back in installments. But the League had handled it for him so that he thought the bike and van were gifts to him, and he had promised to use the van to pay back the "stinking Indians." There was a buried but findable paper trail between the fat man and the League.

Now it was a matter of finding motives. The position of the League regarding a return to subjugation of inferiors was public knowledge as was their avowal that constitutional amendments or even a new constitution had to be legally and non-violently sought. Thus violent acts could not be assumed from what they said but had to be clearly proven.

The League was but one member of a vast confederation of "patriotic"organizations which included survivalists, private militia, and even neo-nazis. The central leadership and coordination came from Jerome Buckhalter who was founder and president of FSN (Free Speech Now!). Links between it and actual activities of subversive chapters and the hooliganism of the skinheads was too tenuous to prove. It was by now a working hypothesis of Chance that the Hidden Valley act of terrorism was not a random act of violence but a test run.

Norman had come to pursue an immediate connection, that of the League being beneficiaries of life insurance. The money motive is always a powerful persuader of Juries. "I'm here to begin processing your claim. You certainly acted swiftly in getting it in."

"Well, we all knew about this because Hump, forgive me, that was an affectionate name for our dear friend. Humphrey came to us last fall and asked advice. He shared our high ideals and wanted to be sure he could keep supporting our noble work even if God took him to his richly deserved reward. So we helped him check out various policies and even tried to persuade him do much less, but God bless him, he had a big heart and went without other things to afford the premium."

"You're right about him being big-hearted. It's a million dollar policy with double indemnity for accidental death. But World Wide Life's legal department has some problems with this case. It does seem as if there could have been an accident, but our experts can't conceive of a load of fireworks going off accidentally, thus setting off fuel explosions. What other explanation could there be?"

Reggie paused and pondered. "I surely hate to speak ill of the dead, but he was a rotten driver, very poorly coordinated. Might not he, tired after a long drive, have crashed into the truckload of fireworks?"

"That's not impossible, but if you carefully read the policy, you'll see that the beneficiaries have to prove the cause of death was an accident. So the double indemnity is out. If an accident is ruled out, it leaves two possibilities. Either Mr. Bogardus deliberately set off some kind of device or such a device had a timer or could be remotely set off. If he did it the policy is void because of the two year suicide clause. He only had the policy for nine months. So if he killed himself by setting off some device, there will be no payment to the beneficiary except a refund of the premiums paid.

"If he did not set it off, it was either an act of terrorism or insurrection and the two year clause refuses payment for deaths due to war, riot, terrorist acts, or rebellion. If it was murder, the beneficiary will receive payment only after the guilty one is sentenced, provided it is not the beneficiary."

At this point Norman gave Reggie an icy withering gaze and paused for an uncomfortable time. "Beneficiaries are always top suspects in deaths involving wills or insurance. Of course your League is entitled to investigate and bring suit against the insurance company. However, it might be very difficult for your investigator since no one may enter the now Forbidden Valley and even if someone could, the locale is flooded and there is great danger of radiation. So the company believes this matter is closed for now. The already paid premiums will be put into an interest earning account until this matter is fully resolved. I must go. Have a nice day."

When Chance left, Reggie was extremely upset about having lost the million dollar windfall for the time being. The League was in great shape financially, its "war chest" amply supplied, but a large immediate infusion of cash could have advanced their time table. The majority of members were students who could not contribute heavily, but there were large numbers of affluent folks who gave hefty contributions and there was wide spread support from wage earners and salaried people.

George Rummler, assistant professor of socio-politico-anthropology was an avid open supporter and member. He fully believed that Caucasians were much higher up the evolutionary scale than other races and were destined to be masters of the world. But as a child a Quaker grandpa and grandma had instilled in him that all violence was wrong. In later years he swore he had totally rejected Judeo-Christian supernaturalism but he clung to the basic ethics and still abhorred violence.

The League's official written position was for non-violent legal methods of bringing about change. George had been very vocal in support of this both on and off of campus. He had repeatedly been offered a position on their Executive Board but had begged off. Said board had masterminded the blast and when the news broke he was absolutely certain it was a deed of the League. There was no doubt in his mind he had been lied to and he was part of a violent organization. It made him sick. He adhered to his basic political philosophy but not the methods being pursued to attain it.

After hearing about the insurance money he also was sure his leaders had planned all along for Humphrey to die. He had never liked the fat man or his odor and had usually avoided him, but he could not be a party to murder. The weekend after Chance's visit George took one of his frequent week end trips, but not to visit relatives this time, rather the FBI. He told what little he knew for sure and what he suspected and agreed to carry a miniature wire recorder to any League functions. He was also given $20,000 in cash he could say he'd solicited for the League. The serial numbers were recorded and could help track cash flow. Upon his return he accepted the Executive Board membership and attended the recruiting rally when Jerome Buckhalter came to speak at the school stadium on Saturday, July 15th.

A private meeting of Jerome with the full Executive Board took place in the office afterwards. A hidden surveillance team recorded everything said via the planed bugs. So did George. Excerpts of the conversation are recorded below.

J.   Great Rally. Your people have been doing a super job.

R.   Thank you, sir. But we have you to thank for the success of the Mikota operation.

J.   That did go well, didn't it? Even better results than we expected. First rate job on that truck. But you'd better be sure to destroy the negatives and any blueprints which show the interior of the van.

R.   We already did, sir. Those working drawings you sent us were very easy to follow.

(Here came talk of construction details of the metal bins that held the oil-fertilizer mix and then the wiring.)

J.   You did use a double ignition system?

R.   Yes sir. Two sticks of dynamite went into each bin. The pairs of sticks were each hooked to separate batteries, six to one battery, and six to the other. (Here a chuckle.) We will never know if one of the batteries failed, but there was a big KABOOM.

J.   It was excellent. And that unexpected fireworks truck was like divine approval of our work.

R.   Could you answer a question?

J.   Shoot.

R.   We received two dozen lengths of lead pipe you sent. Let's see, I believe it was two inch pipe about two feet long and the ends were sealed. We assumed it was radioactive material and per your instructions had Humphrey handle them and place four in each bin before loading in the fertilizer and fuel oil. We told him it was part of a secret stink bomb formula. My question is what was in that pipe?

J.   The pipes were full of pulverized radioactive concrete shielding from a nuclear power plant that was being de-commissioned. The average half life is measured in decades, not centuries or millennia. But it sure did throw a left hook into (expletives depleted.)

   With the above words on tape and a witness willing to verify plus a body of additional information brought to them by Norman Orville Chance, the FBI could have moved. But it was also desired to prove the connections between the many Chapters and FSN and then to make a simultaneous move against all at once, confiscating and freezing their assets in one big move as they arrested guilty leadership. It might take a year but the evidence was solid and it is true the criminals would have no chance.

A New Day and Mokey

It was 8:45 when John began to awaken. As from a long distance he heard little sounds from the kitchen and the crackle of a small fire on the hearth. His pre-conscious state was like a pleasant dream and in it he seemed to smell coffee perking. This smell drew him toward full awareness as the events of the previous day scrolled through his mind. He jerked upright in the lounger and his eyes blinked open. He had that momentary state of confusion that sometimes marks the transition between being asleep and being awake.

Stella saw him move and stepped over to greet him. She was scrubbed and glowing, her raven hair brushed and silky. She had managed to get most of the dirt off the knees and cuffs of her denims and soft shoes. Her smile was broader than he'd ever seen it before as she said, "Thanks to the good Lord and you, it's a really good morning. Cuppa java? I got the makings of breakfast out. I hope you don't mind I nosed in the pantry."

"Bless you, dear heart. I'll get dressed in clean clothes after I wash up and stash my PJ's and be out in a jiffy,"

At the table he said, "Let's thank God together for letting us see the light of a new day." He reached across the table and put his hands over her clasped hands before praying. It seemed very good to her. The rain had stopped an hour earlier and the cessation of its slushy patter outside had awakened her. After the prayer of thanks, while they were sipping the hot brew, the sun broke through. They began to discuss what had to be done that day.

Bernie was the first of the children to be up and dressed. He told how his parents had since Bar Mitzvah allowed him to have occasional coffee half and half with milk. Marian was up shortly after him and declared, "I have coffee lots of time but neither my mother nor uncle will share Irish coffee with me. I snuck some once. It's yucky."

About ten Jojo was awakened by Juliet sobbing for her mother. He started to cry, too, but Bernie told him the man was going to take all of them to town to hunt for their mamas and the doggie. With lots of hugs and a bit of tickling, tears were turned to giggles. Similar tactics by Stella and Marian worked on Juliet. After they were both dressed the boy said to his little friend, "No cry, Juju. We go find mama and doggie." The appellation Juju stuck and from then on it was the team of Jojo and Juju.

Marian helped Stella prepare breakfast which was finally served at 11:00. There was a big stack of pancakes with butter and syrup, pork sausages, canned orange juice, plenty of cocoa and coffee. John was nervous about what the reaction would be by the Jewish lad regarding pork and using the name of Jesus in the table grace. He would not compromise, but he did not wish to needlessly offend. He was pleasantly surprised.

The lad said, "I know Christians finish prayers with Jesus' name but you're trying to talk to God the Creator and I can say amen to that. And my daddy says that when I pay for the food, or am allowed to pick for myself in a restaurant, I can avoid unclean meats. But when I'm the guest of a Gentile and they're paying for the food, I should eat what is set before me. We're not Orthodox, we're liberal Reformed. If there's no Kosher, we eat what's not Kosher. My Rabbi agrees with what your Jesus said about being made unclean by what goes out of our mouth and not what goes in it. Jesus was a smart man but we would expect that because he was a Jew."

The little ones were as happy as could be once they had full tummies, a chance to play with their fuzzy toys, and the renewed promise of a hunt for their loved ones and the dog. It's not sure which one said it first, but one of them commented at the table, "I love panty cakes. Yum!" Then it was repeated back and forth by them. It's also safe to say none of the other four were fearful or depressed once the sun was bright, their appetites satisfied, and they felt secure in their new surroundings.

The next thing on John's agenda was the matter of tending to the live stock. He took Bernie with him but did not just then tell the little ones about the animals. The man wore his own overshoes and lent Lionel's over-sized pair to his buddy Hawkeye to slog through the puddles which would take hours to drain.

Bernie was impressed by the equipment in the work shop and impressed again when John got out the Geiger counter and demonstrated it using the ore samples that had come with it. Knox Farm primarily produced food for those living on it and shared the surplus with others. Aside from a Rototiller and a small garden tractor-mower, there were only manual tools including a human powered tiller with a steel wheel and handle bars.

John did not then own a motor vehicle. In a pinch he would borrow his uncle's Plymouth as long as he was ever so careful with it and made sure it was spotless inside and out upon being returned. It was not a matter of funds, just an unwillingness to spend them. Besides, he could always use the farm truck in the valley. It was a big-wheeled old Dodge Power Wagon.

The truck had a large flat bed made of planks. It had removable side walls and also a canvas top supported by a pipe frame. In low range its lower gears made it a perfect putt-putt for after dark hay rides when the clan gathered. On it could be hauled just about anything the farm needed including awesome amounts of firewood. John started it up, backed it up to the shed where the boat on its trailer was stored, and hitched it, and then pulled up to the door yard of the Honeymoon Cottage.

He explained to Stella and the older pair, "We don't know what happened. We might have to come back here for a while. The old truck has plenty of room to haul us plus necessaries if we really are alone in the valley. We'll want clothing, lamp oil, pantry fillers, honey, candle wax, and maybe even candy."

Stella asked, "What's the boat for? Didn't you tell me once you use a boat to fish on Ribbon Lake?"

"That's the one. If the radiation is low enough we might be able to get to your apartment over the café so at least you and I will have our belongings."

They departed at one after a snack of milk and cookies. The children climbed up in back and the gate was shut. Stella rode in the cab with John. The man slid the rear window of the cab open to call out to the rear passengers when deer were seen near the narrow road. About half way to town he pointed out a number of bee hives in a meadow.

"Zach Lincoln has a Sweet Shoppe in Glasgow that's open all year and a second smaller one here only open during the tourist season. A lot of his candy is home made and features our valley honey. These are some of the hives he collects wax and honey from. His shop occupies the big front porch and living room of his summer cottage a block over from the Red Arrow Mall."

The two adults became very silent and introspective as they approached town. He slid the window shut and said, "Don't get your hopes too high, Stel. God spared us from whatever happened to Dundee and He may be about to lay the responsibility for four other lives upon us. They might be orphans now. We might have to become their guardians. If we do we'll have to work closely together and be in good agreement in front of them. There's also the question of who is in charge of them and has to make the final decisions and govern them. I think it ought to be you. You know umpteen as much about kids as I do. I'll decide on matters of supplies and maintenance. Does that sound okay to you?"

She pondered a while and sighed. She turned away from him and wiped gathering moisture away from her eyes. She then faced forward and took deep breaths. He turned toward her and repeated, "Well, does it sound okay?"

She looked him full in the eyes and said, "No!"

"You don't want to help just in case?"

"I'll help any way I can. I already love them."

"Then why did you say no?"

"Because you have to be in charge. My parents and priest all teach God made men to be heads of families. This would be like a family. I know you'll listen to me but you must be in charge. I completely trust you and it is your farm and I know we're not their parents. But when I'm with Aunt Bonnie and Uncle Ray, he is in charge of me like my dad would be. Maybe we could be an aunt and uncle to them."

He quietly laughed. "I had been thinking I could get out of some things I knew at heart I should be doing by shoving them off on you. I'm hoping it doesn't happen that we'll all have to stay in the Hidden Valley, but if we do I'm sure it will work out well, uh, Auntie Stella."

She couldn't hold back a mischievous snort of laughter as she replied, "Okay, Unca Junior."

In addition to the standard horn the truck sported a trio of long chrome horns on the roof. Lionel had years earlier acquired them at an auto specialty store. Together the three blasted out like a locomotive horn and had been useful for summoning Knox kids back to the Lodge from their wanderings. The ammeter needle would take a big dip every time the horns were used and too frequent use without the engine running could quickly result in a dead battery.

About a mile from the Dundee Grand Hotel John began blasting on the triple horns several times a minute to attract the attention of any people still in the area. A block up river from the hotel was a public boat launching place and John launched and tied the boat here. The hotel's grand opening had not precluded partial advance reservations as evidenced by the number of out of state plates on vehicles in the parking lot. He pulled up to the main entrance and after tooting three more times dismounted.

He made a circular sweep around the building with the Geiger counter before saying, "Okay gang, everybody off. Let's see if anyone is here."

What they saw gave evidence of a mass disappearance and an abandoning of possessions. Only the first two floors of the four-storied hotel had been open to the early guests and vacated rooms had not had maid services nor had clothing, luggage, or personal effects been removed.

The grand dining room was in disarray. Tables had not been cleared of used silverware, cups, glasses, pop cans or dishes, many of which still had uneaten food on them. On a buffet under glass covers were left assorted pastries. John again checked for radiation and then allowed the taking of pastries. In a large cooler next to the kitchen he found cartons of still cool chocolate milk even though the power had long been off. He gave them each drinks of chocolate milk.

He pondered and paced as he ate a Danish and sipped his milk. He prayed silently, "Lord, it couldn't have been the Rapture, could it? It goes against all history that every individual would have been a born again believer and all were taken. Besides, I'm still here and you promised to prepare a place for me and take me to it. I trust you. You always keep your promises and you keep your children. Please let me have some insight."

They mounted a stairway to the fifth level. This was the roof itself with a glass dome over it. It was mostly a lounge with an indoor garden graced with flowers and small shrubs. But at one end was a small carpeted playground. From up here the whole town was in view.

Lionel had always kept binoculars in the cab and John had entrusted them to Hawkeye after dismounting.

They were not needed to see the devastation. The water now covered the eastern third of the town and would be reaching the street just east of the hotel. Its advance would be continually slower as more and more volume would be filling up. But at least the fire was out although there was still haze near the soon to be covered fuel tanks and scattered slicks of oil floated on the lake.

They were standing in a row close together and Marian hesitantly took John's hand and held it tight as she said very solemnly, "Last night I thought it was the Lake of Fire preachers talk about and the end of the world. It's all scary but it's not the end of the world, is it?"

"No Dear, I'd say just the end of most of Dundee. But the valley has over 16,000 acres. The six of us have plenty of room. It does look like the rest have been taken away. We'll have to wait for them to come back. We'll all be okay."

He scanned with the binoculars. "I think there had to be an explosion, most likely behind the Sentinel. It must have blown his cap off. He's shorter now. And windows for the next two blocks have been blown in. It must have been a mini nuclear blast to do so much. But the rain has washed the dust out of the air and must have been washing any other dust into the river off the cliffs and buildings.

"The water is nearly up to the eaves of the front porch of the café. If the radiation readings are low enough, Aunt Stella and I…."

She interrupted, "Kids, your mamas trusted you to our care. So until you see your families again, John and I would be glad to take care of you like good aunts and uncles do. Is that okay? He'll be your Uncle John now."

Uncle John continued, "Aunt Stella and I will be taking the boat and we can float over to the top windows of the café and get her stuff plus any family mementos she might want to save. They'd soon be under water otherwise. Meanwhile Jojo and Juju can play and if we are needed Bernie can toot the horn three times, wait a minute, and do three more."

It was three thirty before the boat was back in the trailer. Juju had been constantly reminding Bernie and Marian about finding her doggie. In her mind it was already hers.

The man drove a search pattern, back and forth on alternate streets, frequently blasting the horn. A couple of door over from Sweet Shoppe II they heard hoarse barking, much weaker than before. They spotted the head of a big dog moving back and forth behind slightly open windows. The side door of the house had a large pet door which was supposed to swing in or out but was somehow jammed so that entrance was permitted but not exits. Apparently the dog had gone for a run, been scared by the explosion, and wandered farther away only returning after what had to have been a mass helicopter evacuation.

When John and Bernie came to the window, the dog snarled protectively, warning them off. Juju saw him and cried out, "My new doggie," and dashed to the pet door. Before anyone could stop her she had crawled in. Jojo tried to follow her but his cousin prevented him. From inside came barks and growls and then a shrill yell from the girl. John pulled out his Swiss Army knife and clicked open the biggest blade and then forced the door with his shoulder to gain entry.

The shrill outburst of Juju turned to uncontrollable laughter. The little one stood with her arms around the neck of the standing dog, a young brown and white Saint Bernard whose tail was lashing frantically as he licked her face. At John's approach with knife hand extended he bared his fangs and growled but the girl said, "No, no, Mokey. That's Uncle John."

The big dog immediately stopped acting aggressive and bounded over to the man, put his paws on his shoulders and thoroughly kissed him. He did the same to Stella, almost knocking her over. The little girl tugged him off for a formal introduction. "Mokey, this is Aunt Stella. Aunt Stella, this is Mokey." She took the dog to each for introductions and each got their faces baptized by the big pink tongue.

The dog was caked with mud and had grease on his back. He must have tried to hide under a vehicle after being scared by the big boom. He was a bedraggled mess not yet a year old but nearly full grown. Such a dog could be a formidable foe to enemies but a very constant friend and protector to his family. John pet him and checked his collar. Necessary medical tags were there but no name tag,

"Honey, do you think his name is Mokey?"

"I dunno."

"Well why did you call him Mokey?"

"He looks like a Mokey."

Marian said, "I never saw a Mokey before. What do Mokeys look like?"

Juju hugged her drooling new friend and said, "They look just like him."

Little children might not have adult logic, but theirs is tied to faith and it is irrefutable. Anyhow, what's in a name for an animal friend? Mokey he would be the rest of his life. Also be aware that children often have a knack for instantly making friends with others, animal or human, and bonding with them with no further ado.

Juju asked Uncle John, "Will you be Mokey's uncle, too?"

"Of course, Sweetheart, and I think Aunt Stella will be his aunt. We'll be a family of seven for now, okay?"

He signaled to the older lad, "Hawkeye, could you hunt up his sack of dog food and load it aboard. If he's out we'll get more on the way. Then our next stop will be at Top to Bottom to get wardrobe items for you four. Then to the Food House to get whatever perishables we can use up before spoilage. We'll be spending one more night at the Honeymoon Cottage but tomorrow we'll move into the Lodge. Then back to town tomorrow to finish stocking up."

He sounded much more confident than he felt. But like Stella he already was loving his de facto family. If ever he had trusted the Lord for help, now would be the time. He could take care of physical needs but he also had their spiritual welfare to consider. During a 48 hour period his whole life had been rearranged. What would the future hold?

Chapter Seven

THE REST OF THE SUMMER

Thursday night, when Stella finally got to bed on the couch at 11:00, John was seated at the kitchen table with his Bible and a couple of study help books. She'd assured him the light wouldn't bother her but also begged him not to be up too late. She had attended to his hands and was pleased at how much better they looked. Though he'd told her she needn't bother, he was pleased that she did.

The children were all soundly asleep. A community effort had been made at the river to clean up Mokey. He had not been very cooperative. There was a small Knox-dug inlet from the Mikota River which made an excellent wading and swimming pool. After the dog had been washed and had a chance to swim to rinse off, it was amazing how many of them had got drenched when he shook his wet fur. He slept on an old rug at the foot of the girls' bed.

Stella had feigned sleep for a while but her act soon became reality. John's last words to her had been, "Jesus said we should not be afraid. He said He'd never leave us alone. He sent his Holy Spirit to comfort us. And he said he was building a mansion for us. What choice have we but to be of good cheer, Stel?" His cheerful assurance opposed and helped conquer the fears and doubts she had.

She roused at about 1:00 and noticed his lounger was empty, the kitchen was dark and there was only one bathroom lamp lit on low. She slipped her robe on over her pajamas and neglecting her slippers, padded barefoot across the cool floor to the windows. There was enough moonlight to illuminate him as he knelt beside a boulder beside the pool. She stared at him for just a moment before hastening back to bed. It seemed almost a sacrilege to intrude on what seemed a holy service. She had trusted his wisdom and capabilities to where she felt very secure associated with him. Now she felt doubly safe to know this good man sought out God like her priest had done.

John had been seeking truth and guidance from God's Word to help him under circumstances which to him were more frightening than any perilous ordeal, that of trying to fill the shoes of parents. He knew that even though the mental, emotional, and physical well-being of a child was very important, the biggest challenge for a Christian was to raise children in the fear and admonition of the Lord. He felt totally inadequate.

The thought had come to him that without God's anointing any task a Christian attempted would be done in vain. He sifted through his Bible in many passages. In Leviticus he saw how priests who were to minister before God were first anointed and set apart. He read how kings such as David were anointed with oil to show God's approval. He read in Isaiah how the prophet after being cleansed with fire was anointed to preach. In Psalm 23 he was reminded of the head being anointed with oil. In the gospels he read of Jesus anointing the eyes of a blind man who then could see. He looked afresh at the passage where a woman anointed Jesus' feet with precious ointment and wiped them with her hair. And finally he looked at Acts where the Holy Spirit anointed with fire to give power.

The man had quietly left the cottage and walked a while whispering the familiar phrases he'd been reading. He communed with his heavenly Father as he mulled over the truths he'd been reminded of. He said very little to God, needing instead to let God speak to him through the sacred book. Understanding had come as he approached the aforementioned stone and it was just after he knelt there that Stella saw him.

"Oh my Father, as I look back I see you leading me right up to this minute. You have set a new course before me, a brand new task. I humbly accept it and ask for a multiplied anointing. I believe you have set me apart to protect, care for, and lead the rest, for how long I have no idea. You did it just like you anointed the Priests and Levites to serve you.

"I also believe your anointing is to show your approval as you did of David as king. This must have already happened for they all, from Jojo to Stella, look to me for leadership and have been doing what I asked. Now like Isaiah I ask you to be continually cleansing my lips and anointing them to say your words to all. Please anoint my head so that my mind, my very thoughts and imaginations will be pleasing to you and I might find wisdom to do what's best. Anoint my eyes to see what a guardian should see and turn my eyes away from what they should not see. Anoint my feet to always stay on your path. Anoint my body that it might be crucified with Christ and die to self will and desire.

"And finally make me a clean vessel that your Holy Spirit may fill me with power as it was at Pentecost. I believe it is so. I believe you have anointed me as I asked. No emotional high this, Lord, but a sure conviction, an absolute knowledge through faith that you have ordained and anointed me in a way you never did before to do a work I never had before. Thanks be to God. Glory to Jesus. Hallelujah! Amen."

John was now best prepared to accept life changes. For the others it took a while. When a person gets a new car it takes perhaps three weeks to get used to it. The same applies to a change of residence. If possessions such as appliances or furniture are accidentally disfigured and not soon restored, after a few weeks the scars are hardly noticed and soon become status quo.

At the Knox Farm in the now Forbidden Valley, John was where he had been all his life and the changes he had to make were in regards to responsibilities and relationships. Mokey adapted immediately. Jojo and Juju had spells of crying for relatives but as the number of days from separation increased, these became less and less frequent. Bernie and Marian tried hard to fit in and help out and both made it a point to avoid solitude. They preferred to always be near John or Stella or each other or even tending the little ones.

Stella was always cheerful and upbeat outwardly. She used constant work, much not necessary, to isolate her from her tangle of uncertainty and sorrow over what might have happened to her relatives and family. She drove herself so that fatigue-induced sleep kept her from thinking.

For the four oldest it was ignorance over what had happened to the rest of the world that brought the most stress. Unknown to John the tuner in the Subaru radio did not work, tuning only to static. After trying dozens of times to receive broadcasts, he had given up. It was true that the mountains and cliffs blocked most transmissions but there were usually a few signals that might bounce in. Depending on cloud layers these might be different stations at different times.

Uncle Lionel had relied on periodicals and newspapers plus the mail to get his news. He had used the phone sparingly. So as far as the Knox Farm group was concerned there was nothing to be heard from the outside world. There were not even any more vapor trails to indicate high-flying military aircraft still flew.

A few days in advance John declared Saturday, July 22nd to be a holiday. "Aunt Stella has been working way too hard. That day she is forbidden to work. We'll all wait on her. And we're gonna go on a picnic and have boat rides on Ribbon Lake, maybe even do some fishing. When we get back we'll have a party and play games. Marian and I will cook and Hawkeye will help us. Now's let all hug her and tell her how much we love her."

The children and Mokey had swarmed over her. When they were through John had given her a fraternal hug, side by side with one arm around her shoulder and said, "I love everyone here and that includes you, Stel. God gave you to us as a special gift. I don't know how I could get by without you. Thank you, Dear." She never stopped whistling or singing that day. He had ignited a glow within her.

At mid morning Saturday the Power Wagon was loaded and ready to chug up to Ribbon Lake pulling the boat trailer. Both gas tanks were full. The farm had a red 300 gallon gravity feed gas tank on stilt legs. It had a similar but smaller kerosene tank. Each were filled in the spring. Although fuels were untaxed and well discounted for Mikota Territory residents and citizens, Uncle Lionel bought them in bulk for the farm for even greater savings. And should the farm supplies run low, there were many untapped sources in the unflooded portion of Dundee.

At the Knox Farm there was a sturdy stone and timber bridge across the Mikota River. In the earliest days of Hidden Valley use there had been well traveled trails on each side of the river, Both had been widened and improved but were yet unpaved rough roads. The northern trail up to the bridge was open to the public; from there to the north shore of the lake it was a private road for Knox use. The southern road was public all the way to its end at the lake. Blue Bird runs into the valley had used the road to the farm, crossed the bridge, and made a scenic run to the lake, then back to town on the southern road which joined the Valley Spur near the hotel.

After crossing the bridge and heading west, Hawkeye, using the binoculars, spotted a sleek wild stallion grazing with his herd. They were on a small plateau two or three stories above the floor of the canyon on which was the road. The road ran alongside a small rapids and water noise fully masked exhaust snorts. They were canopied by large trees and although our picnickers could peek out between the greenery, they were nearly impossible to see from above.

But the stallion was edgy and his nervousness communicated itself to his herd. Perhaps he had caught the scent of exhaust. John shut off the engine and all had a chance to see the wild horses, descendents of escaped domestic horses a few generations earlier. The head honcho kept lifting his head from eating and peered around, prancingly pawing the ground with his front hooves.

After a few minutes John said, "Let's watch 'em run." He blasted on the triple horns. The big black reared up, whinnied a warning to his followers, and kicked with his front hooves as if to declare who was boss, and broke into a graceful gallop. There are few sights that compare to the majestic beauty of wild horses running free.

Once they were out of sight Marian asked, "Who do they belong to?"

Bernie answered with a question. "Who do you belong to? God made us free and nobody owns us. God made them free and nobody owns them either."

It was about ten when the picnic party arrived at the gravelly southeast beach of Ribbon Lake. A small public park had been developed by the Mikotans. It included picnic tables, iron cooking grills, a boat ramp, a unisex outhouse, and a rustic shack for changing clothes. The place was named Saturday Park and its western boundary was a spring which issued forth out of the rock near shore level. All other water entering the lake cascaded down from above. The falls were frigidly cold; the water issuing from the rock had a hot spring as its source. In the Mikota Territory there were many numerous manifestations of geo-thermal activity.

The erosive action of hot mineral water had over uncounted years cut a basin in the rock which was deep enough for wading or limited swimming. The flow from the basin into the lake formed a perpetually warm mini cove in the icy lake. Bathing and water games could be engaged in literally year around. Staying unfrozen getting to the water was the problem. The lake floor deepened gradually but before swimmers got into potentially dangerous depths with tricky currents, they were driven back towards shore by the cold.

Mokey was first into the water and most often in and out of it. But as quickly as they could change into their suits, the six began to enjoy splashing and water fights accompanied by great noise. John was a strong swimmer as were Bernie and Stella. When Stella, Bernie, and the two Jays ganged up on John, it was Marian to the rescue. Nobody escaped being bopped by soft inflatable beach balls. And all this happened on a just right day in a place of exceptional beauty. The happy confusion continued to chow time and even then noise reigned.

As they ate their sandwiches and potato salad Marian asked, "Uncle John, why is this called Saturday Park? Is it only supposed to be used on Saturdays?"

"No Sweetheart, about a hundred years ago back when the tribe was helping my ancestors to build the barn and get the farm started, there was already a small community, a settlement they later called Dundee where the drowned village is now. Divine services where held every Sunday morning in a home. Well you can't go to church dirty or in dirty clothes if you can help it so the tradition of a Saturday night bath was revived. Now there were only men camping at the farm during construction so they'd saddle up and ride up here to wash in the warm water and maybe scrub some duds to wear to church. Incidentally that black stallion you saw and his herd are descendents of horses that went wild back then. So when the time came to name the park what better name than Saturday Park?"

That afternoon was time for the promised boat rides and later as the two Jays were napping, John took Bernie out for a fishing lesson. The lad was quick to learn the mechanics of casting and a bit of fishing lore but the fish in the neighborhood were smarter than the fishermen. But more than the knowledge gained and the experience, the lad treasured the fact that Uncle John devoted so much time to him and it would never leave his mind that the man had announced, "Us men are goin' fishin'."

Finally, before packing everything for the ride back home John had insisted Stella take one more ride with him without the children. He'd opened the throttle wide and did show-off twists and turns all the way to the far end of the lake almost a mile distant. When mist from the falls began to dampen them he turned back and drove slowly so he could talk to the Lady of the Day.

"Stel, you're a marvel. Uncle Lionel and I used to pride ourselves on our housekeeping but since you took charge of it, it's never been more spic and span in the Lodge. One preacher said God made men to use their brains and brawn and be the heads of households, but he said God made the woman to be its heart. Without heart a brain is just a cold computer. It's the heart that brings life and warmth and love to a household. You are that dear sweet heart. I thank God for you and pray you'll never change, Stel."

Men and boys alike had often said good words to her. It was usually flattery to get her to do a favor for them. Even as a young girl whose brothers tried to talk her into something with their wheedling words, she had usually seen through it and stayed clear of tricks or troubles. But there had been men like her dad and Uncle Ray and now John D. Knox who gave her sincere praise only to build her up, and never expected anything back in exchange. She could cooperate with a man like John all her life and never regret it.

That night in bed after prayers, John reviewed with pleasure the day. But most of the images which filled his mind were of Estellita Juarez. Her appreciation and delight for the special attention showed her. Her spontaneous laughter which kept bursting forth causing all others to join her. Her graceful movement in and out of the water. Her physical attractiveness to John whether in casual clothes or her modest bathing suit. He had trouble getting images of her out of his mind. He fell asleep after praying again, "Lord, keep me and her from wrong thoughts or deeds. She is a great help and I'm beginning to care for her very deeply. Keep our friendship and daily association from ever becoming a snare to either of us."

At this point it might be well to take a look at the Lodge where our friends will be dwelling for the foreseeable future. This large log house had originally been built to accommodate the families of two Knox brothers, from one of which had sprung John's paternal grandfather. In appointments, construction, and furniture it had been the standard for the Honeymoon Cottage,

Along the back wall which faced north were five rooms which had started out as bedrooms. The largest one was on the north east corner and Uncle Lionel had turned it into a library and study. It had an impressive collection and particularly paid attention to classic literature, history, natural science, and world religions with particular emphasis on Christianity.

An ell extended out from the southeast corner of the home which more than doubled the space of the sitting room of the early days. The large room was adequate for chapel services when the clan gathered.

Just west of the living room was a large bathroom but there were several outhouses on the farm. The southwest quadrant of the home housed a large country kitchen with a huge table. In the ceiling of the hallway between the bathroom and fourth bedroom were folding pull-down steps which gave access to the attic. This was one huge gabled room which even after giving storage space had room for a couple of dozen Knox juveniles to spread their sleeping bags and allegedly sleep. But the attic, though insulated, was not heated and totally unsuitable for winter use.

The house had woodstoves at each end, the larger being in the living room. There was also the wood-burning cook stove which did most of their winter heating. Lionel and John shut off the living room, library, and both of the unused bedrooms and dressed warmly.

The Honeymoon Cottage was about 100 yards east of the Lodge which in turn was about 35 yards east of the old barn/stable which was now the Great Hall. The dozen stalls along its back wall had been renovated to make eight small bedrooms scantily furnished. The large room was ideal for parties, banquets, or even square dances. Stone fireplaces at each end might do a little to take the chill off the big room in cold weather but they were more suitable for toasting marshmallows or heating big pots of cocoa.

Flagstone paths about six feet wide connected the three buildings. The one between the Great Hall and the Lodge had an eight foot wide cedar-shingled roof over it. This was open on the sides but gave total protection from rain and only allowed a minimum of snow to land on the walk thus eliminating most shoveling.

Beyond the Great Hall were the workshop and various sheds and buildings to house equipment, animals, and their food. Connected to live stock shelter were the pens, coops, and yards the creatures used. It was simple for all to get out to forage or graze if they wished but they always had shelter to return to. And just in back of the Lodge was a root cellar no longer used for the Lodge had a dry cool cellar under the kitchen.

The Friday immediately after the blast had been moving day. Anything John had at the cottage was brought to the Lodge. His customary room had been the west-most. His uncle had used the one next to the study. John moved into it. He purged his former and gave it to Stella. He helped her hang her crucifix and various plaques and religious pictures. Marian and Juju were given the room next to Aunt Stella and the boys the remaining room.

The double beds in the children's rooms were moved to the Great Hall and replaced with double-decker bunk beds. Each of the rooms had mirrors on the closet doors but in addition vanities were brought into the ladies' rooms. Each person also had their own dresser.

All the food and some of the kitchen paraphernalia was brought over from the cottage. In addition to this another trip was made to town to lay in additional supplies. Everyone was caught up in the hectic pandemonium. Even the wee ones from time to time carted over small objects if they could be diverted from romping with Mokey.

As the sun began lowering behind the mountains, about an hour before actual sunset, Bernie asked to talk to the man. "Uncle John. Would it be okay with you if I took a break for the rest of the day?"

"Of course. You're not ill or over-tired are you."

"No sir."

"Can you tell me why you want a break?'

"It's almost Sabbath."

"Yes, I should have thought of it. Certainly you may keep your Sabbath. I would expect it of you. I think I already know you well enough to know you would never use religion as an excuse to get out of work. You're free for the next 24 hours."

"But my family just kept part of it, Friday evening. We'd go to temple together. My father would still work on Saturday. I just want some time this evening to meditate and say some prayers. I'll catch up on my work tomorrow."

"I'm glad you brought it up. I've been thinking there ought to be worship on Sunday. When you and Marian first saw our piano I overheard her say she had taken a few lessons and you said you could help her. Then I heard you give her a tiny demonstration of your skill, a mini-recital. You're pretty good. Would you have any objections to playing hymns at our service? If you have convictions against participating in a Christian service, I would certainly understand."

The lad pondered a moment. "I would be pleased to help you if I had a chance to practice the songs first. I remember one time our Rabbi preached at a black Baptist church on Martin Luther King Day. He preached on how God is a God of justice and hates discrimination.

"And there was the time my cousin. Robert Stein, had a fire in his house. It was mostly smoke and water damage. There was a Salvation Army Church down the street and they were there to help before the firemen left. They gave them meals and temporary lodging and helped clean up the mess and then gave them clothes from their rummage room and loaned them furniture until the insurance money came. After that Robert and his family were always volunteering to help the Army help others and my dad and all our relatives used to put big checks in the kettles at Christmas. How can it be wrong to help one another? Playing Christian hymns for you doesn't mean I have to believe all the words. And I think it would be good for Jojo to start to learn about God, even in a Christian service."

Simple services had been instituted. John always included a children's Bible story and a couple of Sunday School choruses and then dismissed the wee ones to play with Mokey before the more serious part. As time went by

Bernie was glad to do the Old Testament readings. He was even encouraged to comment on God's law. The lad listened carefully as one of the others read from the New Testament and then as John faithfully and simply expounded the Gospel of Grace.

And what is church without an offering? The very first service the man had asked,"How much money did you earn this last week? None? Then your tithe or tenth is zero. But as for an offering, I am certain the Lord is happy to accept kindnesses done to one another as gifts to himself. So let us ever show our gratitude to God for His blessings by how we care for one another."

Summer on the farm was the time of greatest work but none of it onerous. John saw to it that none except he and Stella ever worked alone. As much as possible he and the woman used one or the other of the older children as co-workers in field, garden, kitchen, or for varied tasks. At some times Bernie and Marian would work together. As fruits and vegetables ripened they had to be harvested and stored away one way or another, but not by freezing. Uncle Lionel used to say, "I'll bet we smoke, dry, and can enough to feed a regiment. There must be a couple thousand mason jars in use," which was an exaggeration somewhat.

To name some, potatoes, cabbage, corn, peas, carrots, pears, peaches, apples, cherries, and nuts had to be gathered from various scattered places and made ready for winter. A complete list of cultivated and wild foods would read like a catalog. As for meat there was pork, chicken, venison, small game, and various fishes. Along with this were eggs, grains, and dairy products to round out the menu. But nothing jumped out of the field and on to the table.

One of Dundee's summer families had planted fields of strawberries and raspberries close to town. These also grew wild wherever conditions were right in the valley. At the end of July the family (for so they thought of themselves now) had all gone to pick red raspberries which make delicious jam or pie filling and would be great on ice cream Stella was planning. She had warned that all would take turns cranking. "Everyone cranks. No crankee, no eatee."

The little ones made a game of picking but more berries went in their mouths than in their buckets. John had laughed and said, "When I was little I could make some change by picking but the owner said I had to keep whistling as I worked. Who can tell why?"

Bernie laughed and said, "Because you can't eat berries and whistle at the same time."

It seemed that Marian always gravitated toward the man and as they picked side by side she said, "Uncle John, you said we couldn't mountain climb out of here because it gets worse the farther you go and too dangerous and anyhow we couldn't take the Jays along. But what if we could fly out? Couldn't we build an airplane? Couldn't we take a lawn mower motor from Fix-it's and use it? It already has a blade like a propeller."

Bernie was just one row over and he and Uncle John explained some of the difficulties involved. One problem was that a plane would require forty or fifty times as much horsepower as a lawn mower motor could develop. Bernie had concluded with, "Besides, we don't know how to fly and we could all get killed trying to fly even if we could build one. Besides that, think how much work it would take to clear and level an airstrip. Am I right, Uncle John?"

"Absolutely, Hawkeye, but I'm very proud of Marian for always keeping her brain working and using her wonderful imagination. If we already had a plane and knew how to fly it, we would definitely build an airstrip."

Marian told them, "We wouldn't need to if we had a plane. Isn't the paved highway by the hotel long and straight enough? Or we could put floaters on it and use Ribbon Lake, Couldn't we?"

John replied, "Good thinking. You're one step ahead of us. Yes, either the lake or the highway would work fine. If a plane does fly over them we could signal and they could land. But even though you've given us intriguing ideas, I'm certain we will never leave here in any plane we built."

After lunch that day, the simple picnic variety, came more questions from the red-head, "Uncle John, how come so many things have red arrows on them or are named Red Arrow?"

"Honey, the first John Knox back in 1804 or so arrived with his Bible, broadax, Brown Bess musket, and bow and arrows. That was not all he had but those B's are easy to remember. He seldom used the musket because he did not know when he would ever be able to get more lead and powder. So he mostly hunted with his bow and arrows. He greatly hated losing arrows if he missed, so he tinted all his arrows red to make them easier to find. The Red Arrow name and logo were adopted by the tribe to honor him. Now all the tribe's businesses such as gas stations (remember they own an oil field) are sending profits back to benefit all Mikota citizens."

At home at the supper table came yet one more question from the girl, "Can anyone explain how come a place where we lived is called a Honeymoon Cottage?"

John tried, "What we call the Great Hall was the first building, a barn. Next a small cabin was put up where the cottage is now. Then later on the Lodge was built. Always called that. Matthew, my great grandfather and his brother Mark worked the farm together and needed a home for their families. When Grandpa David was courting, he tore down the old cabin and built the cottage for his bride Eunice. Uncle Lionel was the first one born there and two years later my dad was born there followed two more years later by my Aunt Maude. When she grew up she married Glen McCormack and they live in Elmhurst, Ill. About then great

Grandfather Mark moved to Phoenix and my grandparents moved into the Lodge.

"I hope you're not confused yet because there's more. When my dad got married he and my mom lived in the cottage and I was born there but I have a hard time remembering that event. When I was about five Grandpa David died and the next year Grandma Eunice followed him to heaven, so we moved in with Uncle Lionel. When I was about ten he was contemplating marriage and began to restore the cottage which was beginning to show the wear and tear of years. But when my folks died and he became my guardian, his fiancé bowed out. He had hoped to be the third Knox man to use the cottage which had been the home of honeymoon couples. The clan agreed it ought to have the permanent name of Honeymoon Cottage."

When the children of Israel were forcibly uprooted from their homeland and dragged to Babylon to start new lives, it was roots to their past, ties to their heritage, which kept them from losing their identities. In like manner the four junior members of the new family in the Forbidden Valley had some anchors mooring them to their pasts so that they were not hopelessly adrift under new and strange circumstances.

Visual reminders, snapshots of loved ones were of special help. John's home was full of albums and other reminders and Stella had retrieved the same from above the café. Bernard's billfold was full of photos. He and Jojo had good visual reminders.

But Marian and Juju were unfortunate and had nothing. Providentially Stella had a degree of artistic ability. He hand was steady and her memory of form and detail good. It was unlikely she would ever be good enough to compete in the commercial world and gain fame and fortune, yet she could make sketches that could be recognized for the person drawn. She got supplies in secret from the Paper

Place and drew Corinne O'Connor and Bernice Eberhard so that the girls recognized their mothers. The memories would not die.

Another thing that ties us to our past and helps bring continuity is the tradition of yearly birthday celebrations. All that is needed is a calendar and a birth date to keep track. But Juliet's was not known for sure. An educated guess was made when she told of her birthday party a week (or maybe two) before the fateful trip. Bernard was certain of Jojo's date. As of July's end, 2000, ages and birth dates are as follows.

1. John D. Knox. 25   June 10th, 1975
2. Estellita Juarez. 18   November 1st, 1981
3. Bernard Krause. 13   August 3rd, 1986
4. Marian O'Connor. 12   December 14th, 1987
5. Juliet Eberhard. 4   June 23rd (??), 1996
6. Joseph Krause. 3   August 10th, 1996
7. Mokey. 1 (??)   1999

On Thursday, August 3rd, came the first party. Shopping had been done on the sly and Bernie's most treasured gifts came from Uncle John. Two of them were volumes 1 and 2 of Christian apologetics which presented evidence and asked the reader to pass a verdict. They were scholarly works, yet easy to understand and drew from the Old Testament, contemporary history, and even science to defend the deity and resurrection of the Lord Jesus Christ. It impressed the boy that the man never tried to push Presbyterian faith down his throat and also was challenged that he could by intellect and logic evaluate the evidence and come to his own conclusion. Both doctrinally and as lived day by day Christianity was being held up for inspection.

The third gift was not wrapped but given verbally. "Well Hawkeye, (John was the only one to use this nickname on a regular basis.) you are fourteen and more and more a man each day. Since I'm the only citizen who can vote in the valley, I have elected myself Governor, Chief Justice, Sheriff, sole legislator, etcetera, etcetera of Knox Valley, I am granting citizenship to Estellita Juarez and appointing her as second voice in all the aforementioned. We have decreed that driver's licenses may now be issued to those 14 or older and Mr. Bernard Krause will begin receiving his driving lessons as soon as he dries the supper dishes. Later on Aunt Stella will get her's too."

When the young man began to slowly and cautiously navigate the Subaru and later the truck, it raised his status one or two notches. For a change Miss O'Connor's admiring eyes were fixed on him instead of the man.

A week later Jojo had his birthday party held at Saturday Park. As birthday boy his food requests were honored. Cake, ice cream, and his favorites, "peambuddah Jell-o samwiches" were served. His vocabulary and use of words was improving, but when excited he sometimes regressed to earlier days. He had been delighted with the water fun and excited by his cousin's driving even though Uncle John had to help find the right gears in the truck.

By the end of August the family functioned smoothly for such a mixed group. None would ever forget from whence they came nor would relatives be forgotten even though family ties had been severed. Unanswered questions about missing faces or what had happened or was happening in the outside world would never cease coming up from time to time but the necessary daily tasks and convivial atmosphere promoted by Stella and John effectually dispelled gloom or depression for the children.

On Saturday, September 2nd, after the children were in bed, John escorted Stella to a plank bench which had been set up by the nearby pool. They sat still relaxing and enjoying the sounds of the river, breezy whispers in the trees, and the night calls of birds. After about 15 minutes of just listening and thinking, the young lady began to fidget.

"John, I'd better go in. I still have work to do."

"Work is like the applesauce we canned. It'll still be there tomorrow. Sit with me a while yet."

She did give in and it was pleasant, too pleasant. It made her nervous. After a few more minutes she said, "Unless there's a good reason for me to stay out, I'd better get back in."

"Actually there is a good reason but I wanted us to enjoy a few hassle-free moments first. We've been here over two months and I think we ought to discuss where we are and where we're going. I've done a lot of meditating and praying and I wanted to be sure we were both on the same wave length. Like about the kids for instance. Let's talk about Bernie first. What do you think about him?"

"Oh. Well he sure is smart. He knows way more book stuff than I do and he's willing to tackle anything I ask him to do. But he doesn't have much practical skill like on household chores. They're a far cry from book-learning, but he is always willing to try and he learns fast. I suppose that must be true about things outside the house with you. He's a good boy and he thinks the world of you."

"That's mutual. He's untrained but very strong. The only sport he ever went out for was swimming and it makes every muscle in your body strong. If he was a bad boy or had a bad temper or evil disposition, he'd be very dangerous. I think we have to stay very alert about his adolescence, his rapid maturing. He's becoming a man and it's a time of raging hormones. I'm concerned about fending off bad possibilities. At that age boys may be silent or afraid to mention their innermost feelings about the opposite sex but they're beginning to really notice girls and women. It's a perilous time. What do you think?"

"I'm sure you're right, John. In High School my brothers suddenly went girl crazy. They never went too far but I think there were some pretty close calls. Are you worried about Marian?"

"Yes, I am. And about you, too. As for her, we can't isolate them from each other but we can be sure they don't have privacy combined with leisure. She wants to be a good girl but not for the best reason. She wants me to be pleased with her and that's fine but the best reason for what we want to be or do should be to please the Lord."

She paused to ponder before answering. "John, you're quick to hug all the kids and except your buddy Hawkeye you let them sit on your lap. It might be good to phase that out with Marian. I've been talking to her about hygiene and female matters like I used to with my sisters. One of these days she won't be a girl any more but a very impressionable and easily led young woman. I want you to be very cautious with her."

John tucked away her words and inflections and wondered if something akin to jealousy was at work. He tried to lighten up and said very jokingly, "Well if you were sitting on my lap I might get nervous." He added very seriously, "She's just a lost lamb who desperately misses her father and uncle and she's accepted me as a poor substitute."

She replied, "I desperately miss my father and uncle too…..Just do be careful. I love that little redhead just like you do. Every day she either has a crush on you or Bernie. It keeps jumping back and forth. I can tell. It's more than just a longing for a parent. Every girl is born with the skill of turning one male against another to get what they secretly long for. I just want us to be very careful."

"Stel, I'm not blind either. I'm aware of how adoringly Bernie looks at you sometimes. We both have to stay alert and careful and seek out God's wisdom and guidance."

They were silent again for a few minutes thinking about possible implications of their mutual concern and feelings for each other. He finally broke their silence with, "What about Jojo and Juju?"

She broke into a broad smile. There was enough sky light so he could see her sparkling teeth and flashing eyes. "I love those little imps all to pieces. The day after it rained last week I washed and waxed the kitchen linoleum. They wanted to come in and I told them they had to first take off their muddy shoes and wipe off Mokey's paws. As soon as I turned my back they came scampering through with Mokey, muddy paws and shoes and all, tracking up my clean floor.

"I grabbed Jojo and turned him over my knee and gave him a few swats on his butt. He was more surprised than hurt and as he wailed, tears as big as jelly beans rolled down his cheeks. I went after Juju. She had been the leader. She usually is. Mokey came between us and actually growled and showed his teeth for a few seconds. I snatched that big wooden stirring spoon off the cupboard and yelled at him to get out of the way if he knew what was good for him. He quit growling, put his tail between his legs, ducked his head, and hunkered down. But he stayed between Juliet and me. He was ready to take a beating to protect her.

"But she knew she was in the wrong and she told him to stay put and she came over to get her spanking. She took her swats and they both cried and said sorry Auntie Stella. I made them both help me clean up their tracks. They are quite the kids, aren't they? And Mokey is quite a dog."

John said, "That's quite remarkable. I wish I had seen it. I know I don't want to be in range when you start swinging spoons or anything else for that matter. But that wonderful dog! Ever think what might happen to any stranger who tried to hurt us? I believe Mokey is part of God's plan to keep us all safe here.

"I just wish Mokey would keep her from climbing all the time. She loves to scramble up on rocks or trees and it makes me very nervous. On easy climbs Jojo follows her and I don't like that either. After that church service when I told them about angels, she said an angel was going to teach her to fly some day. She has no fear of height. I wish we could put a leash on her and have Mokey walk her.

"What about you, Stel? How are you holding up.? You work and work as if driven. How can you keep smiling all the time? If you're like me there have to be a lot of times when it's hard to keep from crying instead of smiling."

How could he know? Could he see inside her? "I'm doin' better all the time. We really have it pretty good here." She steered the talk away from any inner thoughts. "I'm even getting used to doing laundry by hand."

He replied, "In spite of our ingrained frugality, that was one thing we had done for us by a laundry in town. We also had most of our firewood delivered by Malcolm Firecloud and his sons. We have axes, mauls, wedges, and hand saws, but no chain saws. We also have a buzz saw in the work shop and a hydraulic splitter. I have been thinking we'll have to get a couple of chain saws and start laying in a supply. There is almost enough stored up in the Great Hall but we like to double up so it's had a whole year to dry out well before we burn it.

"Now back to the laundry. I'm sure we could get a machine out of the hotel or one of the homes and also a generator from Fixit's to run it. And with a small generator we can use electric lights on a Christmas tree,"

They discussed plans for Fall and her forthcoming driver's training. They discussed how to hold school and were glad Uncle Lionel had stashed away all of Junior's books ever since first grade. They made mental lists of things they had to attend to. And then they rambled on at length sharing likes and dislikes and happy memories from the past. The time flew by and it was well after one when they went in.

He whispered to her at her door, "We'll have to have more conferences like this. We've been like the proverbial ships that pass in the night. This has almost been like a date."

He opened his arms to give her a hug and she squeezed him in return. He released her and said flippantly, "Good night, Auntie Stella."

She giggled and replied, "Unca Junior, sleep tight. Don't let the bed bugs bite."

On that same Labor Day weekend Mr. Lionel Knox departed from O'Hare on his long dreamed of vacation to Scotland. He had been boarding with his sister Maude in Elmhurst. He had accepted what had happened in the valley as deeds permitted by his Sovereign God. He was a staunch Calvinist and had accepted that he had been predestined to continue to send out the gospel through the media of Christian fiction for children.

After the disaster he had met several illustrators but had been most impressed by a fellow Calvinist (Christian Reformed not Presbyterian but close enough) who was blessed by having Scottish ancestry. This Aaron McDougal had been born near Dundee, Scotland and had migrated to America after marrying an American student studying overseas. His brother-in-law Albert Holmes and sister Margaret had a small book-selling shop in Glasgow and were prominently involved in a literary guild.

The end result was that canny Lionel would be able to board with them and give lectures at various chapters of the guild. He could also do a wee bit of evangelizing while touring Scotland and some points of interest on the continent. He would have plenty of free time to finish his current book and perhaps outline another. He expected to be back to the Mikota Territory the following Summer to begin to build a home near the Aberdeen Forest.

Chapter Eight

AUTUMN INGATHERING

Summer officially ends on or about the 21st of September, but unofficially it ends with the start up of school just before or after Labor Day. On Labor Day which was the occasion for another festive outing at Saturday Park, John informed the children of the opening of Knox Valley P.S. #1.

"Aunt Stella and I have lined things up for all of you to learn before the school year ends next Memorial Day. Classes start tomorrow. We hope to teach Jojo and Juju to count to 20 or higher, to be able to read the numerals, and to tell time. We also want them to learn the alphabet song and learn to read all the letters, and they can be learning as they play with clay, use building blocks, and draw pictures with Crayolas. They're not Kindergarten age yet but this will give them a head start. Now, Aunt Stella, would you tell Hawkeye and Marian what we have in store for them?"

"I'll be glad to, Uncle John. You older kids know there is no way we can have proper grades as in Junior High or High School. So we've eliminated numbered grade levels. Marian, you finished seventh, and Bernie finished eighth but now you will be in the same grade, whatever that is. Your subjects are Algebra, General Science which will include the study of plants and animals in the valley plus astronomy, and John will be teaching History, a blend of U.S. and Mikotan from his uncle's book. Finally we will both continue to teach you practical home, kitchen, farm, and field skills which we're calling Home Economics for want of a better name."

John said, "Marian is going to keep developing cooking and domestic skills and Hawkeye will try to become an all-around mechanic and farmer. Rural folks usually end up as Jacks-of-all-trades. And we mustn't forget one other subject, Spanish. Tia Estellita will teach this as time permits."

Schooling would be during a pair of two hour sessions each week day for the older ones and two one hour sessions for the younger. After hour assignments would be kept to a minimum. Daily chores would indeed be a part of the curricula. Stella and John were determined that each day would also give the children free time for recreation and personal interests. With no electronic media for use or entertainment, athletic activities and board games could give wholesome entertainment to all.

Marian was apprehensive about Algebra. She said to Bernie later, "I have no clue how to work equations or find X. I just don't know if I can do it."

The teen boy assured her, "Well, I'll help you. I already know a bit about it. It's all logic. You're more logical than any other girls I know and more than most boys. You ask good questions. You can easily do it. I have confidence in you." For the next several days Marian's concentration was on the Hebrew lad rather than John.

The following Saturday after breakfast John had Bernie drive him to town in the Power Wagon. Their destination was the home of Malcolm Firecloud on the outskirts of Dundee. They went immediately to his workshop in back. John appropriated an assortment of Husqvarna and Homelite chainsaws along with spare bars and chains. They included lubricants and files and jigs for sharpening chains. There was also a pile of seasoned firewood, almost two cords, which they loaded aboard.

They had taken the south road to town and had detoured first to Saturday Park in order that the man might point out varieties of valley timber. On a sloping higher level not far from Ribbon Lake was an old stand of Ponderosa Pine.

"Some of them were cut off for building material when the first buildings were erected at Knox Farm, but they're off limits now by Council decree. There are none under a hundred feet tall and some reach a hundred and fifty. In high country in other ranges they have reached one hundred and eighty. The bottoms of trunks go from three to four feet wide. You could build a cottage from the lumber in one tree. But these great grandparents will not be cut.

"The same goes for any of the mature taller timber such as Lodgepole Pine or Douglas Fir unless they die or are diseased or very crooked. But of any species of healthy trees, be they crooked or not, if they're more than eighteen inches across at the bottom, we let 'em grow unless they're in the way. We do cut Quaking Aspen (Some folks call them Popple) but mostly for kindling. And we cut some Rocky Mountain Juniper and even willows. But most of our better fire woods are Birches, Elms, and Maples, but not our sugar maples. But Bernie, we always start out by harvesting fallen or dead trees and limbs."

The lad had asked, "Aren't there any oak trees? Grandpa Krause had a summer cottage with a fireplace in Wisconsin and he used to burn oak. It burnt well."

"There are a few here and there but we leave them alone to seed more and feed squirrels. And we never cut down healthy Walnut, Apple, Pear, Peach, Plum, or Cherry. They feed us and wild life. Those that don't feed us can heat us."

"What about those Christmas trees we saw? There was a big field of them."

"Those are Scotch Pines. No, they're not my relatives. They were planted on purpose to supply the Territory with Christmas Trees. They can grow pretty tall. I've heard past forty feet but they're usually crooked trees. They are mostly useful to control erosion and give us Yule decorations."

When they got back, Marian rushed out and donned work gloves to help unload the truck before lunch. After eating she wanted to go along to help John cut wood. He thought this would be a bad idea but wished her to come to that conclusion without him ordering it.

"Okay, both of you put on goggles and ear muffs and gloves." In turn, starting with Bernie and using the smallest chainsaw, he had them start the motors. Then he had them make practice cuts through branches.

"Keep your left arm straight and keep a good grip on the balance bar. Lock that elbow. Keep a tight grip with your trigger hand and ease down onto the wood. If it kicked back and your left arm was bent, the saw might pivot up at your face, but if your elbow is locked, the saw could rise up but not pivot toward you."

The noise and potential danger scared the girl and although she did not chicken out, she was secretly relieved when John said, "I've been thinking. This works best with a two man team. Honey, would you be terribly disappointed if I asked you to do me a different favor than logging?"

"I'll do anything you want me to, Uncle John."

"Swell! Would you bake some of those delicious apple slices you made last week? And maybe you could whip some cream to put on them to feed my sweet tooth."

As they gathered wood they several times came across coyote tracks and once a smaller canine track John identified as that of a fox. They discussed the night sounds they'd heard of coyotes gibble-gabbling back and forth in the distance, for all the world sounding like a drunken party with words too slurred to understand. There had also been the frequent "huu huu" of the Great Horned Owl.

And a few times when the wind had carried sound just right there had been the unmistakable yowl of a Mountain Lion, a sound sometimes mistaken for the scream of a woman. John had promised he would sometime tell the tale of the Puma Uncle Lionel had named Lady Regina.

The two came home at suppertime with a full truck. They had only been garnering fallen wood and had only done enough sawing to make pieces short enough to easily handle and haul. Cutting to stove size and splitting could be done at any time.

On Saturday morning, September 16th, Bernie drove the Subaru to town and back with the rest of the family except Mokey as passengers. The big dog was chained to one of the posts which supported the roof over the flagstone walk. He was usually free but had gotten used to being restrained at times. The ride was a test of the lad's ability to drive with the stress of distraction and noise Jojo and Juju were so capable of supplying.

When they got back John said, "Congratulation buddy, you're a licensed driver now. You must drive with Aunt Stella or me along except if there's an emergency or we send you on an errand. We trust you and your discretion. Welcome to the world of licensed drivers."

That same afternoon John received quite a surprise when he asked Stella if she would like to start her driver's training. She had snatched the keys from his hand, raced over to the car, buckled into the driver's seat, and waited for him. As soon as he was buckled into the passenger seat she started the engine and threw dirt getting up speed. She went zooming over the north road much as he used to do in the Plymouth once out of sight and sound of his uncle. She expertly controlled the vehicle through twists and turns over bumps and ruts,

After about five miles of sporty driving during which he kept a grim grin on his face, she slid the car to a stop and turned it off. Before he could say a word she said after one of her infectious laughs, "You asked me specifically if I had a license. You never asked me if I knew how to drive. I passed Driver's Ed. before I graduated and my cousin Charles DuPres had been giving me extra coaching here. I do have a Mikota learner's permit but you never asked me that. I would have been taking my road test after the 4th of July. Well, did I pass? Am I able to drive?"

He couldn't help but laugh at how she had put one over on him. "Well, I should scold you, but how can I? Yes, you are definitely licensed. I just wish I had known in case there had been an emergency."

"I would have told you if there had been but it sure was fun keeping it a secret."

"Hey, Lady, are there any other things I should know about you? Any other secrets?"

Stella became very thoughtful and her jovial mood vanished. She said very seriously, "There are lots of things. And you have secrets too. Maybe a day will come when we can share our secrets,"

Within each of us are many secrets that ought to remain private. This is not to say they are wrong. But we may have legitimate wishes, yearnings, and desires for things that do not seem likely or even possible. And there may even be moments of intimacy for believers that are not meant to be shared with others in this life. In Heaven the day will come when the time of secrets will be past. In this imperfect world we so imperfect people will always have secrets.

Little children are more open and transparent. After they come to Jesus it is exhibited openly by their words and deeds. People who are converted after they are mature can often point to the specific incident when they accepted the Lord Jesus Christ as Savior. But when faith and trust open up like a flower in a young heart it is often impossible to pinpoint the exact initial yielding to the Lord. Many people who began to trust as young children cannot tell the exact time, but the testimony of their lives declares it to others and the witness of the Holy Spirit within them assures them they are children of God.

Such was the case with both Jojo and Juju. On the girl's part it was declared by a better heeding of John's instructions not to climb up high. She would still climb up several feet and then jump onto tall grass or wind heaped leaves. She also became quicker to obey about muddy shoes and the like. Whenever she quickly obeyed, John or Stella would always tell her she was making Jesus happy and a huge smile would light up her face.

Jojo took to imitating John. In the morning he would stretch and yawn the way the man did when first out of bed. One night when he'd drunk too much water in the evening before bed, he had to go to the toilet after the other children were asleep and through the window in the pale moonlight he saw John kneeling to pray at the big rock. The next night after putting on his pajamas, but before bedside prayers, he had scampered out bare foot to run to the rock to kneel like Uncle John had. Stella was right behind him and heard him say loudly, "Jojo loves Jesus. AMEN." Then laughing with delight had jumped into his auntie's arms and hugged and kissed her all the way back as she carried him to bed.

When John came in from a late chore that evening she had told him and he said, "Well praise the Lord. I believe both little ones are trusting Jesus. If a child is able to love and trust those around him, I believe he's able to love and trust the Lord. And I feel sorry for anyone who tries to hinder them spiritually. According to what Jesus said it would be better for such a person to hang a heavy millstone around his neck and jump in deep water and drown than to offend one of Jesus' precious little lambs."

Little ones have always been attracted to fires. Had they been staying in the Honeymoon Cottage the open fireplace would have had to have its screen up constantly but all fires in the Lodge took place behind iron. After one or two scorches from brushing against hot metal, the youngsters learned to keep a safe distance. There was the added protection of Mokey. He would come between them and fire or intense heat even at the risk or singed fur.

He also herded them away from the Smokehouse when it was in use. This was a tiny building with brick walls and a corrugated galvanized roof supported by angle iron. It had a flagstone floor and a metal door, but no windows. A small potbellied stove was just inside the door in the corner but its chimney, its only vent, was in the diagonally opposite corner. The room was full of metal racks and shelves.

When used for smoking fish or meat the stovepipe was removed and smoldering fires were used. The smoke would becloud the chamber before venting out. For use as a drying room the stovepipes were replaced and any soot wiped off the racks and shelves. Meat, fish, apple slices, peach slices, herbs, various berries, and even mushrooms, would be dried for future use. Such dried things could be kept indefinitely.

Fish were not a substantial part of their diet but smoked or dried fish gave an interesting variety to their snow season menu. Although Ribbon Lake and the Mikota River were the only fishing places (too much radiation in Blast Lake), there were over forty five plus miles of shoreline plus they had the boat to use. Pikes, Walleyes, and various Trout made for good action fishing in the cool waters of the lake and much of the river.

But not all of the Mikota was cold and fast. At several places where the valley floor was nearly flat, the water slowed way down and sprawled out to form quiet shallow places where the water would get warmer and weed beds grew. These places were where the pan fish thrived. Such places were like miniature bayous. Uncle Lionel had called them restaurants where the bigger fish dropped in for dinner.

Although John and Bernie were the ones to fish most often, no one was completely left out. Even Jojo and Juju sometimes landed a few pan fish with their cane poles. Marian was in her glory when both males showered attention and instructions on her, but not so happy when she had to dig her own worms and bait her own hooks.

When Marian O'Connor had arrived at the Knox Farm after the blast, she had brought with her very little precise knowledge of the Bible or organized religion. Her father had been brought up as a Roman Catholic and to his very last breath insisted it was the true religion. His practice, however, of very spasmodic attendance did nothing to substantiate what he said he believed. He supported his church with his checkbook, not his presence.

Corinne, Marian's mother, had been nominally Catholic but had adopted the attitude that children should decide for themselves when they were old enough. Catechism and First Communion had never been promoted. Both adult O'Connors had poured their efforts into their construction business but did try to set aside some time on Sunday for family activities. They were devoted to Marian but alas, their devotion had not usually including worship.

So Marian had been like an empty sponge ready to soak up God's truth under the patient ministration of the Presbyterian man. Stella tried to help her along regarding a moral life but the girl's polite attention masked a shunting away of anything that did not come from the man. Marian concentrated on John's words and life. Because she thought it would please him she did faithfully read the Bible and tried to learn many of the historic hymns he loved.

By the middle of October John felt compelled to have a serious talk with the girl about her spiritual condition. He set it up one Sunday afternoon while the Jays were napping and Stella and Bernie were playing Scrabble on the kitchen table. The man and girl retired to the study and sat at the little reading table. The door was wide open but their quiet conversation could not be distinguished by the noisy Scrabblers.

The girl was thrilled to be alone with him but apprehensive that he might be going to scold her. "Did I make you mad or disappoint you, Uncle John? I always try hard to do what you and Aunt Stella tell me so you won't stop liking me."

"Honey, nothing you can do would make me stop loving you. I love the whole family and it doesn't depend on what you do. If you were bad it would make me sad and I might have to require some kind of punishment, but the love would still be there. And I hope you have a little love for me."

"I do. I love you with all my heart. I'll do anything you ask me to, no matter what it is."

"Well I would never knowingly ask you do anything evil or that would hurt you. You're my precious niece now. A niece is the very next thing to a daughter. That's how precious you are."

She was glad when he said such nice things to her but her soap opera view of life coupled with romance movies she should not have seen had left her with misconceptions of what love was really about and gave her no understanding of cravings that could never be satisfied at that point of her life. She did need a man, a righteous man, a biblically-oriented father figure to protect her, to preserve her, and to prepare her for a proper fruition of her maturing femininity when the time was right. God had given John the task of being that man and had anointed him for it.

Her brow furrowed. She waited silently for him to go on. "I'm very concerned about the relationships we all have for one another here. But I'm even more concerned about our relationships with God. In order to have a proper relationship with God, we first need to know some things about him and what He has done and what He expects of us. Does this sound reasonable?"

"Yes."

"Have you been learning about God from our church services and our Bible readings?"

"Yes, lots."

"Would it be okay then if I ask you some questions? I'll be glad to help you with the answers if you're not certain."

"I'll try very hard for you."

"Fine. Where does the universe come from? Who made it?"

"God did it."

"Right. Did God give us a set of rules to live by?"

"Yes. Bernie knows them by heart but I don't yet. The Ten Commandments."

"You're right. Have I kept all of them? It's sin when you break them."

"You're good. You don't break them."

"Thank you, but you're mistaken. Maybe I haven't broken every one of them but most of them I have at one time or another. Lying is a sin. Have you ever lied? I have."

"I guess so. Uh. Yeah, I have."

He showed her Romans 3:23. "According to this, who has sinned?"

"All. Would that be everybody?"

"What does it say?"

"All."

"All of us? Everyone? Is that what it says, Marian?"

"Yes."

"Both of us, right?" She nodded her head not knowing where he was going but knew it was true. She had been feeling more and more unright with each service and Bible reading.

He showed her Romans 6:23. "What are the wages we get for our sinning?"

She read it several times and then said very softly with a tremor in her voice, "Death." She pondered it and felt very panicky. "Does that mean we go into the Lake of Fire?" The image was before her of fire moving toward them on the porch of the Santa Fe Café."

"Yes, it's what we deserve. But God could do something about it and He did. Read the rest of that verse. His gift to you is eternal life. He wants to give you a life that never ends. And may I tell you why?"

"Yes, please."

"Because He loves you. Remember John 3:16 I've read so often? Look here. Read it aloud, but since you are part of the world he loves, put your name in where it says world or whosoever."

She read it several times as he asked and it was obvious the Holy Spirit was beginning to illuminate her even as He had been convicting her of sin. A look of wonder came over her face. "God loves me? Really?"

"Yes. Really and truly. He loved you so much His only Son died for your sins on the cross so you could live eternally."

John then showed her John 1:12 about receiving Jesus and becoming God's child. He spoke quietly, almost in a monotone. He was sure he could have talked her into a fake conversion where she just parroted his words to please him without real inner change.

But she initiated the crucial part. "I thought I was pretty good, but I know I'm not good enough. I'm a sinner. Do you think God would let me receive Jesus?"

He answered, "Jesus invites us to come to Him. He wants you to invite Him in to become your Lord. He wants to forgive you and make you clean inside and give you eternal life and now is the right time to do it. Do you understand? Are you willing to do this?"

He took her back through it quickly and made sure she wanted to pray and accept Jesus as her Savior. Would she let her uncle help her with words of a simple prayer? Tears came out of both sets of eyes as another Lamb came home to the Good Shepherd.

When the prayer was over, he asked her what she had done. She told him she had invited Jesus to be her Savior. He asked what happened when a person sincerely did that. She declared that she had become a child of God and had eternal life.

"How do you know, Marian?"

She reverently touched his Bible and said, "Because God says so right in here."

"So you know you have the gift of eternal life? What are we supposed to do when we get a gift?"

"We're supposed to say thank you."

They had been seated on two sides of the table but at the same corner. She had held onto his hand as she had prayed and he had not released it after. He gave her a gentle squeeze of encouragement and said, "Go ahead, Sweetheart, tell God thank you in your very own words."

"Dear God, I just accepted Jesus as my Savior and you said I would have eternal life if I did and I know I have it and I want to thank you for your gift and that you loved me so much Jesus died on the cross for my sins." Here tears began pouring out afresh as she concluded, "Thank you again and I love you, Amen."

John immediately showed her from Romans 10:9&10 how after believing in the heart we must confess with the mouth. He said, "I already know about it. Who else is there?"

"Aunt Stella and Bernie!! She jumped up almost tipping over her chair but paused as the man got up to throw her arms around him and give him a kiss on the cheek just like she used to do to her father. She said, "Thanks a million, Uncle John." She raced down the hall to the kitchen.

"Bernie! Aunt Stella! I just accepted Jesus as my Savior. He gave me eternal life."

She was so excited she hopped and danced and jumped much as game show winners often do. The nappers were about over napping and the commotion fully aroused them. They scampered out stocking footed to join in. Marian was a volatile person like her mother but this time her exuberance was fueled by high octane. Her excitement was so contagious that everybody joined in and outsiders would have thought a hugging contest was going on.

When it had quieted down the redhead said, "Jesus loves me and I love Jesus and so does Uncle John." She dropped to her knees and encircled Jojo and Juju with her arms and asked, "Do you guys love Jesus?"

Jojo's eyes were like saucers as he said loudly in a tone reminding the others of John's preaching voice, "Jojo loves Jesus. Yes, yes, yes."

Juliet became quite shy and hugged Marian around the neck and said softly in her ear, but loud enough for all to hear, "Me too. Yes, yes, yes."

Marian struggled to get up with her double burden and Bernie relieved her of his cousin and helped her up as she asked, "Do you love Jesus, Aunt Stella?"

She hesitated. She could not remember a time she did not believe that Jesus was God's Son who had died for our sins and rose again. She had always tried to live so that she never brought reproach to the Virgin's Son, but she had never thought of it in such a personal way as loving Him. She began to smile and said quietly, "Yes Marian, I guess I do love Jesus."

To the Jewish lad was delivered the same question, "Bernie, do you love Jesus?" It shook him. After a long pause he gave a circuitous answer.

"You surely know I embrace the Jewish faith. We believe there is just one God, not three. I do not believe Jesus is the divine Son of God any more than I am. But he was a very good Jew. He did good deeds and gave very good advice. I have great respect for him. And I must admit that Christians who follow his teaching do a great deal of good, even for us Jews. Well I suppose I have a brotherly love for him the way one Jew ought to love another. In that sense I love him."

Bernie would not come out and say that the books John had given him and the Christian New Testament had been more and more declaring to him that his ancient faith was incomplete or that it was beginning to look to him that the Nazarene seemed to fulfill the words of the prophets of old. But Jesus could not be the Promised One, the Messiah. Or could he?"

John was a straight shooter with the truth of the gospel. He was also a straight shooter with a hunting rifle. A couple of day after Marian's conversion he took his stalwart companion Hawkeye aside for a council of war.

"Most of our supplies are safely stored for winter. We'll soon be having light snows but usually we do not have a big buildup on the ground until well into December. But in the meanwhile hunting season is on us. We'll soon be going after a few migratory water fowl such as geese and ducks and maybe a few pheasants. We'll take squirrels and rabbits as opportunities arise. But our serious hunting will be for deer. It would be good to get two or three. Don't get me wrong. Even if we got no game at all, we would not be in any danger of running out of food until next summer but we'd appreciate the extra variety. Have you ever hunted?"

"No sir."

"Do you have any ethical or moral objections to killing wild creatures for food?"

"No. I wouldn't eat any meat if I thought it was wrong to kill animals. God put them all there for our use. And when you taught me to kill and pluck and clean chickens, I didn't particularly like it, but I knew it had to be done. I just don't know if I could shoot any game because I never fired a gun. All I know about guns is what I've seen in movies or on T.V. and that's pretty hokey."

"Well then it must be time to give you training about gun safety and proper use."

They went over to the Great Hall where the firearms were stored. Although most of the sleeping cubicles had pushbutton locks on the doors which could be opened by inserting a skinny screwdriver or a finishing nail, the door to the gun room had a stout lock. Within was a steel gun vault which also was securely locked. John opened the double vault doors to reveal thirteen assorted rifles, shotguns, and hand guns.

John took out what looked to Bernie like a museum piece. The man said, "This is a black powder percussion rifle of .50 caliber. It is patterned after the old Hawkins rifles. The Thompson Center Company manufactured the kit this was constructed from. Uncle Lionel and I blued the barrel and I sanded and finished the stock. We assembled it; test fired it, and then carefully cleaned it and oiled it for storage. It has not been fired since I was in High School."

John next showed him a Ruger .44 caliber black powder Old Army six-shooter complete with powder horn, bullet molds for both guns, both sizes of percussion caps, and bar lead ready to be melted down and cast into bullets. "We have enough makings for over one hundred rounds for each of them."

He pointed out a Vanguard model of a Weatherby Magnum rifle in .460 caliber. "My uncle got this from a bank in Denver for purchasing a large long term C.D. He survived firing it twice and once was enough for me. It's a shoulder buster. It kicks two or three times as bad as a 12 gauge. It's retired."

Bernie asked, "If it's too awful to shoot, why did he get it?"

John laughed, "We Scots are so tight that sometimes we're suckers for bargains. And it was. But it's an African big game gun. And if a T-Rex came charging at us, we could stop it. But it's been quite a while since there have been any around. However it could also work on charging Rhinos and Uncle Lionel said he'd keep it in case he ever went on an Africa Safari.

He continued, "This is his bolt action Remington 30:06 and the one next to it is my Marlin lever action chambered for .35 Remington cartridges. It's a great short range gun and a terrific brush buster. I'll explain that later. We have a total of over sixty rounds for them.

"Now these are the first ones you'll learn to shoot. They both use .22 caliber long rifle cartridges. Uncle Lionel prefers this bolt action Winchester. I like my Ruger 10/22. We also have this Ruger Mark I semi-automatic pistol. Let's see, we have eight of these 100 round boxes with only a few used from one, almost 8oo rounds. That could translate into hundreds of rabbits or squirrels.

"But much game is taken by shotgun, particularly water fowl or pheasants. This 12 gauge and this 20 gauge are both Remington Wingmasters. Next is this .410 Stevens single shot. I used to get a lot of game with it. We don't have many boxes of shotgun shells but most residents own them and we ought to be able to scrounge a lot of boxes from town."

The man concluded, "Finally there is this WW II souvenir, a German officer's 9 mm Luger Parabellum. We have no ammunition for it. Its value is historic."

Asked Bernie, fascinated by the modern day versions of old-time guns, "Do you ever use the black powder guns for hunting?"

"No. And as long as we have cartridges for the long guns, we won't need to. But that day might come. It depends on what has happened outside the valley. We don't have a clue now of what has transpired outside Knox Valley."

"Knox Valley?"

"Well, since the Knox Farm is the only habitation and we do not know for certain of anything beyond the cliffs and mountains, I consider the whole valley a little world God has given us. Thus I renamed it."

"Uncle John, is it possible that like Noah's family we're the only ones? It scares me but I never talk about it because I don't want to scare Aunt Stella or Marian. But before the blast I'd see on T.V. about suitcase bombs, the atomic kind, and about secret viruses and diseases and about chemicals like nerve gas. I feel safe here but I hurt inside to know if Mom and Dad and my sisters and Jolene are alive and okay. Is there any way we can find out?"

"Maybe in a couple of years. The last time I checked, the radiation level was much lower at the west end of the flood area. I don't know how it is down past the Sentinel. When it's low enough we can go by boat to the far end and scale the cliff, you and me. But only after I teach you what I can about rock climbing. From on top we can see for miles and maybe we'll find out what has happened. Who Knows? But like you said, God has indeed made us feel safe where we are."

John continued, "Which brings me back to the use of black powder. If we do remain here the time will come when we run out of modern cartridges and then we'll takes up what some call charcoal burners. After that, bows and arrows."

"Uncle John. I don't mean to contradict you, but I think it might be wiser to do some of our hunting with the Hawkins right away so when we run out of shells we'll be pretty good with it."

The man tousled the lad's hair a bit and said, "You're a good thinker. I believe you've got a good idea. Okay. You carry these shells and I'll carry the bolt action .22 Remington. After you understand gun safety, you'll carry the guns. Let's go, but first we lock up everything we're not taking along."

October 22nd, the Sunday after Marian's conversion, was an unseasonably warm day, so much so that after dinner

John asked, "Who would like to go to Saturday Park for one last swim before it gets really cold?" He then helped Stella in the kitchen with the dishes so the kids could get out of their Sunday clothes and into swim suits under their play clothes. He said to her, "Stel, I'm hoping we'll have some free time for a little chat later today. Sound okay?"

When that later time came, after the fun at the park, and after the two Jays' naps, and after their light supper, while the little ones were out playing and the older ones doin chores, the man and woman had a chance to sit and sip tea. After normal chit-chat there came an uncomfortable silence. She said, "Well?"

"Uh. I'm at a loss for words,"

"Mr. Preacher Man, I can hardly believe that. It must be pretty complicated if you can't launch into an explanation."

"Well it is. Sort of. Stel, I'm beginning to be afraid of you."

Incredulously, "What?! You're putting me on. This has gotta be a joke. You've several times said you wouldn't dare get too close when I'm swinging the big wooden spoon or my rolling pin. Well, I assure you Unca Junior, I could never purposely hurt you."

"No, that's not it, Stel. I know you'd never attack me or try to hurt me. But I am afraid...."

He was cut off from finishing his statement as they heard Jojo yelling at the top of his lungs. "Uncle John! Auntie Stella! Juju is hurt." This was accented by Mokey's frantic bark from just beyond the Honeymoon Cottage as he made a canine call for help.

Juju was trying to get up as John arrived at top gallop with Stella at his heels while Bernie and Marian were racing over from the pig pen. The little blondie was gasping for breath. He face was scratched, her nose was bleeding, and she would have a small black eye. As soon as she caught her breath she began to cry and Jojo wailed in sympathy. Her crying was more for fear of the consequences of disobedience than from any severe pain. She had climbed too high and had fallen.

She had fortunately landed on the big heavy furred dog and this broke her fall but a branch had snapped like a whip and hit her across the face on her way down. Mokey limped for a few days but soon completely recovered. She had fallen face downward and landed on her belly on her dog's strong shoulder. Everyone praised the dog for being there where most needed. Juliet loved Mokey even more when she realized how his body had saved her from serious hurts.

It was quite a while before she had calmed enough and was able to talk without those ragged intakes of breath which often follow a child's crying. She was sorry and the reason for her disobedience sprang from her active imagination tied to woefully misunderstood Bible truth.

"I'm sorry, but I saw an angel. And he knew I want to fly. He was flying to show me how. So I climbed up high to talk to him and he just flew higher and went away and I slipped and fell on Mokey."

Jojo insisted, "I ain't seen no angel and Mokey ain't either."

Once things were quieted down to the usual buzz in the Lodge, the little ones were readied for bed and John told them a couple of bedtime stories which emphasized angels such as their appearances to Mary and the shepherds. He stressed that angels were usually invisible guardians who protected us, but the girl was emphatic that she had seen an angel flying. He was quite sure it had been her imagination at work but what she said was not an impossibility. And the providential presence of Mokey beneath her in the exact place at the exact time hardly seemed coincidental.

After the little ones said their Now I lay me downs and God bless prayers, they were soon asleep. Marian then requested that she be told more about angels. Before the Bible study was over, she asked Bernie if Jewish people believe in angels and whether he had ever seen one and whether he thought Juju had seen one.

"Well. Father Abraham certainly met angels before Sodom and Gomorrah and Jacob wrestled with one. What Uncle John said about angels being God's messengers who do special things for God and protect God's people is surely correct. I do believe in God's angels. But not like on T.V. where their hair glows or their faces light up and they always have to tell who they are and what they're doing. My pals in Bar Mitzvah thought they were like Secret Agents for God and seldom let people know who they were,

"So any of us may have seen them at one time or another and didn't know it. But I have no way of knowing if I have. And maybe God did send an angel so Mokey would be there but he always tries to stay close to her anyway. Did she see one? I don't know. But haven't we all noticed how if there's a number on the chalkboard on the far side of the room, she squints and tries to move closer? My sister Liz used to be that way. Near-sighted. Myopic. Isn't that the word? But she got contact lenses. Maybe Juju saw a funny shaped cloud or a big bird."

John was beginning to yawn and get heavy-lidded even before the older children retired. On Sunday he customarily got up two hours earlier than his normal early hour in order to prepare for Sunday School and Divine Service. He apologized to, "Stel, I'm really bushed. I'll have to get back to you. I need to be wide awake and have enough time for our discussion."

John fell asleep thankful and rejoicing in God's care, comfort, provisions, and protection. Stella went to sleep wondering what in the world there could be about her that frightened the man. Or did he feel that she was inferior because she was partly Hispanic and also Catholic? Well they were both part Mikotan and she believed in God like he did. She vowed she would not lose any sleep over it but her vow was easier made than kept.

It was not until Wednesday, November 1st, Stella's birthday that she and John were able to finish his "fear" dialogue. There had been a surprise party in the Honeymoon Cottage. There had been mysterious and suspicious goings on for several days and she had astutely not pried. After supper the children and John and Mokey had one by one slipped away. Marian had come running in the front door yelling, "Aunt Stella, come quick. We need you."

Almost before she had opened the door to enter the cottage Jojo had begun yelling, "Soup rice. Soup rice." The rest had joined in with the proper pronunciation except Mokey's barks never came close. They had seated her in the Barca-lounger in front of a cheery hearth fire. It was a nippy day. One by one they brought little gifts to her. She had of course to play Pin-the-tail-on-the-donkey which the wee ones had chosen. She was feted with the birthday song and cake and punch. She knew now why John had taken her to town to make up an inventory of things left in the shops. Marian had needed time to bake the birthday cake.

After a festive hour the older children and dog took the Jays to the Lodge for bedtime. Uncle and Aunt were first hugged and kissed and "night night" said. She thanked John for the mini-celebration of her 19th birthday. He led her into the kitchen for a cup of chamomile tea as they had the first night. She was quiet and expectant.

"Stel, I'll be blunt. There's a biblical mandate that believers are not to be unequally yoked with unbelievers. The question is asked whether two can walk together if they are not agreed. I have no idea how long you and I will be continuing to share responsibilities. There might be a sudden revelation and a rescue and we could all return to our former family relationships. Or we all might be here for the rest of our lives. An unequal yoking could be disastrous. I'm not concerned about unimportant things but about essential spiritual matters. That's where I'm afraid."

She pondered it and was on the verge of anger. "Oh. So you must be thinking I have to be a Presbyterian or I'm wrong. I have to quit being a Catholic; they're inferior. I shouldn't even want to receive the Lord's body in Holy Communion at Mass. I ought to forget about the Blessed Virgin and the Saints. I shouldn't even want to go to Confession. Well, I have no intention of forsaking my religion."

She realized she was getting loud and shrill and paused to regain composure, and then spoke quietly again, "I'm sorry for the outburst, John. But I've seen no conflict in what our faiths both teach on how to live and treat others. And look at Marian. It wouldn't matter if she was Catholic or Protestant because she's all wrapped up in Jesus, just like Mother Teresa. I just don't understand what you're driving at. It ought to be obvious to you that I try to follow Jesus and be like him and do what's right. Like you've said in your sermons, he gave everything for us and we ought to want to do anything we can for him."

As she had spoken the last few sentences, his solemn face had acquired a smile. "I think I was fearful over nothing. I'm sure now we are both fellow followers of the Lord Jesus Christ. I cannot see how any association we had could be an unequal yoking between a believer and an unbeliever. But may I ask you a couple of questions? Are you sure your sins are forgiven? Do you know you're going to Heaven?"

She lacked certainty about those matters but she had declared how after Marian's question she had realized she did love the Lord. The man got a Bible from Lionel's former cottage bedroom and showed her assurance verses. The Holy Spirit gave her enlightenment with God's truth and it shined in her face. "Yes! That's it. I see it now. Thank you so much, John."

"Wouldn't it be better to thank the One who gave us His truth?" They knelt by the sofa and Stella declared to God her trust in His Son. She reaffirmed her desire for Christ to live in her life and she thanked them both. She could not point to the exact moment when she had invited the Son to be a resident in her heart, but she knew she had. Waves of assurance rolled over her and glory broke through. Like Marian she felt compelled to tell others and they went to the Lodge to tell the two older children. The younger were asleep and would hear on the morrow.

After the older children were abed, the exuberant pair slipped on jackets and took a long walk. They strolled in silence and without even thinking about it were hand-in-hand. Under the pale moon light they became very conscious of each other and also very self-conscious. He finally stopped and faced her and took her other hand, too.

"I have something to say."

"I'm listening, John."

"Good. I was not sure if you really believed or just had a form of religion and I found myself in a quandary. I was not really frightened of you but of what was in me. And I was scared of the consequences between us if you weren't one of Jesus' sheep. Schooling never prepared me to say what I need to say. God knows I shouldn't get rattled at a time like this. Confound it!! (This was the closest to an oath she'd ever heard him come.) I love you, Stel. That word gets used so much. We love food and things. Relatives. Friends. God. But those are different. I'm thinking about the love of a man for a woman. The kind of love that starts in an instant, keeps growing, and lasts a lifetime. If you have that kind of love for me I want you to consider the possibility of an equal yoke between us. A joining together in marriage some day. I almost don't dare to ask for an answer."

"John, the first time I saw you in the Café with your uncle I mentioned to Aunt Bonnie that a good looking man like you could be a real heart breaker for the unlucky ones who didn't get you. And as I got to know more about you and got better acquainted with you I began to hope I might some day be fortunate enough to have a husband like you. After you got us out of the Sentinel I really admired you and thought how lucky and safe your wife would be. And soon I discovered I was not interested in a man like you, but you yourself. Each day my love grew but I was sure it was impossible. My secret love could never be told. And that's why I talked about laundry and washing machines that day instead of what was in me.

"I can't name the exact times when it changed from liking to caring to loving. But it's no secret love now. Yes, John, I do love you. And yes, I have considered it. And yes, if there's a way for us to become husband and wife, I want to. I just never thought a plain Catholic girl like me could ever have this happen."

"Plain? You're a beautiful senorita. There's nothing plain....." He would have gone on and on but her lips got in the way. We will retreat from the scene until their embraces were over and they were nearly back to the Lodge. She had laughed in delight and said, "Unca Junior, does this mean we're engaged?"

The pair told the others the following morning of their desire to become man and wife as soon as possible. They were warmly congratulated and Marian summed it up, "I think married aunts and uncles are better, don't you, Bernie. It'll be even more like a real family then."

When Thanksgiving came our hunters delivered pheasant and duck to be roasted since there were no turkeys in Knox Valley. These were deliciously acceptable. Before dinner all shared what each considered a blessing to be thankful for. John summarized it all in table grace.

"Dear Heavenly Father, you have so richly blessed us we can't begin to name it all. There is much more feed than is needed for the livestock. Our pantry overflows with food. Our firewood supply is doubly adequate. We have sufficient candles and wax to make more plus a several year supply of lamp oil. And you have been gathering lambs into your flock. All of us have more and more love for each other and for you. Knox Farm has never had a more abundant ingathering spiritually and materially. For all these gifts we bless you in the name of our Lord Jesus Christ. Amen."

Chapter Nine

A WINTER OF LOOKING BACK

Marian became a teenager on Thursday, December 13th. At the breakfast table John announced it, congratulated her, and led the rest in singing the birthday song. He commented that even though the calendar showed another week until winter, the foot and a half of snow on the ground with some drifting over three feet, pretty well proved the season was under way.

"But today is a beautiful sunny day we've been hoping for. Aunt Stella and I have planned on declaring a school holiday and having a winter outing to celebrate Marian's birthday. As soon as she has received her gifts and after the necessary chores are done we're all going over to Swede Henderson's cabin. It's only about a mile from here over the bridge and on the road to town. Mokey is going to pull the toboggan to give the Jays a ride and haul our lunch and stuff over. The rest of us will be using our cross country skis. Aren't you all glad I've been giving you lessons? Swede taught me when I was ten. He's the one who fixed our skis so they wouldn't backslide."

The man was referring to an improvisation which allowed the skis to slide forward but retarded backward motion. In essence the idea was very simple. The last few inches of the trailing ends were cut off and refastened with a spring loaded hinge which kept the end from flopping up but if the ski went backwards, the hinged end would dig down vertically and help prevent sliding backwards on a sloping surface. Thus there was less strain on shoulders and arms for the poles were not needed as much.

The children were glad that the winter barn where the critters were housed was only about ten yards from the west end of the Great Hall. No shoveling was needed between the Lodge and the Hall due to the covered walk. To get to the winter barn from the Lodge, one went through the Great Hall and only a minimum of shoveling was needed between there and the barn. That day the chores were completed in record time.

By ten the six snow warriors were having snow ball fights near the Henderson place. After the uncle and aunt had been pelted enough, they retreated into the never locked cabin to prepare the birthday lunch. Outside a snow fort and snowmen were being constructed. Mokey seemed very happy to jump on things to knock them down.

The former resident, old Swede, had died in early spring of '86. John's father and uncle had noticed a lack of chimney smoke and had gone to help. The old man had died peacefully in his sleep. No had lived there since. His wife's family had inherited the furnishings of the home and had emptied it of what they wanted that summer. They left behind the massive oak table and its two benches, a couple of oil lamps, the cast iron cook stove, and the wooden bunk he had slept on between heavy quilts.

The 18 by 24 cabin had one large room that served for cooking, dining, and as a combination sitting room and studio. A lean-to addition behind the kitchen had served as bedroom and there was a nearby outhouse for the plumbingless home. The river was the source of water. A low-roofed front porch sheltered about a cord of old bone-dry firewood.

John and Stella immediately devoted themselves to kindling fires in the cook stove and also in the fireplace at the opposite end of the room. Either was adequate to keep the house habitable in winter but since it was about 20 degrees it took about a half hour to raise it to shirtsleeve temperature.

After dinner and an impromptu party the Jays, all tuckered out, napped on the bunk in an over-sized sleeping bag John had brought along. Before Bernie and Marian went back out to ski along the blanketed road with Mokey chasing them, they first sat and sipped cocoa as John told them about Swede Henderson.

"I first met him when I was about five. I was amazed at how life-like his carvings and paintings were. He did that one in our living room of that deer getting a drink on the shore of Ribbon Lake with the mountains and falls behind him.

"He came to the Mikota Territory in 1945 on a sick leave. There was a problem with asbestos at his job in Duluth. That might not have been so bad but he was also a two pack a day cigarette smoker. The pure air here was just what he needed. He liked the place, liked the people, and had a chance to turn his wood-working hobby into a new livelihood making furniture and cabinets. He began attending Lutheran services when he got settled and soon transferred his membership. It was in church activities that he became acquainted with the Redfeather family.

"Love bloomed between him and one of the Redfeather girls, Constance, and a year later they were wed. She was 21, ten years younger than the vigorous Swede. She knew he was a fellow believer in Jesus. When he proposed she told him she could marry him as long as God would be the only person he would ever love more than her and on condition he quit smoking. With God's help and her encouragement he did quit. He said later as his lungs improved dramatically that she had saved his life.

"They lived happily in Glasgow and in 1950 she became pregnant but had a terrible miscarriage with resultant health complications. In '55 there was a second pregnancy which seemed to be completely normal. During the summer when she was about six months along they decided to go for a picnic in the Aberdeen Forest. The Jeep ran smoothly on the way out but a short in the wiring drained the battery while they were there enjoying their pleasant afternoon. And then trouble came. It's not known why. She hadn't fallen and the ride had not been bumpy, but a second miscarriage occurred. Swede ran and jogged nearly killing himself going ten miles to the nearest phone. Help arrived much too late to save the baby and almost too late to help the hemorrhaging mother. They lost their child and any hope of another chance.

"From then on she had a haunted look about her always feeling she had been to blame and that she had somehow failed her man. His love never faltered for a moment, if anything grew stronger. In '70 he obtained permission from the Tribal Council to build this cabin as a summer hideaway and his constant devotion made their months here edenic. That was when he began to do serious carving and drawing, mainly to please Constance. She learned to laugh again and was able to forgive herself. But in '76 her fragile health failed and God took her home. On their double tombstone it was finally revealed that his long hidden name was Gustav.

"The man forsook their former Glasgow home and began to live here year around. He learned there was a more lucrative market for his artwork then there had been for his cabinets and furniture. He did most of his carving right at this table. He had many friends and much family on the Redfeather side. During frequent visits no one ever found him idle, ever working even as he entertained.

"His brother-in-law, Jethro Redfeather, youngest of Constance's siblings, used to often come out with his family. That's how I met Wanda. We were both in second grade. She's a cop now. You may have seen her at the gate. She was a real cutie then."

He winked at his fiancé and the kids across the table and added, "She still is."

Stella knew he was trying to get a rise out of her and she played along by jabbing her elbow into his ribs saying, "Watch it, Senor."

That night after the others were abed, the couple paused at the table for herb tea and a talk time. This was becoming a daily habit before going to their own beds. John's memories about Constance had put great concern into his mind for if they wed, no medical help would be available for his bride or bairn.

"But John Dear, all my relatives have histories of safe and fairly easy birthing and many babies. Why should I be any different? But even if I am, I love you so much I'd gladly risk it for you."

His reply, "But because I love you, I don't think I could let you risk it. Besides, we don't have a preacher to join us."

She sipped in silence before responding. "When our Mikota ancestors chose a mate and agreed together, they made private vows to one another first and then had a public ceremony. But it was the private vows, the agreement between two hearts that made it genuine. Are you getting cold feet, Sweetheart?" He averred he was not, just felt they must act with caution and without undue haste but that they both knew their union was inevitable.

Because Christmas is of vital significance on the Christian calendar, its first celebration at the Know Farm was much like millions of other family celebrations all over the world. The songs were sung (many as solos by Marian), the grand story was told, gifts were given, and treats such as cookies were gobbled. All the pictures and photographs they had of absent family members were displayed. There was a time of remembering the past and sharing it. God was thanked for all the good those not present had done for those present. The Christmas tree had electric lights powered by a generator. Marian and Bernie gave piano recitals and even did a couple of simple four-handed pieces. The Jewish lad participated and considered it a late Chanukah holiday but paid special attention to the story of the birth of his kinsman, Jesus.

It was during the snow season that Mikota/American history was being taught in Knox Valley P.S. #1. John's approach was that history was a sequence of events about people and although dates were important pegs on which to hang happenings, an understanding of flow or cause and effect was more important, as was knowledge of circumstances which influenced deeds. We shall draw from what he said but not quote him.

In the 1900's ethnologists tried to trace the origins of the Mikota tongue. By then it was saturated with words of Spanish-American origin and with a great deal of Scotch-English. The United States has been called a melting pot of language and culture and to a great degree this is true of the Mikota Territory. But the basic language was discovered to have been derived from Uto-Aztecan, Algonquian, and Athabaskan.

Dates and events before John's birth in 1774 are very obscure. His fragile family Bible, now preserved by the Glasgow Historical Society, gave some dates. But the journal he kept during his travels had been partly destroyed in a fire. The earliest accounts had been passed down by word of mouth and may have been somewhat embroidered.

It is known that his paternal grandparents had migrated from Scotland to the Virginia Colony at the end of the 1600's. They had established themselves as farmers and within the clan was an endowment of other skills and crafts such as working with wood or blacksmithing.

What had put John's life on a different course was when his parents, his fiancé, and most of his kinfolk had died in 1799. Scholars differ on the cause of the deaths. Some say people who had been loyal to the Crown in the War of Independence had been denounced by the Knox clan and retaliated by instigating Indian raids. Others thought it was downright malice by lazy malcontents who were jealous of Knox industry and prosperity. But Uncle Lionel in his writing about it theorized it was the result of an outbreak of disease carried over from Europe by immigrants.

Whatever the reason, Knox sold out his inheritance and left to go westward, perhaps to fabled Kaintuck. The famous Lewis and Clark expedition was still in the planning stage when he left in 1800. He traveled with a group that was predominantly Cherokee. From them he learned a smattering of language and gained skill in basic sign language.

His inheritance bought him a string of saddle and pack horses and a good supply of trade goods such as knives, hatchets, and simple farm and carpentry tools. Being a strict God-fearing Bible Presbyterian and named after a distant earlier relative who had been a prominent church man, he spurned alcohol and would not consider trafficking in it. His knowledge of farming and simple medicine was also valuable trade material. But his most valued cargo was a treasury of various seeds in small sturdy air-tight casks. He would not trade these. He planned to use them once he was able to settle. Farming was in his blood.

It is history that the steamboat New Orleans between Sept. 11, 1811 and Jan. 12, 1812, traveled the whole Mississippi ending up in the town for which it was named. But this must have been about ten years after Knox somehow crossed over. The place and date of crossing was lost along with the burnt pages of his journal. However, it is certain he crossed the Appalachians through the Cumberland Gap for this was mentioned later in his journal as he reflected on how far God had led him to where he ended up.

The rigors of his several years of travel and what perils he faced after parting from the Cherokees are a matter of speculation. His words about the Cherokee later were that they were an honorable people whose words and deeds could be trusted but this was not true of everybody you met. He did know they were a tribe who once had a vast geographical dispersion although the focal point of their culture was in the area now called the Great Smoky Mountains. This chronicler doubted this until he learned there had been Cherokee living as far north as Grand Island in Lake Superior near what is now Munising, Michigan.

When Knox arrived in Mikota land in 1804 he was down to two nearly worn out pack horses, but still had most of his personal possessions. It could not have been the Cherokee who had left him with barely a tithe of his goods. The real story will probably never be known.

It is most likely his losses were the result of unfortunate encounters with rogue strangers, possibly renegade Indians, for he was leery of seeking to gain acquaintance with his new neighbors. He had heard from the Cherokees about them and there were many similarities between the two nations. Both preferred permanent dwellings and an agricultural life-style, but they did not abandon foraging, hunting, and fishing. They both believed waste was evil and if we are wise enough to properly use them, all plants were given for food, medicine, and other useful products. Both tribes stressed monogamy and traced family trees through the maternal line.

But referring back to his losses on his exodus it may be said that once burnt, ever shy of the fire. He set up his camp about 15 miles south of the Mikota village which was in the place where Glasgow now is. He found a cave-like den overhung by a big slab of rock which kept off the weather. It was only a short walk to the river and in a heavily wooded area.

At the entrance he built a semi-circular ring of rock about waist high to serve as a fireplace. He could cook in it and it reflected heat inside. The smoke rose up and followed the up tilting ledge away from the den. He could readily step around the ring to enter his bedroom but he was sure no marauding animals would come near while the fire burned or even embers glowed.

The exact calendar date in which Knox arrived is uncertain but he had been sure it had been about the end of October. He had been so involved in stealthily preparing his camp, foraging for food, and foddering his horses, that he had neglected his journal. The normally bountiful supply of wild food in the Mikota River environs had been decimated by a hot drought summer. The Hidden Valley had been much less affected but crops raised near the village had done very poorly even with laborious manual irrigation.

So the Indians had entered the premature snow season with a much smaller supply of the grains, fruits, and vegetables they mainly subsided on. They had intensified their hunting and fishing and drying of meat. They seldom went after buffalo in the prairies to the east but this year it was necessary. They might have to skimp, but no one would starve and the children would have plenty.

Not so the outlook for Knox. His salt pork, beans and corn meal were running out. The nuts and berries he'd gathered would never sustain him. The fish he'd dried would not be enough, and for his horses nothing had been gathered. He faced the gloomy prospect of butchering them and living off them for they would starve anyway.

A lesser man might then and there have called it quits and thrown himself on the mercy of the unknown Mikotas. But he was a stern and stubborn Calvinist who would not change his course without a clear mandate from God. He was convinced that when the fullness of time was come for his first encounter, God would lead him into it. And if he died from the winter or his first meeting, he would enter death undismayed trusting his Savior who had promised resurrection and a heavenly home. Whatever God had predestined for John Knox was perfectly acceptable.

It so happened that an old battle bruised grizzly that had come on hard times had wandered down from the high country. He should have been well fattened up for that year's hibernation, but this was not so. The drought had greatly curtailed his food supply. He'd ranged far from his accustomed feeding grounds and never had enough to show for it.

His attitude was surlier and fiercer than usual due to continual hunger pangs and also a fierce tooth ache. Spring had come later and colder than usual and when he aroused and came out the first time the temperatures had been well below freezing. He had scented meat and had found a mountain lion's half consumed kill, a goat. She had come back and he'd driven her away and tried to eat the iron-hard frozen remains. A weak old tooth had snapped and had soon abscessed and continually pained him.

During the Fall as the snow was fast approaching the grizzly's instinct and hunger told him he must gorge on food to survive. He'd made a couple of forays into the outskirts of the Mikota village lured by the scent of cooked food and living animals. Be they animals, dogs, horses, or humans he would be eating. But alerted by their dogs, the men had driven him away with torches and lances.

He tried again late at night but again the dogs warned the village. Once more he was driven away but this time with an arrow piercing his shoulder. In his frantic crashing through the brush the shaft was broken off but the arrowhead caused a festering sore. Men had never before been his natural prey. Up to then he'd avoided them. Now he was not only hungry but angry and getting reckless.

The big bear did become much bolder and a constant threat but he was not stupid. He avoided the main community and began to terrorize small outlying settlements. In their nation it was common for compatible groups, not necessarily related, to work together for crop-raising or for raising domesticated goats or geese. They would build their homes and other buildings around a communal square. Then the old bear began to brazenly and systematically raid them, eating what he could and killing as much as possible that he couldn't eat. The Chief immediately called for volunteer mounted hunting patrols to destroy the menace.

This new concentration of highly mobile weapon-wielding warriors near the little settlements drove the grizzly south to the more rugged foot hills of the Bittersweet Range where new growth timber land gave him better cover and better ambush places. This was the area where John Knox was camping.

It was the end of November when their paths crossed. Knox was despairing of keeping Nibble and Buck, his remaining old mare and her brother alive. The two horses, named for their habits as foals, would soon have to die. If he let them suffer and die of starvation, there would be that much less meat to feed him. About 50 yards from his shelter there was a little clearing surrounded by sheltering trees and undergrowth. He kept them tied here with long ropes so they could browse for whatever was edible.

He had been a very busy man. He had woven pine boughs to make a screen over half of the opening to his den. Once snow covered it, it would effectively block chilling breezes. He planned to use his horses' hides to curtain the rest of the opening up to his fireplace. He would be able to just shove it aside for egress and regress. From inside he would be able to look out through the open space above the fire wall. Said open space also let the smoke go away. In front of the woven screen he'd heaped up gathered wood for later fires. Outside of the fire ring was a pile of brush and pine-needled branches for kindling. Inside he kept a little pile of cut wood and would cut more as needed.

About two hours before first light while the wind howled and a hard snow, almost hail, was peppering down. John was awakened by the screams of Nibble and Buck. In an instant he was adding brands to his fire. He slept fully clothed in cold weather and his scabbard with big keen knife was always on his belt or within hand's reach. He scooped up his Brown Bess flintlock musket, always loaded and ready, and cautiously moved into the dark on the very familiar path to his impromptu corral.

The tethers were snapped. The horses were gone. And then he sensed rather than saw an immense presence not 50 feet away. He was noticed at the very same time and a roar such that John Knox had never heard before trembled his ears.

He knew it had to be a bear more horrible than any he'd seen on his travels. He remembered having heard that if he yelled right back it might make the bear pause for an instant so John could get his long legs going for a head start retreat. At the top of his lungs he yelled, "A mighty fortress is my God." This for a second or two puzzled the bear and its brief hesitation let the man race back to his refuge. He instantly began tossing firebrands over the fire wall onto the kindling pile in front of his window. Combustion began even as the beast approached.

The big creature feared fire, indeed had been scorched in the past but there seemed to be a clear path to the man where the small beginning fire could not reach it. It rose up on its hind feet to advance.

John bellowed out, "You're not welcome in my house, you devil," and raised his musket to fire. A gust of contrary wind raked through the brush pile fanning life into the tinder. Sparks and fiery bits of pine needles went flying at both the man and the grizzly. Fire coming toward the man's eyes made him flinch and the muzzle rose as he fired. The heavy lead ball flew over the bear's head. At the same instant sparks came at the bear's eyes and he swatted at them as at hornets. Then he backed up as the shifted wind blew flame across his path. Snow on the screen snuffed out sparks there.

When it was clear for John to go out, his gun of course reloaded, he saw no sign of the animal's presence. He made a brief reconnoiter staying where his fire prevented an unseen attack. He deemed it wisest and safest to wait for the pre-dawn glow. He spent his time sharpening his axe and knife and gnawed some of his leather hard dried fish. He was determined to find his horses or their remains and also deal with the furry predator. He'd be hanged if anyone but himself would slay his beasts.

At first light he set out. He had his gun slung on one shoulder, his axe on the other. He saw bloodstains on the shrubbery where Buck had been tied. Apparently the bear had crept up during the snowing and had come against the wind and attacked. Buck must have lunged and kicked but been unable to avoid the awful claws. In terror both horses had snapped their ropes and fled. There were spots of blood here and there but snow on top of the tracks made tracking a big puzzle game. The bear's tracks were hardly covered for he must have lurked a long time in the darkness. It was also easy to see where he had crashed through shrubs and thickets. He had waited and then must have decided a wounded horse was easier game than a man who roared and threw fire.

John tracked the beast south as the pale light slowly increased. Ominous black clouds and a brisk breeze threatened the onset of a blizzard. He lost the trail for a while and had to zigzag right and left to pick it up again. The deteriorating weather made him think it might be wisest to go back ere long and drag as much firewood with him as he could.

And then he drew near to a clearing next to a drought-dried creek bed that usually drained into the Mikota River. He'd been there before. He had been careful to leave no sign of his visit for it was obviously near a Mikota hunting camp. A substantial old lean-to showed signs of frequent improvement over the years. In front of the lean-to was a fire ring of smooth river stones.

Knox realized his first sighting had been about four weeks earlier, a couple of days after he'd arrived while he was scouting out his environs. Could it be the end of November so soon? He again admired how the shelter was situated to receive maximum protection from the nearby trees. The prevailing breezes would be kept off the backs of four or five braves.

John was out of sight in a pine thicket and looked carefully before crossing the creek. He leaned against the opposite bank, hid save for his head. He was almost ready to proceed when the breeze pushed a smoky haze out of the fire ring, evidence that there'd been a very recent fire. He peered more intently under the low lying shrubs and he could just make out objects back in the shadow of the lean-to.

Then he heard snapping noises of branches being broken. He watched as a young brave came around the lean-to with his arms full of wood. The lean supple man selected a few smaller pieces and knelt by the fire ring to blow on embers and ignite his new additions to the fire. Smoke swirled in his face and he changed his position so that his back was facing the nearest trees.

The brave was dressed in buckskin from top to bottom and his moccasins had leggings that laced up to protect his ankles and shins. He wore a buffalo fur cape with a hood covering his head. They were about a hundred yards apart and John was getting ready to cautiously back track and make a wide detour around the camp when he detected motion in the pines in back of the brave. Snow fell off disturbed branches.

The scientific name of the Grizzly is Ursus Horribilis, the horrible bear. Those who have been charged and survived the attack insist the name is woefully inadequate. The bear smashed through his cover like a bulldozer. Even with his badly infected shoulder, his gait was unbelievably fast.

John gasped, momentarily paralyzed by the suddenness of the assault. At the very first sound the brave jumped to his feet and wheeled around to face his opponent drawing his stone knife to defend himself. In what looked like a mere twitch the bear was on two feet and his unhurt right paw was swinging. The awful impact of claws and paw threw the man aside much like a petulant child might fling a rag doll.

Onto the fire fell the man and rolled quickly away, then up he sprang to his feet. His left arm hung down numbed and useless by the blow it had received. The blood flowed freely where the claws had slashed through buffalo hide, buckskin, and then went deep into flesh. Even had a way been open to flee with no more damage to himself, he would not have. He let out a war cry and charged, knowing he would surely die but hoping he could so damage his tribe's enemy that it too would die.

This was contrary to any past experience the bear had had from its prey. He looked down at the man coming at him, roared and again swung his mighty paw, this time aiming at the head. The brave swung his knife to fend off the blow and tried to dodge it. The blow connected but less squarely and the claws did not find flesh.

The force was still enough to knock the stunned man onto the ground and he banged his head briefly knocking him out. Disregarding his sore shoulder and the new gash on his foreleg, the bear went down on all fours for supper. No bear law says supper has to be dead first.

At first sight of the bear, John had the idea it would be wisest not to get involved. What did the death of one more savage matter? But then his life long knowledge of the gospel reminded him that God loved every soul and Jesus had died for all and he had sheep in other folds. John had to do what he could. He tossed his axe back to the bank behind him and clambered up to make himself known.

He yelled at the bear as he charged, "Get ready to die. You'll not eat one of Jesus' other sheep."

The bear knew John's voice and turned to attack the one who had thwarted his hunger. His anger was like a ret hot iron prodding him on. When about 40 feet away John stopped and the bear rose up. The bear roared and John roared back, "My God is a consuming fire." He cocked his Brown Bess, aimed, and squeezed the trigger. Click!

At their best, flintlocks are none too reliable. Flints get dull and fail to shower enough sparks in the pan. Powder in the pan may get damp and instead of instantaneous ignition may burn slow or not at all. Powder in the barrel may do the same. Even when ignition takes place there may be noticeable delays between the trigger pull and the flight of the projectile. This delay is called a hang fire. The Brown Bess had one just then.

The delay was only a second or two and John tried to keep holding his aim and his breath, not easy to do after a fast and emotional dash. The gun fired. The bear fell. "Hallelujah!" The man drew his knife to cut the throat as a safety measure.

And then the bear got up on all fours and shook himself with an awful headache. Smooth bore flintlocks are not only unreliable, they are noted for inaccuracy. The heavy lead ball had ricocheted off the bear's forehead but the blow had been far from lethal. He stood again doubly mad at the one who had hurt him.

John's big heavy well-balanced knife was in his hand. Similar knives were immortalized by Jim Bowie. Through constant use of it the past few years the man had acquired considerable skill with it. He flung it with all his might at the bear's chest and it sank in several inches. The man ran back to the creek bed and retrieved his axe. He was sure the knife would be eventually fatal but not soon enough to save his own life.

The brave had seen most of what happened after John's charge. He forced himself to his feet and staggered to the lean-to to get his lance. He was determined to help the fearless pale face. But blood loss and shock made him so weak all he could do was lean against the corner post of the lean-to resolving to yet fight the bear should it come back to him.

The bear pawed at the knife and managed to dislodge it. If such wild creatures could think like us he would have wondered how the man could have used such a big fang on him. The bear was in awful pain but no less determined to kill and eat this thing so much smaller than himself. Ignoring the pain the bear advanced toward the man who now stood on the edge of the far bank of the creek where his elevation would put him eye to eye.

The bear clambered clumsily down into the bed and then again stood up to look at his puny challenger. He roared and advanced. John waited silently gathering his strength. He prayed that his God who had given David victory over Goliath would give John Knox victory over this giant.

There was a short pause of silence as they looked into each other's eyes. For the first time in the bear's life he began to feel fear, an emotion foreign to him. When the distance was just right John brought up his axe from his heels in a great sweeping arc over his head. The brave saw only a blur as the axe came crashing down on the beast's skull. John had swung with every bit of strength in his body and his aim had been perfect. The axe handle snapped off near the head and John's hands stung for a great while. The iron had driven into the skull and cut the brain in two. The beast tottered and fell dead in a heap. John said later it took several days for his body to quit aching.

John was quite sure grizzlies were loners but quickly retrieved his Brown Bess and carefully reloaded it just in case. Then he rushed back to the wounded brave, picking up his knife on the way. They smiled at each other and made peace signs. They both spoke to each other and each thought the other was using gibberish. John saw the bleeding and quickly tightly bound the upper arm with the cleaning rag from his possibles bag. The blood still oozed but the flow was staunched. The Scot helped the Indian to get comfortable on furs in the shelter, covered him with others and built up the fire. He promised by signs he would come back.

John quickly gutted and skinned the bear and used the hide to make a curtain which blocked most of the wind. He made two trips to his camp to bring over food, clothing, utensils, and of course his weather proof pouch in which he kept his Bible and journal. He cached his casks of precious seed, the remainder of his trade goods, plus a small chest of keepsakes from his original home.

When the things were moved, he performed an impromptu surgery on the brave. He was concerned because the wounds were still oozing blood from the deep claw cuts. John prayed that what he did might somehow help. He got out some fish line he had made from animal intestine and a needle he used to patch leather or canvas. The gut was too stiff from the cold and he boiled it in some water to soften it. There would be awful scars later but the man would retain most of the strength and mobility of his left arm. Sealing the wounds with stitches did stop the bleeding which would have eventually killed the man. Amazingly there was no major infection.

While he had stitched the stoic brave he had been melting snow in his kettle brewing a bitter tea of ground up bark the Cherokee had taught him could ease pain. He poured in the last of his honey to make it palatable. The brave slid in and out of consciousness for several hours. Whenever he was alert John served him more tea.

Later John made sassafras tea for both of them and that afternoon they shared the broiled bear's liver which was supposed to impart some of the beast's strength to the eater. When evening came and a growing storm they were as snug as could be. They had a good pile of firewood and had sustaining roast bear for their supper.

During the five day storm, they got well acquainted. They communicated with signs and gestures and the words common to both the Cherokees and Mikotans. They each learned many basic words of each other's language. John learned that he was in the company of Chief Gray Wolf's only son, Little Wolf. The head medicine man was Thunder Cloud, brother of the Chief's wife. Little Wolf's youngest sister was Running Doe and her garrulous other sister was named Magpie for her chattering. Little Wolf pronounced John Knox as Shah Nock and dubbed him Bear Chopper. To preserve this memory in the 20th century the public campground was called Bear Chopper Campground.

Four of Little Wolf's companions, those on the hunt with him, had been sent back for additional supplies while their leader had stayed behind. They had left shortly before John had gone looking for his horses. They arrived back at the lean-to the afternoon after the storm ended. When they heard the story they treated Shah Nock with reverence.

They marveled at his Betty Lamp as it lit up the bear hide shaded interior of the shelter. These lamps are palm-sized brass boxes with hinged tight-fitting lids and an inner tube which hinged up when the lid was opened. In the tube was a wick. Any kind of fat or tallow would burn to give a small flickering light.

Two of the braves raced back to the village and returned with others the next day. They pulled conveyances some would call sledges. But sledges normally have some kinds of runners and these were more like miniature canoes with greased bottoms so they'd slide easily on the snow when heavily laden. Cushioned and covered with furs, Little Wolf was brought home.

All of Shah Nock's things from both camps came along. The bear head with axe buried in it was put on public display so all could marvel. The several hundred pounds of bear meat was enough for a great feast for the whole village.

Thunder Cloud examined the stitching up of the wound and declared Bear Chopper to be a mighty shaman sent by the Great Spirit with powerful magic. The people held John in awe but were also afraid of him. What if such a mighty one was cruel and turned against them?

The day after the feast, Shah Nock was shown around the village. When he was brought to the paddock of horses, he spied Nibble and Buck. Buck's wounds were minor and had been treated. The two by instinct had come to the village and been cared for, fed, and groomed. He called their names and they whinnied and trotted over to him. He hugged them both around their necks and they nuzzled him affectionately.

He raised his arms and looked up to Heaven giving thanks and praising God for preserving them. Those near him knew he must be talking to the Great Spirit in his peculiar tongue. Tears ran down his face and they could see how much he cared for his animals. His unknown prayer and his tears wiped away their fear. Surely someone who loved his animals and talked to the Great Spirit must be someone you could trust.

In the following days John used up the remnant of his trade goods as gifts. He had three knives in scabbards similar to his which he presented to Little Wolf, Chief Gray Wolf, and Thunder Cloud. He had three little mirrors in brass frames which went to the Chief's wife and two daughters. He had a bag of copper pennies and gave one to each child in the village, the balance to the medicine man.

He was a much loved celebrity and hero. As he learned the language he became friend to all he met, especially the children. By the end of the Winter he was considered a full member of the tribe and his advice was sought by the tribal council.

When the proper time came for planting he began to raise squash, peas, beans, melons, and wheat. These were new to the tribe and in years to come would be valuable additions to their diet. In addition he planted apple seeds but it would be many years before these would be generally available to the people.

From his youth Lionel Knox had been fascinated by the story of the Mikota Nation. His most intense interest had been in the period when his ancestor had arrived and become Bear Chopper until Shah Nock's death in 1851. Lionel had been inspired to write a comprehensive and definitive history of that period but had continued it to 1951 to show the after effects and continuing good influence of John Knox's life. What follows now will just show some of the significant events.

1805. September. Running Doe was the first of the people to receive the Great Spirit's Son Jesus as her Lord and Savior. She was soon followed by her brother Little Wolf and after that by the remainders of the Chief's and Medicine Man's families. With these highly placed endorsements of Christianity Shah Nock's message of salvation spread like wild fire.

1806. June. Running Doe and Bear Chopper were wed. She is thought to have been about 16, half his age. But these Indian women matured early and took on adult responsibilities. As a wedding gift John gave her a carved box containing a hair brush and set of combs. The hinged lid was mirrored on the inside. Such things were quite common in the colonies but absolutely unique in Mikota land. They would make their possessor seem wealthy beyond imagination.

1808. John and his wife began teaching children and interested adults the mysteries of the English ABC's. The Bible was their textbook, indeed the only book they had for several years. Chief Gray Wolf, Thunder Cloud, and their families all had such high esteem for this man they were sure was the voice of the Great Spirit that they all became diligent students.

1812. While war was being waged elsewhere, the ever growing group of believers founded the First Presbyterian Church and appointed John as Chief Elder and Pastor. He was well aware of his limitations but did his best to faithfully tend the flock.

1817. Rev. Melvin Chandler was installed as Pastor.

1820. A public school was organized for redskins and palefaces alike. A pioneer family had decided to settle amongst the gentle God-fearing people. The mother had been a school marm, the father a far better scholar than farmer. Clara Miller and her husband Malachi long served the community. It was they who first heard of Sequoyah who had invented a syllabary for the Cherokee which had propelled them into literacy. The brilliant man who did not know how to read or write any language devised a phonetic system still used by the Cherokee. Clara and Malachi adopted this so the Mikotas had a written language of their own.

1840. Trade with pioneers and settlers kept growing. Beadwork, baskets, leather and fur goods, and grain and produce could be used to gain hard money. The silver and gold could bring in books, metal goods, and fabrics. But because John Knox well knew the rapacity of which humans are capable, he made sure the tribe acquired the means to defend their land, goods, and persons.

The goal was for each family to have at least one firearm in addition to traditional weapons. These were intended for hunting and self defense, never aggression. After the story of the Alamo battle in 1836 the council decided they should have cannons to defend the Hidden Valley should refuge from invaders ever be required.

A wagon train had been sent to acquire ordnance. Two six-pounders and four four-pounders were brought back. These were all of Austrian manufacture, some dating back to 1760. The carriages were in serious need of work but the barrels were in prime condition. The six-pounder barrels weighed in at over 600#.

1850. March. A Constitution was ratified for the Mikota Nation. All members of the tribe 21 or older, both men and women, had the right to vote. Over 95% exercised their right. Of ballots cast, 87% approved. This document had been worked on for years by Shah Nock and the Tribal Council. It preamble boldly asserted that God instituted governments to protect the lives and properties of all society members who obeyed God's Law as given in the Ten Commandments. It forcefully declared that all people must be equal under the law and free as long as they obeyed the law. It denounced slavery. It insisted that equality meant that all citizens had equal rights to vote, own property, and to have the final word as to whom they would marry.

1850. August. A delegation of well-schooled Mikota representatives went to the Capital of the United States to hammer out an equitable and binding treaty. John Knox's son Charles, schooled in a prestigious Eastern University's College of Law, was the primary spokesman. Territory boundaries and the right of self determination were recognized. Since there was growing animosity between

Slave and Free states it was expected the Mikotans would side with the North should there be hostilities. But Charles informed the Federal negotiators that neutrality was the only course open to them. No battle would be waged on their land but they would offer refuge and medical help to any wounded who came to them as long as weapons were laid aside.

The Federal negotiators were amazed at the wisdom and legal expertise displayed by these "ignorant savages." They were further astonished that the delegation was fluently bi-lingual and presented documents in both impeccable English and their own written language. The Indians were bargaining from a position of strength for they were a small well-armed nation ready to die for what they believed and also honest, well-informed people who sincerely wanted kind and friendly relationships. The Treaty of 1850 was signed.

1851. July 4th. There was a combined church picnic and celebration. By now there were Baptists, Lutherans, Methodists, and the biggest congregation was Presbyterian. There was also a small parish of Roman Catholics. All gathered for fellowship, praise, and celebration. The Bear Chopper, now getting quite feeble, insisted on getting up to make a speech to thank God and the people for the good which had been done over the years. And then one last time he recited to them the story of God's love and Calvary. He faltered before he was through, said a few incoherent words, and fell down unconscious. He peacefully passed in his sleep, probably the victim of a massive stroke. His funeral had the largest attendance ever known in Mikota History.

1877. September 11th and 12th. Colonel James Madison Montgomery had a dazzling military coup in mind. He was a contemporary and rival of Custer who had died so ignominiously the previous year. His assignment had been to maintain law and order in Indian lands and to prevent outbreaks of trouble. He interpreted this to mean he was to dominate all Indians and he was determined, contrary to the Treaty of 1850, to make a name for himself as the man who brought the Mikotans under U.S. Calvary control.

At the head of a column of 200 riders he brazenly advanced through Mikota Territory toward the Hidden Valley. His route was almost precisely the one which the fat man had taken but not over improved or paved roads. The troopers rode four abreast in a column a little over a tenth of a mile long. Every man had a rifle, a six-shooter, and a saber. Colonel Montgomery was sure this display of military might would be more than enough to cow these craven savages who always seemed to avoid battles.

The steep single lane unpaved approach up into the Hidden Valley was blocked off by a stout stockade fence about fifty yards from the bottom. It closed the gap in the rock. A white flag appeared behind the double gate which when wide open allowed wagons to pass through. One gate swung in enough to pass three horsemen. The gate swung shut behind them. The Colonel was about three hundred yards away.

The Colonel and his Lieutenant watched through binoculars. There was a white man dressed like a banker and two Indians who looked like store keepers. The Officers passed the order for their men to dismount and rest their horses. They were sure the white flag meant surrender but forgot it also meant a desire to parley.

A grandson of Shah Nock, Charles Knox Jr. and his two attendants dismounted about ten yards away from the officers and waited for them to dismount before meeting them half way. Very little is known about that conversation but it is known for sure the cocky Colonel, over-awed by his own genius and importance, demanded an immediate surrender. He was very politely informed that a strongly worded protest would be lodged with his superiors and the proper government agencies because of the blatant violation of the 1850 treaty.

The rebuke by Charles Jr. had not been expected. "Colonel, had you come openly as customers to trade with us, or as strangers wishing to get better acquainted and become friends, we would have gladly welcomed you. But you tried to sneak in intent on violence. You are all trespassers and we have the right and duty to defend ourselves. If you surrender your weapons, you will leave in safety."

Colonel Montgomery and his Aide laughed aloud at how this fancy dressed half-breed was trying to bluff them and said as much. "It's best you take a look around before you decide what to do," and nodded to his flag bearer who held it high and waved it from side to side.

None of the mostly green troops had seen signs of even one brave on their trek in. In response to the signal camouflaging brush was moved aside from four fortified gun emplacements above them on the foot hills at their right. The gates were flung open and a fifth cannon guarded the approach road. On the top of the cliff above Knox Rush a sixth emplacement was uncovered. The last two were six-pounders and the gun on top had a special carriage so that the muzzle could be elevated high enough to drop the cannon balls almost straight down onto the approach road.

The six-pounders and the four-pounders were trained on the column. The two farthest back could maul the escape route. But a troop of 80 mounted Mikota Militiamen had come up behind the troopers and had moved into cover on that same route, their only escape path. In addition about 20 or more unmounted Militiamen stood and let themselves be seen at each gun emplacement. The Colonel's men were actually outnumbered and could easily be outgunned.

Speaking very loudly so the U.S. Cavalrymen could hear him Charles said, "You are all guilty of trespass and treaty violation and you have two options. You can surrender your weapons and we will treat you as friends until you leave. Or you can resist. Let me give you an example of what could happen."

The signal flag was waved again and the two six-pounders spoke very emphatically. The gateway gun dropped a ball about 20 yards in front of the parley party. Just far enough from them so there was no danger. The upper gun arced a ball high over their heads so it fell about twenty yards behind the column. This was when the only two casualties happened and damage was minor. One of the horse at the end of the line, not yet battle hardened, reared up kicking and two troopers were knocked down.

The Colonel was a proud man, perhaps a bit cowardly, but wise enough to know he'd been stupid and also wise enough to surrender and not follow in Custer's footsteps. His career in the Army was soon terminated and it was reported he had found employment training troops in Brazil.

The Mikota Militia brought up three wagons and collected all weapons and ammo. The intruders were led to Glasgow without further incident. The two bruised men were tended to. All were fed and treated with kindness. With no language barrier friendships got started.

Glasgow by then was a thriving community much like other frontier towns. It had many stores and shops but not one liquor establishment. About 400 families lived in and nearby. Enough of the families offered a night's lodging to the troopers that none had to camp out.

The men were given hearty breakfasts before leaving. They were then escorted to the edge of the Territory sans weapons or flags. These were later delivered to the nearest military outpost along with a detailed report of what had happened.

One happy after effect was that there was never again any such military incursion. It was also true that after some of the men finished their tours of duty, they migrated to the Territory and found themselves wives from amongst girls they had met.

When the students at Knox Valley P.S. #1 got this far with their history studies, Uncle John read a line Lionel had written about Bear Chopper. " One needn't look far to see the profound effects of the life of this man who lived with his feet firmly on the ground but had his eyes fixed on Heaven."

Chapter Ten

JOY IN THE SPRINGTIME

Winter had been quite severe but situated and provisioned as they were, not a time of hardship. Nonetheless when the snows ceased falling and the average temperatures began climbing, the family's good spirits became excellent spirits. By the end of March most of the lower land snow blankets had disappeared and the Mikota River was running loud, fast, and high.

Uncle John, now sometimes jokingly referred to as Shah Nock, had suggested they take lunch and eat at Swede's cabin. It was cool and the air was crisp and the sun bright, a delightful day for a walk. Juju and Jojo rode most of the way in a dog cart. John and Bernie had repaired and refurbished this in the Great Hall close to a blazing fire during days of howling winds.

Bernie insisted on showing off his learning by naming trees for Marian. "That's a Salix Babylonica." "You mean a weeping willow?" "Yes. And up there are Pinus Contorta and Pseudotsugo Menziesii Glauca. Shah Nock interrupted Bernie, "Use the common names, too. Marian, he mentioned Lodgepole Pine and Douglas Fir." But the lad kept on and mentioned Pinus Ponderosa and Ulmus Americana, etc, etc, ad infinitum, ad nauseum.

Marian soon had enough and after spying a shaded bank of snow scooped up two handfuls and washed Bernie's face and yelled, "Enough! We're not in school. Lighten up!" Of course Jojo and Juju joined in the ensuing snowball fight. It was a wind free day and it was certain their noise carried far for from down the valley came the distinctive yowl of Lady Regina again sounding like a screaming woman.

John had said, "Praise the Lord. She made it through the winter. I didn't think she would. That makes me happy." At the table at lunch they shared memories of the one close encounter they'd had with the mountain lioness.

The first part of January after blizzard conditions had died down there had been a calm bright day and small game was moving around. John had taken his Ruger .22 and his skis to see if he could get fresh meat for a stew. He had seen motion in back of the Lodge and had headed north after lunch before afternoon classes were scheduled.

Mokey was running back and forth on the unplowed road tugging the toboggan with the Jays aboard, often turning fast and dumping them in the snow. Bernie and Marian were racing back and forth on their skis and Stella was enjoying a time in the fresh air after many days of being bound in cabin-fever-inducing activities.

Juju was unceremoniously dumped near the bridge. Jojo was laughing and squealing and hanging on for dear life. The little blondie decided to look in the pretty rushing water. The Mikota never froze over in winter but grotesque ice formations did form along the shore and against the pilings of the bridge. Stella was not concerned about the little one falling in for there was a high plank railing with gaps between to look through.

When at bridge center the girl had looked at the undergrowth on the far bank and had uttered unheard words due to water noise. They later found out she had said, "Kitty! Let me pet you." She had pushed her way through the snow that came up to her waist and before Stella could begin to come after her had left the bridge and gone out of sight.

Then came a warning growl and a roar from Lady Regina and a scream of fright from Juju. Mokey had stopped in his tracks and the curved prow of the toboggan had run into him. He spun around snapping the light tow cord. Little Jojo, well padded by his snowsuit had tumbled off and rolled in the snow. Mokey, running at maximum speed, passed Stella at the far end of the bridge.

She saw Juju a few yards from the "kitty." At the snarling Puma's feet was a fresh kill, a large raccoon, probably close to 40#. It must have sold its life dearly for the big cat had several bleeding wounds, the worst of which was her eye. She was hungry and angry. Fortunately she was not cornered.

And then the big dog, many pounds heavier than her, collided with her and both were knocked sprawling. Mokey and the big cat were simultaneously on their feet. Both danced from side to side. The dog blocked the path to his mistress. They jockeyed and feinted. He eluded her claws, she his fangs.

By then Bernie and Marian were beside Stella and Jojo was trying to push past them to see what kind of fun was going on. At first sound of the cougar John, who had been successful hunting and had been nearly back to the Lodge, went to top cross country speed to get to his family. From the mid-point of the arched bridge he saw the two animals getting ready for final mortal combat. He fired his rifle into the air twice and called out, "Stel, get Juju away. Everyone back up. Juju! Call Mokey."

John whistled between two fingers and called out as loudly as he could, "Mokey. Mokey! Guard Juju. Guard Juju." In spite of growls and snarls, the big dog heard the whistle and heeded the command. He retreated to the center of the bridge and blocked the way to his family. He barked a volley of warning to the cat.

John advanced to the far end of the bridge and was only about 15 yards away from the carcass over which the cat stood, poised and ready to attack. She snarled and kept her head cocked to stare at him through her remaining good eye. She took particular heed of the thunder stick he held in front of him with both hands. He very slowly slung it on his shoulder freeing both hands. She warily watched his every move.

He spoke slowly and distinctly to her. She cocked her head more and listened intently to this man she recognized. "Lady Regina, old girl, you look much the worse for wear. Your ribs show. Your fur used to be so sleek and now it's mangy. That eye looks terrible, too. Don't worry about me trying to take your supper. We've got plenty."

He took the two snow shoe hares out of his game bag and tossed them half way to her. "In fact, we have much more than we need. Why don't you take these for dessert? And one more thing, don't ever come near my family or I'll come after you. There's plenty of room for all of us in this valley. You hear me? Good bye. Good fortune." Dumb beasts may not understand words but they do have the ability to somehow perceive malicious intent or fear, either of which might signal a threat to them. She read him as no threat and as he backed away she turned her attention to her supper.

Back in the Lodge the older children wanted to know why he hadn't shot her. "Well first of all I only had one shot left in the rifle. Secondly, a .22 long rifle cartridge is definitely not the thing to use against big game. And thirdly, we were the trespassers and threat to her need to eat. She was just trying to stay alive."

He continued, "I'm really proud of Mokey. What a great dog he is. I do believe he had her scared. After a while we'll go back and look at her tracks. Her right forepaw always leaves a blurred outline. Several years ago she thought she could take one of our shoats. Uncle Lionel went out to scare her away. He fired his 12 ga. And some of the buckshot lodged in her foreleg. He had not meant to hit her but she moved the opposite way he expected. The shot must have stayed in and damaged a tendon. Whenever she puts weight on that paw it twists a bit as it lands.

"Anyhow, she started and jerked when it hit and then stood stock still as if to reproach him with her eyes. It was as if she was saying she'd stay away from his den and territory as long as he stayed away from her den and territory. She had then turned and walked regally away, ignoring any pain. She knew she was the queen of the valley. Uncle Lionel named her Lady Regina. Regina means queen. I hope she makes it through the winter."

The survival of Lady Regina was a small matter in the grand scheme of things, yet still something to cause folks who loved Nature's Creator to rejoice in His providence. But this was a pivotal point in a matter of eternal consequences, a matter that is said to cause rejoicing in Heaven. When John had taught the Scriptures that speak of angels rejoicing over one sinner who is saved, Marian had chimed in, "They must have had a party when I asked Jesus into my heart. I know it was like a party to me."

So we could probably say that this next section is a prelude to a party. The first sound of Lady Regina's survival had been heard on March 31st, about two and a half months after the encounter near the bridge. John had been the most happy as they had been reminded of the incident, but it had set Bernie to brooding. It did not hamper his lessons or chores. It did make him less responsive to the others except Stella and positively aloof, almost to the point of rudeness, toward John.

John and Bernie were working on chores in the barn before supper on April 4th. After a long stretch of sullen silence on the boy's part John had stopped everything and asked, "What's the matter, son?"

"I'm not your son," snapped back the lad.

"I know. It's meant to be an affectionate term. What's wrong with you?"

"With me nothing. With you a lot."

"You're mad at me?"

"Yes."

"Would you tell me why? What have I done to hurt you?"

"You haven't done anything to me. It's what you're doing to Aunt Stella."

John was dumfounded. He was not aware of anything he'd done to hurt his beloved. It had to be a big misunderstanding on the boy's part. John replied, "We are all often blind about our own faults. God often uses someone else to show them to us. Help me to know what wrong I've done and I'll fix it if I can. Tell me."

"Uncle John, you say you love her and you ignore her. You're more concerned about a dumb old mountain lion than you are about her. You hardly even talk to her. Marian and I have been comparing notes and she says the same thing. What happened to all the hugs and kisses? The ones we weren't supposed to see but peeked at? They're gone. You treat her like a stranger. And Marian said she sometimes hears Aunt Stella crying in bed ever so softly late at night. What's the matter with you?

"All my sisters are married and I remember how every one of them acted to their fiancés. Hanging on each other. Squeezing each other's hands. Hugging. Kissing all the time. Whispering and giggling. The two of you hardly talk to each other and never hold hands. Hardly ever a hug or kiss. You won't even sit by her on one of the sofas or next to her at the table. Why did you stop loving her? You're breaking her heart."

How could John explain it? It was nothing to do with him not wanting her. She was never out of his mind. He could hardly keep his hands off her or his arms from going around her. But she and he were very well aware of how powerful the chemistry between them was becoming. In pre-blast situations people would live in separate places, not just a few feet away from each other.

The very way she felt to him went through his mind. Before their mutual declaration of love there had always been a firmness to her putting him in mind of jocks at school who kept their muscles taut around those of the opposite sex. But now Stella was relaxed and yielding, the essence of softness, not rigidity. Their kisses had become longer and longer and it was almost impossible to break away from a hug.

She had told him they were becoming like teens in an isolated parked car, almost out of control. And so by mutual consent they had made sure their only contacts were under the scrutiny of the family. It was either restraint or constraint or there would be intimacies forbidden by God. How could John explain this, indeed why should he bring out a private matter? How could Bernie really understand that it was the couple's love of God and each other that held them apart?

"Bernie, let's sit on this bale of hay a couple of minutes. That's better. First of all Aunt Stella and I love each other more each day. And we are more and more powerfully drawn to each other. But until we are married we have to stay apart. We have to be very careful. We must be bound by God's commandments."

"So why don't you get married and solve the problem?"

John reminded the young man about Swede's wife Constance. He tried to explain how he could not risk any danger to Stella should an emergency arise without a doctor

213

available. "So you can surely understand why I'm afraid to go ahead. If you were in my shoes, you'd be thinking the same way."

Bernard Krause pondered this in silence for several minutes. Then he twisted around to speak eye to eye with John. His words were totally unexpected. "Mr. Knox, you keep talking about this fellow Jesus, a very good man I'll admit. And I was almost beginning to believe he might really be the Messiah, the Anointed One. If I did believe in him it would be 100% the way you say you do. But you don't. You faith is just an elaborate fairy tale. It's play acting, a big happy game."

John was shocked. He was not aware of any glaring inconsistencies in his life. "How can you say that? I do trust the Lord."

"Hah! In Proverbs it says you must trust the Lord with all your heart and not depend on your own understanding. In every detail you must admit God's control so he can steer your life. You say you love Aunt Stella but you depend on your own understanding and choose your own path. Why did the Lord bring the two of you together and kindle a hot love between you if He did not want to join your paths together? How come you refuse to go ahead with His plans because there's fear in your understanding? How come you can't trust Him? Is Jesus a fake or are you?"

As soon as the last few words were out of his mouth he regretted them. "I'm sorry. I was out of line. But how can I trust Jesus if you can't?" He picked up his pitchfork and went into a frenzy of work keeping his mouth shut and his back to the man.

After the kids were to bed, John said to Stella, "Honey, I need to take a little walk. I need to be alone to pray about some thing but I have a feeling I already know the answer. Would you wait up for me and make some chamomile tea like we had the first night when we arrived at the Honeymoon Cottage?"

Some basic matters were settled once for all as they sipped tea and held hands. In the small hours of the morning they adjourned to the living room and John kindled a small fire in the parlor stove and moved one of the over-stuffed chairs closer to it. He sat down and patted on his lap for her to sit there.

She teased him a bit by reminding him of his words, ages ago they seemed, when she'd cautioned him about Marian always sitting on his lap. "You said if it was me, you'd get nervous. I wouldn't dare make you nervous."

His reply was to pull her down onto his lap and kiss her. They sat tangled in each other's arms, her head on his shoulder. They whispered back and forth, often giggling, until they dozed off and fell into a deep restful sleep.

Juju happened to be the first one up. As she came out of the bathroom, she noticed that one of the lamps was lit in the living room, but it was turned down low. She peeked around the corner, saw the sound asleep couple, said, "Oooo," then clasped her fingers over her mouth and quietly woke the rest to come see. They all looked in quietly except Mokey. His canine exuberance could not be restrained. He bounded into the room with wakeup woofs. When the two sets of sleepy eyes opened he put his paws on John's knees and lavished slobbery tongue greetings. Both John and Stella would have put the dog on the bottom of their kiss-wish-list.

She said to John, "Shall we tell them now?"

Says he, "Naw! After breakfast," and gave Bernie a conspiratorial wink. The Jewish lad had a strong inkling of what was to come and felt good inside.

After pancakes and fried eggs the couple deliberately dawdled over their coffee. Jojo was the least patient. He began rapping his empty cocoa mug on the table chanting, "Wanna know now. Wanna know now." The rest picked up the chant, "Wanna know now. Wanna know now," accenting each word with raps of their mugs.

The man laughed and said, "Okay, hold it down you clowns. Well..... You'll be glad to know Thursday. May 31st, is the last day of school."

Marian exclaimed, "That's your big announcement? We already knew that."

"You did. Imagine that. What else was there? Oh! I remember. Aunt Stella wants to be a June Bride and I guess that would make me a June Groom. Friday, June 1st, is the date we set for our wedding. Sound okay?"

There was a minor epidemic of pandemonium for a few minutes. Once the laughter and cheers and congratulations wound down John continued, "Aunt Stella and I want to get away for a couple of days. We thought we could maybe honeymoon at the Dundee Grand Hotel. We have every confidence in Marian and Bernie to tend to chores and care for the little ones."

Stella spoke, "Miss Marian O'Connor, I would be greatly honored if you would do some favors for me. I need a woman to serve as wedding consultant and planner. And John and I would be privileged to have you sing O Promise Me and the Lord's Prayer. But most importantly, would you be my Maid of Honor?" The red head jumped up and dashed around the table to hug the bride-to-be to show acceptance.

"And Miss Juliet Eberhard, sweet Juju, I really need your help, too. Will you be my flower girl?" The child's reply was a copy of Marian's although she had not the faintest notion of what she had to do. But she'd do anything she could for her Uncle and Aunt.

John spoke next, "Mr. Joseph Krause, my good buddy Jojo, I have a very important job for you. Will you be my ring bearer?" "Yessir! Amen!"

"Finally, last but not least, Mr. Bernard Krause, my faithful companion Hawkeye, who God used to help me see things better. I can't tell you what a great honor it would be if you will read the service and act as God's man to declare us husband and wife and also to be my Best Man plus maybe be our musician to play the piano."

The usually vocal boy was almost too choked up to speak. He and John gave each other bear hugs and manly pats on the backs. He later said privately, "I'm really sorry I got mad at you. I acted like a jerk. What would Jesus have thought of that?"

"I'm sure he would not have been happy with the anger part, but I know he would have been glad about your motivation. I think he would have said well done about your tender hearted concern for Aunt Stella. And I thank you for putting me on the right track about trusting my Savior 100%"

Good Friday fell on April 13th. The afternoon school session were cancelled and a short service held in their place. From the wedding announcement on the fifth until then Bernie had been doubly cooperative and pleasant to everyone but also seemed to be doubly introspective and thoughtful. After supper that Friday he came to John requesting a private conference in the Library.

"Uncle John, my logic was all twisted when I asked how I could trust Jesus if you couldn't. My father often told me that even if everyone around me did evil, it was not an excuse for me. And even if everyone else refused to do what was right, that was not an excuse for me to refuse. He said every person has to stand on his own two feet and do right even if the whole world is against us, because God is for us."

"Hawkeye, your father is a man of great wisdom. But I still have to practice what I preach."

"Yessir, Uncle John, and I know you try super hard to do just that." He paused as if to gather strength to say words which came out only with great effort. "I think I've known deep inside for several months now, at least since

Christmas, that Jesus really is God. I don't understand it. I can't make heads or tails of it. But I know it's true. Jesus is God. He is our Messiah. He lived a spotless life so he could be our sacrifice, the Lamb of God who died for our sins. And he did rise again. He is alive today. I'm sure of it. But you never argued or pushed me into believing it. Now what must I do? Would you please show me like you did Marian?"

That hour, to put it in Marian's words, the angels must have had another party. The circle was now complete at Knox Farm. Although Bernie immediately told everyone how he had invited Jesus to be his Lord, he insisted he be allowed to give a formal testimony at the Easter Service. When he did this, he even mentioned he was glad like Uncle John that Lady Regina had survived another winter.

It had been an evil event which necessitated the sojourn in what the residents called Knox Valley. But God had brought great good out of evil. Joy was blossoming abundantly with more to come. In like manner Lionel Knox had come through days of sorrow but was moving on into days of joy. After the storm comes the rainbow.

He had arrived at the home of Albert and Margaret Holmes where he'd be boarding during most of his time overseas. He arrived a few days after our Labor Day. Bad news had just come to the family. Albert, brother-in-law of Aaron McDougal, Margaret's brother and Lionel's new illustrator, had been faced with steadily decreasing health and with bouts of pain. He had finally gone in for a complete physical. The big C was taking control of his body. He was already at the point where no treatment could offer any real help. It was a matter of killing the pain until the cancer killed the man.

As soon as Lionel learned of the circumstances he wished to make other arrangements. Albert was adamant that nothing be changed in their previous agreement.

"Lionel, you said you'd board with us. I agreed. I hold you to it. Whether I am on two feet or my back, my word is a bond I will not break."

So Lionel stayed there whenever his lecture tour did not require him to spend time elsewhere. There was plenty of room. Holmes Books Ltd. Had a large bookstore with quarters in back and two comfortable apartments upstairs. In addition there was a sideline, a specialty print shop next door for those wishing handbills, booklets, business cards, or sundry items printed to their personal specifications.

The oldest son Henry, 25, and his wife Maureen lived behind the store and managed it. She was pregnant and as soon as they needed extra space they'd move upstairs and move the inventory stored there.

Albert and Margaret were semi-retired and had the front apartment over the store. There was a sunny spare bedroom Lionel could use which had a small adjoining sitting room which made him an ideal study. He would be dining with them when present.

Son Michael, 22, and his wife Ann already had 6 month old twins. They lived above the print shop which he ran. It was a busy and profitable undertaking and he even had an apprentice who would soon be his full time assistant. Financially the whole family was in great shape.

The youngest son Kevin, 17, was an honor student finishing his last year of schooling before University days. He was the only family member not consumed with a passion for literature and producing and distributing it. He was a plant lover and had a green thumb. He wanted to learn all a person could learn about all food plants and how to increase yields and quality. His dream was of a world where all people had enough to eat. As he had read the Red Arrow stories and later questioned Lionel, he had concluded it would be a must in his education to spend summers in the Mikota Territory and learn from experts.

Lionel spent about 2/3 of his time with the Holmes family. Albert's physical decline was rapid but he was able to keep up a semblance of normalcy through October. He managed to get to Divine Services almost every week accompanied by his family and Lionel who responded to their use of Len as his name. The two men ministered to each other spiritually up to the end. When Al was bed-ridden, Len whenever present in the home willingly helped with the unpleasant physical aspects.

By the end of November Al's lucid moments were becoming very infrequent. During times of clear-headedness he enlisted Len to take dictation and type up final letters to his wife and sons to be delivered after his demise. He also extracted a solemn promise from Len to stay the full agreed time and help the family make the sorrowful transition.

Two weeks before Christmas he called them all to his bedside to sing Yule Carols and read the Luke account. After their very simple Christmas celebration he said, "It's nearly time. My next celebration will be at Jesus' feet. But you must celebrate as usual on Christmas Day. I'll be praying for you up there. I love you all and that will never end…. Ohh!...Oww!...Go now. Meg stay. Gotta say something…. Oww!" His short farewell to Margaret was his last words on earth. He had slid into a deep, untroubled sleep and within 24 hours was gone.

Lionel helped in every way he could. Meg and her three sons assured him they wanted him to stay on in accordance with the dying man's last letters. The lingering sorrow over the loss of six in the Forbidden Valley and the new sadness over separation from a new but dear friend were both somewhat submerged and assuaged as he tried to bring comfort and cheer to the widow.

In the process of running errands with her, escorting her to church, having meals with Kevin and her, going out for tea, and later on restaurant meals, he began to discover depths of feeling akin to how he had felt for his fiancé before his brother's death. He almost felt guilty, but reminded himself she was a widow. He confided in eldest son Henry who first had smiled enigmatically and then later on confided that his father had considered Len as a proper candidate on a mental list of possible second husbands for his widow.

This chronicler is not a proponent of arranged marriages. He believes that such matters are decreed in Heaven. But under these circumstances?

On Tuesday which was May Day there was a church social to which Len escorted Meg. On the walk home he gave a rambling dissertation on age. He was 57, Meg 50. He rattled on about the uncertainty of life, how their candles were burning low, and how folks with Scotch blood hate to waste time or resources.

"So get to the point, Len. You're wasting both time and breath."

He paused and swallowed and cleared his throat several times. "Uh, Meg, I'm growing very fond of you and I am hoping you might perhaps care for me."

She smiled and said, perhaps a bit coquettishly, "Well, perhaps I might be a wee bit fond of you." As she said it she slid her hand down from where she held her escort's arm and took hold of his hand and squeezed it. Over late tea they had a long and earnest conversation. Sorrow's shadows were being dispelled by the light of growing joy.

On the following Sunday in Knox Valley the church service was held at Saturday park. After Bernie's conversion he began inquiring into when he could be baptized as penitents had under the prophet John the Baptist or converts after Pentecost. Stella, Marian, and John had been baptized as infants. Jojo and Bernie had not and it was not known about Juliet.

But although John had been baptized as an infant, he also felt that his Baptist friends in college had a compelling argument for born-again believers to be baptized as a testimony of their identification with Jesus. The immersion process seemed to him to give a better visual reminder of Jesus' burial and resurrection. So in college he had been immersed.

In the name of the Father, Son, and Holy Ghost he had baptized all three with the Jays and Mokey as witnesses. Marian declared afterward that she was sure there must have been a crowd of angelic spectators cheering them on. She herself felt joy similar to when she had invited Jesus into her life. The whole day was a time of exceeding great joy.

On Saturday, May 26th, Lionel and Margaret were wed with full family approval at a private ceremony in her church. Some so-called friends were excluded who had denounced the whole idea and had chided her for not having the decency of having a proper period of mourning, one year being the minimum.

From Albert's last words to her she knew he had not wanted her too long alone. She was right with God about it and she was much more than a wee bit fond of the fine man. She had responded to meddling critics perhaps too tartly as she expelled them from her presence.

She had said, "If you loved me you would be glad I'm finding happiness. If you really cared for me you would not be dictating to my heart. Jesus answered opposition by telling Satan to get behind him. Draw your own conclusions and tend to your own business. Good day."

Sunday afternoon on May 26th, John and Stella demonstrated a very simple Mikota ritual hardly ever used any more. Up into the early 1900's it had been a standard procedure. After a man and woman agreed between themselves to be married, this very simple ceremony was used to announce their engagement to the tribe in advance of the public wedding.

When the family had gone to town to prepare the hotel's bridal suite for the soon-to-be-honeymooners, faithful copies of the original type of garments used were seen in a display case in the hotel's small library.

Ornamentation was the opposite of wedding garments for the woman's dress and moccasins had no beads or fringes. She would however wear a small beaded head band. Her wedding clothes would be very ornate, the man's plain.

But for this ceremony the man's buckskin trousers and tunic were very elaborately beaded, as were his moccasins. A large feathered cape would be fastened around his neck and to his wrists. On his head would be a carved hat made to depict a Golden Eagle's face. The beak would jut out from his forehead like the bill of a baseball cap. With arms outstretched the man would have a bird-like profile.

After Sunday dinner the couple changed into the Mikota costumes. When they were ready and their audience seated on lawn chairs in the front yard, Bernie began to beat on a tom-tom slowly and steadily. In the very early days this might have gone on for hours to summon the tribe. At a pre-planned moment the drumming stopped and John who had been out of sight around the corner of the Lodge did a reasonable imitation of the shrill keening of the Golden Eagle. The drum beat resumed and Stella stepped regally out of the Lodge,

She moved as gracefully as a ballerina twirling as she made a great circle of the yard looking ever skyward. She stopped in front of the door and kept looking expectantly upward. The drum beat ceased long enough for another shrill call.

And then John glided into sight reminding us of how children extend their arms and pretend to be birds. He slowly flapped his wings as he majestically twice circled Stella. Then he moved in front of her, lowered his arms as he jumped upward, and landed in a crouch. He lowered his arms as he straightened up. After a moment of staring into each other's eyes, he extended his arms toward her. She pressed against him and encircled him with her arms even as he enfolded her so the cape wings hid her.

During these several minutes Marian had been snapping photos with an old Polaroid camera that had been abandoned in the hotel along with several packs of very hard to locate film. The bride would have a wedding photo album.

John explained the significance of the ritual. "The Golden Eagle is held in great respect by the Mikota people. It is brave, fierce if the need arises, and mates for life. The good strong qualities of this noble bird are much desired by men of the tribe. The little dance signifies the hope of the bride that her husband will be fearless in protecting her and their children and providing for them. It indicates that the couple is willing to bond for life and share all they have."

Although it would not have affected the outcome of the wedding had all dressed in their better casual wear, it had been possible to obtain semi-formal wear from one of the shops off the lobby of the hotel. The shop, named Just Right, was not yet fully stocked for the blast had come before its final shipment which was due just before the Grand Opening. Nevertheless the three ladies each got new gowns and Jojo and Bernie nifty suits. John had his rarely worn best suit.

There is a cliché that all brides are beautiful. Stella had a natural wholesome beauty which life in the valley seems to have enhanced. But her radiance as she stepped up to her groom in the service was beyond his comprehension. How could anyone so beautiful love him?

Juju had exuberantly strewn wild flower petals around perfuming the whole house. Jojo had pompously paraded with the ring box before presenting it to John. Marian had never sung better and Bernie's playing seemed to exceed his capability.

Bernard Krause officiated by reading a slightly revised copy of the exact service which John's father and mother had used. He could have made a good Rabbi or Cantor for he spoke distinctly and with proper emphasis, never stumbling over the words he'd almost memorized.

The conclusion was, "John David Knox and Estellita Juarez, in the presence of God and His angels you have both declared to us as witnesses that you both love each other and vow to be faithful to one another until death parts you.

"Estellita, you have promised to obey this man. But you will never be his slave or servant. You will be his co-worker yet will understand that at times he must have the final word.

"John, even though you will have the final authority it must be like that of Christ over His church which is His Bride. He would never do anything to hurt his bride and He gave all He had for her including his life blood. You must never lord it over her but serve her best interest with all you are and have.

"Finally, Estellita and John, you must both love each other more than anyone else on earth. But you must love God more and worship him with your very souls and spirits. And you must also worship each other with your bodies.

"All this having been said in the absence of clergy, I will act as spokesman of us all and declare that God is joining the two of you together and His wrath could be revealed to any who tries to break this bond. We all now acknowledge that you are husband and wife. Amen."

The lad expelled a sigh of relief and then said, "So will you guys please kiss so we can go over to the Great Hall for dinner and our reception? I'm hungry."

When Mr. and Mrs. John D. Knox returned to the farm just before dark on Sunday evening, they expected to immediately take possession of Stella's room as their own. During the week before the wedding they'd refurnished it with a double bed and an extra chest of drawers. But Bernie and Marian forbid their elders to use it and shunted them to the Honeymoon Cottage which they had stocked and prepared for them.

Marian explained, "It's already decided. You should have more than a weekend honeymoon. We can handle all the chores for the next couple of weeks. You can come over for any meals whenever you want to or just to visit a bit. But the cottage is off limits for the rest of us except to bring you food or firewood if you ask for it. Okay? We all love you both to pieces."

About the time the newlyweds were settling into the Honeymoon Cottage for their fortnight sojourn, Mr. and Mrs. Lionel Knox were on their way back to the Holmes' holdings in Glasgow. Len had rented a car and they had wandered northward past the Grampian Mountains and somewhat followed the northern coast past the Firths of Moray and Dornoch up to the north tip of Scotland as much as roads conditions allowed. They had no set itinerary, stayed at out of the way Inns and one night when no public accommodations were available, were taken in by a jolly hospitable Anglican Vicar.

Len was smitten by the rugged beauty of the highlands but seeing such country made him feel homesick. Before their vows he and Meg had agreed that what she teasingly called the "uncivilized colonies" was to become their home together. Her sons could capably run the business and Kevin would be spending time in the States anyway for he had been accepted at Texas A&M.

When he was informed of their plans to sail as soon as possible on a cruise vessel in order to sooner begin construction of a home in the Mikota Territory, he was doubly excited that he would not have to travel alone. "It will be great traveling with Len and you, Mum. There are so many questions I have for him."

Putting on a stern face she replied, "Ach! It's not my husband you'll be pestering on my honeymoon. Who ever heard of such a thing as a bride taking along one of her brats on such a trip? We'll not be seeing you until we land. We have a fine state room booked. We've arranged to stow you in the cargo hold. They'll give you a hammock to sling between some crates and we can have a steward bring you one or two sandwiches and cups of broth. That is if we happen to think of it. Newly married people have more important things on their minds."

At this point she had turned her back on him for she could hardly keep from laughing. Kevin had stepped around her and hugged her and given her a kiss on the cheek. "Mum, I'm on to your little jokes. Beware. It's my turn next."

The truth was they had booked a small suite with bath, two compact bedrooms, and a sitting room where the threesome could have breakfast and high tea together. On the actual cruise the high point to Lionel was when Kevin, after a private conversation with Meg, asked for permission to call the man Dad instead of Len.

Years later when reminiscing, all six of the valley people and all three of the voyagers would name Spring of 2001 as perhaps the happiest they could remember. They would also admit that the good things and blessings were there to help them later on when evil days came, as often they will.

Chapter Eleven

SUMMER DARKNESS

Even when there is bright illumination, whether from the sun or man-made lights, it is possible for there to be great darkness which has nothing to do with photons of energy. Even on brilliant Summer days unfortunate accidents or deliberate evil deeds can have the effect of throwing deep shadows over the human spirit and may bring depressing gloom. Unexpected events often overwhelm the psyche. Even folks who are usually filled with the joy of the Lord may on occasion be temporarily plunged into sadness and have black hours of doubt and despair, even terms of spiritual blindness.

Even a succession of troubles, though most are small, may weaken us to the point where the arrival of a big misfortune nearly destroys us. A little jingle says, "It's the little things that bother and the little things that rack. You can sit upon a mountain, but you can't sit on a tack." There's more truth than humor there.

Inside and out of the Forbidden Valley many things happened that Summer to bring days of darkness. Then near the end of the season a whole nation was plunged into darkness. Following will be told some events which had particular impact on people with whom we are already acquainted.

John's 26th birthday anniversary was honored after Sunday dinner on the 20th of June. Juliet's date was not known for certain but was thought to be about the 22nd, just as Summer was starting. A picnic/party/playtime was set to be held at Saturday Park in the afternoon. The Knox Valley Percussion, Rhythm, String, and Reed Band was going to give a concert. It had been organized during snowbound days.

It was a singing band except for John who played his uncle's old Hohner harmonica. Marian sang a strong lead and clicked castanets. Stella sang and played her Spanish guitar. The adults had taught Bernie to strum a ukulele as he sang. Jojo vigorously beat the tom-tom and Juju slapped and shook a tambourine. It was sometimes harmonious and on the beat. At other times it was a discordant cacophony. But it was always jolly good fun. There was an air of expectant excitement until Jojo made an announcement shortly after lunch.

"Uncle John, the toilet broke. Won't flush." The lad was tearfully fearful that he had somehow broken it. John opened the tank lid. The reservoir was empty. He checked all bathroom faucets as Stella checked the kitchen taps. There was no more than a dying trickle of water.

The man said, "Our tank must be empty. There must be something wrong with the windmill. Jojo, my little buddy, you didn't do anything wrong. You're a good boy."

The windmill was behind the Great Hall and higher that its ridge pole. Adjacent to it and about six feet shorter was the water tower topped by a 500 gallon tank. Water was pumped up and when the tank was full overflowed into a pipe which carried the surplus water to the cows' watering trough which overflowed into the hog trough which flowed into the chicken trough and from there to the river. Whenever the wind blew the critters had fresh water.

Blow it always did save for an hour or two each day. At night chilled air from the ice fields flowed down but the rising of the sun, even on cloudy days, created thermals which reversed the direction. Also, changing weather brought wind but the funnel effect of the valley forced these to be either easterly or westerly.

The windmill was a home-built-one-of-a-kind designed by David Knox, John's Grandfather, and constructed under his supervision before our John was born. In essence it was very simple. A simple rotating circular carriage on top supported an axle/differential assembly from a junk yard. The drive shaft hung down suspended by a U-joint. One axle was welded immobile and to it was hinged a wind vane. On the axle's rotating end was a wheel to which were welded the blades which fought the wind. There was no brake mechanism.

An ingenious centrifugal governor would have no effect on the vane in modest breezes and the vane would keep the propeller facing directly into the wind. As the wind increased and thus the RPM's, the governor would swing the vane to the side so that the fan would face the wind from an angle thus preventing it spinning too fast which could damage the system.

At the bottom of the tower was a solidly mounted differential. Its driveshaft of course pointed up. One axle was locked as above. The other had its brake drum bolted to a heavy machined plate on which was welded a section of a automobile crankshaft. Through a long connecting rod the up and down motion of the crank empowered the double acting pump.

Pipe couplings had been welded to the ends of both drive shafts and between them were two lengths of heavy duty galvanized pipe. These were joined in the middle by a two piece bolted sleeve which could be undone to separate the sections for service.

Each short stroke of the piston sucked up about a pint of water and pushed the previous pint up the pipe to the tank. Depending on wind speed as much as five gallons a minute could be sent to the tank. But the average was about half that much which meant about 2-1/2 a minute or about 150 an hour. About 3000 gallons a day were normal with most of it continuously purifying the stock water and then returning to earth in the river.

The family had hurried out to look. The big blades were whirling away as always, but the vertical shaft was not turning. It was leaning against the inside of the riveted angle iron framework. The upper U-joint had broken, possibly the previous day.

What would the average city dweller do if no more water was available to flush toilets, prepare food or wash away dirt? If a metropolitan area is cut off from its water supply, it is a major disaster. At Knox Farm it was an awful inconvenience, not disastrous. The old pitcher pump in the winter barn could supply the animals. The pure Mikota River was flowing by. There were also a couple of seldom used but fully functional outhouses, but these were not convenient, especially for the little children or after dark. The Knox couple considered it mandatory that the windmill be fixed.

Fixing it would involve climbing to the top and working up there. The simple issue of the degree of risk or hazard contained in this simple task brought on the first real quarrel John and Stella had after their marriage began. On John's instructions Mokey was pulling the dog cart to transport jerry cans of water up from the river. The children were filling jugs and none of them heard the disagreement.

"John, I forbid you climbing up and maybe falling. It's much too dangerous."

"Honey, I've climbed it dozens of times. I'll go get some tools and get started. No problem."

"You're wrong. There's a big problem. If you fall I could be a widow."

231

"Don't be so foolish. I'm a pro at climbing."

"Sure you are. Just like Juju. And don't call me foolish. I'm not foolish. I'm not the one ready to climb up there. You're the foolish one. Climbing up there is foolish."

They were both under stress which certainly can affect behavior. Little sparks can ignite big fires. Back and forth went the dispute heating up as it went. Then Stella said, "If you really loved me, you wouldn't want to take dangerous chances."

"Well, if you really loved me you'd trust me to be careful and you might possibly believe I knew what I was doing."

Simultaneously they realized the total unfairness of the phrase, "If you loved me," for they were both totally convinced of their mutual love. After a long embrace which cooled their anger but warmed their ardor, they both apologized and were willing to accept the other's viewpoint.

He said, "Let's not get an argument going over who was the most foolish. It was me. I don't climb like a kid anymore. It is dangerous, very unsafe. But I think I have a solution. The Dundee Utility Co. which managed the operation of the water plant and maintained the gas and electric networks had a truck with big extension ladders on a rack and also safety harnesses for high work.

"Bernie and I will make a run into Dundee. We'll take the Power Wagon. We can haul anything we need on it. We can still have the music party for Juju later. We should be back in a couple of hours but we could be held up hunting for their truck if it was on a job when the blast happened. Don't fret if we're detained."

It was 3:00 when Shah Nock and Hawkeye went on their hunting expedition. Stella held supper until 7:00. Afterwards she kept her happy face on and served the birthday cake and the four played some child games. When the Jays were safely bedded, she said the men might be quite late. Her reassuring hugs belied the dread she felt.

At 9:00 she and Marian shared how very nervous they were. The wife considered bundling up the kids into the Subaru and going after the men. Marian pondered and asked, "But how would we know which road they'd be on? What if we took the north road and they came home on the south road? You know Uncle John doesn't always go the same way. And what if they came and we were gone? They might come looking for us."

"You're right. Best we stay put. For all we know they might have run out of gas. Let's pray for their safety and then you'd better get in bed. I know you're extra tired after doing Bernie's chores too. I'll stay up and have sandwiches ready for them."

The one o'clock chime of the grandfather clock roused Stella. She had dozed off in the dark living room in the chair in which they'd made their wedding plans. A kitchen lamp was lit as well as lanterns by both entrances. As she sat up she thought she heard a distant motor.

As the noise was approaching, Stella could tell from the much brighter headlights and less raucous exhaust that it was not the old Dodge. After warm greetings the late comers ate as John began to relate events. Bernie gulped down a sandwich and a glass of milk and then hit the sack. He was asleep almost as soon as his head hit the pillow. John, at his wife's bidding finished eating before going on, knowing talking with a full mouth was not proper.

"So we were a little over halfway to Dundee and the truck began pulling to the side. I first thought it might be a flat but the right rear wheel was barely turning. Something had jammed up in the brakes. You knew the brakes needed to be overhauled if we could have found parts. But you know we hardly ever drove over 25 and used compression to stop us. Anyhow we stopped for quite a while to let it cool off but that didn't do any good and the nearest tools would have been in Dundee so we decided to keep on.

"Well, we ran it in its lowest gear and fought the steering wheel to stay on the road. But the drag kept getting worse until the clutch began to slip. We waited quite a while for things to cool off and tried again. This time the clutch burned out. It's toast. We were overdue for a new one. Now there's no way to fix it or the brakes. No auto parts place in the Valley. No other Power Wagon we could cannibalize. End of Power Wagon.

"So us Braves began to wear out our moccasins. We were eight miles from town and ten from the farm and we did need those ladders. We arrived about seven and as I said might happen, so it did. The Utility Office and garage are by the water tower and that's the first place we looked. No soap. We ransacked the office to find some record of calls or service or a schedule of runs to be made.

"I have two reasons to think God was directing us. First, in the manager's desk drawer we found Granola bars and some M&M's which after our walk we really needed. Secondly, next to the candy, we found a notebook with the schedule of where the truck crew was last supposed to have been. It was about a mile and a quarter to hike. We took the spare keys from the office. Good thing we did. The crew must have taken them along when they left.

"So we get to the truck and the battery isn't completely dead for the dome light glowed when we opened the door. But all the response we got from the starter was a click from the solenoid. There must have been just enough acid in the battery to keep it from freezing solid and bursting in the winter.

"Now a mile walk back over the bridge to the Red Arrow Mini Mall to get a light weight Honda generator. But we had no gas to run it and it was getting dark. So into Paradise Outdoors to get a Coleman lantern and fluid. Then back into Fixit's where we'd left the generator and located some plastic hose we could siphon gas with and a gas can.

And then into the Food House to get a grocery cart. You remember there's no food left there. We needed the cart to tote all our gear. Weren't we having fun?"

She replied, "Men have all the fun while their wives are slaving at home. Next time you go shopping, take me along, but not for automotive parts." She spoke with good humor but knew how deeply stressful John's time must have been.

"We siphoned gas out of one of the cars in the hotel parking lot and gave the generator a test. After all that we didn't want to get to the truck and not have the generator run. It ran. I forgot to mention we also got a battery charger at Fixit's but there weren't any heavy duty ones and he had to keep it going over an hour before we could start the truck. I can't tell how thankful we were when the motor started.

"We hauled all the stuff in the truck but dropped off the cart at the empty Food House. We had to go that way anyway because we intended to use the tow chain to dray the Dodge off the road where it blocked the way. I do intend to get Uncle Lionel's air horns off it."

He finished off by explaining that the only truck in town on which they could haul a reasonable load of firewood, even if only half which the Dodge had hauled was a ¾ ton GMC but it was not four wheel drive. "This Utility Company truck has storage bins on both sides and hardly any other cargo area but it does have a hitch to haul our boat trailer. As for a U-joint for the windmill, I do believe the one on the Dodge was replaced just before I graduated. I'm sure I can machine adapters in the shop.

"We'll be fine. Nobody's hurt. God is good. It's been a long harrowing day but not threatening. Things are bound to improve. We can have our little celebration tomorrow. Oh. That would be Sunday. Okay, Sunday it is. We have to celebrate Juju's birthday together."

Although it would take John until Tuesday evening to get the pump going, lack of running water did not dampen their spirits. But what they found out on the way to Saturday Park did. It was necessary to use both the Subaru and the Chevy Utility Truck else there would be no room for Mokey and what fun would it be without him? So John and Mokey filled the truck seat, the furry friend filling 2/3 of it, his drooling head out the window. He suddenly stood on all fours and began barking furiously, his thrashing tail slapping the man in the face.

John halted the truck. They were next to a sloping meadow which gave an easy path to the little plateau where they had seen the wild horses. They were coming up to the wooded stretch where they had watched from concealment. Something was crawling through the grass toward a big tree at the edge of the meadow. Tufts of grass swaying back and forth marked the slow passage.

John left Mokey in and went to see. Those in the following car bailed out and came running toward him. As soon as he could clearly see what was happening, he ordered them all back so they would not see. It was Lady Regina, but not how John wanted any of them to remember her.

Apparently her scent had stampeded the wild herd for hoof prints abounded on the dirt road and a lane had been trampled across the grass. It was also evident that the puma had not been quick enough in her old age to get out of the way of those awful pounding hooves. Her back was broken, her hind legs twisted to the side and paralyzed. She gasped for air fighting against a crushed rib cage. She was desperately clawing the sod trying to get to the tree. Mountain cats' instincts drive them to climb to safety whether on rocks or trees but she was past her last climb.

John told Stella to take the car and kids to the lake and he would soon join them. He returned to the farm for a rifle and a shovel. They soon heard a shot echoing in the valley. He never spoke about it except to his wife. There was no way he could have let the noble Lady Regina die a lingering painful death. There was a solemn damper on the entire birthday party.

Some believe in luck and think that luck, good or bad, can run in long streaks. Some think misfortunes lead to one another. In the valley that summer there were bruises, cuts, burns, scratches, bug bites, hunts for straying critters, broken and misplaced tools, etc. yet no more than the previous year. But the incidents of the windmill and the Dodge and the cougar seemed to set up the four older residents to link each new mishap to the preceding ones. There was always background gloom shed by the unspoken question, "What next?"

On Thursday, June 28th, a year to the day after the blast, the combined forces of the U.S. Attorney General's office, the FBI, and the IRS, were openly launched against the interlocking network of hate organizations which had conspired together for the act of terror in the Hidden Valley. The most prominent legal assaults were against Jerome Buckhalter and Reginald S. Vander Maas III. Jerome was the charismatic unifying force for all the various associations but legally only the head of one, FSN (Free Speech Now!) Reginald was president of the League of Purity and Justice.

Due process was followed to obtain the financial records of all the various groups which would have to prove their right to non-profit status or cough up taxes. Personal financial records of all members and contributors were sought. Even as it had taken the IRS to drive the coffin nails in Al Capone's career, so now a day of reckoning was coming but every bit of procedure would be by the book.

Yet there are people in high places or on the staffs of such people who love money more than truth, justice, or personal integrity. These will leak information if the price is right. Mere hours before arrest warrants could be applied, Buckhalter and Vander Maas were seen in D.C. entering an Islamic nation's embassy. In an embassy limo, operating with diplomatic immunity, they were transported to the airport where an embassy jet whisked them away from powerless Federal agents.

From an unknown place overseas Buckhalter masterminded a legal counter-attack. Vast sums of money had been discretely siphoned out of all the various treasuries over the last several months and were lost in an intricate series of electronic transfers believed to have ended in the coffers of Islamic terrorists. The best guess was that they were headquartered in Afghanistan, but enough money was left behind to finance a dazzling defense. The ACLU was eager to defend these innocents and defend the right of the various so-called patriotic organizations to do what they pleased.

Nevertheless there were scores of arrests over the country of those whose culpability was real. The Attorney General called the evil network a house of cards. Topple a few and the whole house would fall.

But Morris Langford, a radical judge and bitter enemy of Aaron Knox was in a position to torpedo the Federal case. He was in a position to rule on evidence and first ruled that the tapes the FBI had obtained through electronic surveillance were not admissible since the court order by Knox only specified phone taps and not other devices. Any information obtained by means other than phone taps was illegal.

Secondly it was the taped information which told of the truck driven by Bogardus being a bomb. Since no on site investigation had been done which might prove this, to say that what had happened was anything but an accident was purely speculation and thus inadmissible.

Thirdly, since those accused had not had an opportunity to conduct their own investigation at the alleged bomb site, their civil rights were being infringed upon.

The prosecution countered all this by saying there had been another tape made independently which had a witness that could verify it and also experts could verify the voices to be those of the accused. It had been hoped that the FBI mole, George Rummler, who had subsequently witnessed and taped much more, could have been held in reserve. George was never able to testify.

The evening before his scheduled pickup and protective custody was to start, (He was still supposed to be a secret witness.) there were two busloads of skinheads which arrived in Maryvale, George's hometown and the college locale. County Sheriff Hayes and the town's Chief of Police pooled all of their forces to prevent a riot at the school stadium where the Neo-nazis and League members were holding a rally to denounce the government for trampling civil rights.

During the rally a van-load of skinheads roared into George's driveway, broke into his house, and beat the bachelor with truncheons, leaving him for dead. As they left a neighbor called 911 and it only took the police 20 minutes to make the three block run from the stadium. The battered man did cling to life but entered a deep coma from which he did not recover.

The CIA dug up quite reliable information regarding ties between the Muslim militants and the Buckhalter confederation for both wanted to see the U.S.A. destroyed. But the Jihad view was that non-Muslims were to be used and discarded when their usefulness was over. It took a number of months before Jerome had put all his resources at the feet of those he thought were benefactors and allies. Once this was done the uneasy alliance was over. Jerome and Reginald might just as well have fallen into a bottomless pit in the sand, for they were never heard of again.

Norman Chance was among the prominent witnesses for the prosecution. Threats came against the lives of himself and his sister. Around the clock protection had to be provided for them until the conclusion of the matter.

Many of the accused pled guilty and many testified against their leaders in exchange for immunity or reduced sentences. It took many months for the "house of cards" to fall but inevitably it did. However an event near the end of summer required an immediate diverting of resources and delayed the outcome.

One of the goals of terrorism is to bring a nation to its knees financially. The price being paid would likely never be fully added up because of the immense commitment of human and other resources needed to investigate, apprehend, and convict enemies of the state. So in this sense the terrorist act in the Hidden Valley was a step in the right direction regarding terrorist goals.

On July 15th, the third Monday, an Energy Symposium was held at the State Capital which was about 400 miles from Glasgow. Simon Hawthorne, CEO of the Red Arrow oil Company, drove his great aunt Esther Crowe to the two day gathering where they would jointly represent the Mikota interests.

It was a two day media circus. Oil producers were attacked by radical environmentalists. They were pilloried over the sudden and extreme price changes and accused of price fixing and profiteering at the expense of the American public. Red Arrow Oil, which had kept a constant price and worked with narrow profit margins, was irrationally included in the diatribes. And since it refused to put in more wells and only a small surplus left the Territory, was also accused of monopolistic hoarding. Only a few voices declared that it, the smallest of the oil companies, was the only one above reproach. These voices were drowned out by both left and right wing radicals.

Just before noon on Tuesday, with several hours yet scheduled, Esther had had enough. She got the floor and declared bluntly, "I can not see how all the contradictions, arguments, and misrepresentations can in any way produce any solutions to our nation's energy problems. A few here are honest and fair, but their voices are drowned out. The rest speak with forked tongues. Our position is clear. You have it in black and white and so do all the major networks. We will not be wasting any more time here. Farewell."

Esther and Simon checked out of their rooms at the Ramada where Lionel had first heard of the blast. They were on their way by one. Esther had been a widow a little over five years. Her husband had purchased a shiny red Ford Escort shortly before his death. It was in pristine condition and had low mileage on the odometer. She preferred not to drive any more and her grand nephew enjoying taking her in the peppy and economical car.

"Grandmother?" This and Grandfather were customary terms of courtesy Mikotans used to show their respect for senior men and women whether or not they were kin.

"Yes, Son."

"We'd better have lunch before we leave town. I was curious about that place we saw on the way in, Yooper Pasty Shop. Want to try a pasty?" He pronounced it paste-ee, not its proper pass-tee.

"That might be a good way to get the taste of that Symposium out of our mouths. Yooper? I think that refers to northern Michigan people. Miners used to have their wives bake a pasty for their lunch in the mines." She pronounced it correctly. "Isn't it just a few more blocks? You could run in and get us each one and some pop or juice and we could stop at Jefferson Park at a picnic table."

They were on a one way street with diagonal parking on both sides. Yooper Pasty Shop was on the left side, the last place before an intersection. As they approached, the vehicle in the last spot backed out and left. Simon smiled at their good fortune and pulled in near the entrance.

Esther said, "Be sure to get a receipt, Son." She cranked down the window to wait. She clicked on the key to the accessory position and turned on the radio to scan stations to find some good gospel music. She heard the two tone tune of a fast approaching emergency vehicle. As was her custom she paused to offer a silent prayer for whoever was involved. She then realized the siren was that of a police car.

A new Ford Crown Victoria was coming from the right on the intersecting street at more than double the limit. The light changed. A man in a Winnebago, who was stopped for the light, not seeing the speeding vehicle a block away, crossed the intersection. The driver of the Ford, a drunken teen-aged boy trying to impress his girl friend, could not stop, swerved to the left to miss the Winnebago, lost control and flew bumper first into the Escort.

The two youngsters were protected by belts and airbags and had no serious injuries. But the boy had just ruined his life and would have to face his father, his conscience, the judge, and some serious jail time, plus a criminal record that would not go away.

Esther survived. The media called it a miracle. The door of the little car was hardly protection against the mass of a heavy machine speeding. Esther's pelvis was broken and there was serious spinal damage. Her right arm was paralyzed. Once she left the hospital she would spend the rest of her life in bed or a motorized wheel chair. She lived two years after the accident.

Her body could be battered and bones broken, but her spirit could not. A deep abiding faith in Him who had died for her sins was evidenced by the first words she said when she regained consciousness. "The people who ran into me, are they okay?" When told the circumstances she said, "Tell the young man I forgive him and I'm going to pray that he finds God's forgiveness.

She had been planning to announce her resignation in the Fall. Lionel and Meg came to visit as soon as they could and she prevailed upon him to serve as temporary General Manager of the tribe subject to Council approval, until such a time as an election could be held. Perhaps no other man knew as much about Mikota history and tradition as this historian whose ancestor had been the Bear Chopper.

On Friday, Aug. 3rd, 2001, the Tribal Council formally appointed Lionel Knox as acting General Manager. An election would be held a year later to either elect some other eligible candidate or affirm his appointment.

On the same day this decision was being made known, John was giving the Jays permission to play in the attic of the Lodge. It had six gables in front and six in back. With these twelve windows open pleasant breezes made it a comfortable play place. But John laid down a few simple rules and rued it later that he had not thought to add one more.

"You mustn't play on or near the step. If you find anything sharp or with a point like a knife, don't touch. Tell me if there are any bullets or guns hid up there and don't touch. Just tell me. But you can play with any toys you find up there. And you can wear any old clothes you find and there's a mirror in the room on the far end over the kitchen."

He repeated his instructions and made them recite them several times. "No playing by the stairs. Don't touch sharp things or bullets or guns."

And so they had played that afternoon. The fold-up stairs were steep and Mokey was poor at climbing. He did a doggy pout when ordered to stay down. The children did find trunks of old clothes and played "dress up" rolling up cuffs and sleeves and donning too big hats. They giggled at their images in the big mirror. Then they came across other trunks full of discarded toys which over the decades visiting Knox kids used during their visits. But the supper call was made before they could properly ransack through them.

The next day they could hardly wait to get through their simple chores so they could return to their treasure trove. It was not that they lacked a goodly supply downstairs, but these were different and new to them. And at the bottom of one of the old battered trunks, wrapped up carefully and hid away was a box of matches and a few fireworks some mischievous child had filched from Uncle Lionel's Fourth of July supplies. These must have been hid away at least ten years earlier when John was in his teens. In the damp- free attic they would have kept indefinitely.

To the ignorant Jays these were odd candles. Jojo said, "Let's light one." John had sometimes allowed them under adult supervision to light candles at the supper table. He and Stella figured this would squelch their curiosity so that they would not hide and experiment.

Juju observed, "Uncle John only lets us use candles when it's dark."

Jojo agreed, "Yeah, let's take some with for when it's dark."

But they couldn't carry such things in their hands and still play with toys and their pockets were way too small. They solved this problem when Jojo remembered a large old purse with a shoulder strap. Juju brought it to the head of the stairs and called Aunt Stella to see. "Can we keep this? We can carry our stuff in it."

Permission given, the purse was loaded and Mokey and his wards went for a walk. They immediately made their way to the smoke house. Had it been in use and the stove lit, the huge dog would have barred their entrance. As it was he was willing to patiently wait in the shade outside. There were no windows and it was fireproof but the former fact was the only one that mattered to them for when the door was shut it was dark inside. Also there was no way to get locked in.

They left the inward swinging door open a tiny crack to let a sliver of light in. Juju got out one with a broad base and narrow top while Jojo opened the box of matches. She set her "candle" on the stone floor and they both crouched over it.

Jojo got out a match, carefully shut the box, and struck the match. It was as bright as a candle. They were half laughing with glee and anticipation as he, gingerly holding the match stick as far from the flame as possible, brought it to the fuse and saw it ignite. He turned away shaking the match the way his uncle had shown him.

Juju wondered why the fuse was sputtering and hissing instead of burning like a candle. She bent over and looked straight down on the fuse. And then it erupted like the volcano it was patterned after. An uncountable number of minute incandescent particles accompanied by super heated red smoke hit her in the face. There was a smell of scorched hair and she screamed as she tried to twist away from the fountain of fire.

Jojo dove at her to push her away. She fell and was momentarily knocked out as her head rapped against the stone floor. Mokey crashed in almost knocking the door off and caught a shoulder strap of her bib overalls and dragged her out and away from the scene of danger. Jojo whimpered as he scampered out. He was too petrified to call for help and just bawled. John and Bernie were there in a moment summoned by Mokey's loud call for help. Marian and Stella came running out of the Lodge immediately after.

Cooling cleansing water was the best first aid that could be offered. A little later salve on tiny burns of Juju's forehead, nose, and cheeks was applied. Her eyebrows were singed off but would grow back. None of the little burns to her skin were likely to leave noticeable scars.

But her eyes. How dreadful. The hot gases had clouded the right cornea from clear to translucent, looking like a full cataract. From then on that eye could only detect variations in intensity of light and predominant colors. The left eye fared a little better. There was just enough clear cornea that the girl would have a very narrow tunnel vision and with her extreme myopia would be able to see enough up close to navigate around nearby objects and able to fuzzily recognize the family members and her beloved Mokey.

Endless prayers went up for her eyes to heal, but as the days went by there was no evidence of this happening. The previously exuberant and free-spirited girl became very subdued and thoughtful. But it was obvious the little lamb's Shepherd was holding her close to his bosom, for a week after she announced to Aunt Stella, "It wasn't Jesus' fault. It was mine. And don't blame Jojo. He always does what I ask him to. I told Jesus I was sorry and we both cried."

The speed was remarkable with which the burns of the little one healed. The emotional trauma also faded way quickly as she was surrounded by loving care and concern. But the impact of the accident would long shroud the minds of the older four, particularly John.

He and Bernie devised a simple harness such as are used by seeing-eye dogs so Mokey could lead his mistress around the grounds, Her big furry companion seemed to understand he was expected to keep her from wandering away from the immediate environs of the Lodge. Jojo was also expected to be at hand when Juju was outdoors. Even with her very feeble vision she was soon galloping around hanging onto her noble steed's harness. The dog cart also got use but she had to let Jojo or one of the others drive it.

Within a couple of weeks Juju was almost as active as she had been before. One thing she started to do caused John to sternly intercede. The two Jays and Mokey happened to be playing under her favorite climbing tree. By feel she started to climb, not intending to go too high. John spotted her and ran over, snatching her off the tree before she was higher than his shoulder.

"Miss Juliet Eberhard, climbing is something you must not do. I forbid it and so does Aunt Stella and I'm sure Jesus does not want you taking any chances. No more tree climbing and that goes for big rocks too. Jojo, you be sure she doesn't climb rocks or trees, and you both better always be careful going up or down steps, even porch steps."

Before that day was over all five of her valley family had given her the same message and it was frequently repeated in the days to come. She promised over and over she would not climb although she yearned to get up high where an angel could teach her to fly. The commandment laid on her was to never climb trees or big rocks and always be careful on steps. She strictly adhered to the letter of her law.

But on the warm Saturday evening of August 25th, after supper but an hour before bedtime, obeying the letter of the law did not keep her from harm. She and Jojo were playing on the grass by the windmill behind the Great Hall. He was shoving toy trucks around and making loud motor noises. Mokey had been tied to a corner post of the windmill because if free he would chase and pounce on trucks the boy sent rolling. She sat on the ground quietly crooning to Huckleberry Hound, her favorite doll, the one given to her the first night they came to the Honeymoon Cottage.

Jojo had been fidgeting for a while and suddenly got up and ran into the house. "I gotta go. Be right back." As youngsters do (perhaps learning this from oldsters) he took his good time and hummed as he sat on the throne. The others were exiting by the front door as he came in the side kitchen door.

For a moment we will go back to the days of windmill repair. John had adequate lengths of metal extension ladder and safety harness to use with it. But he would only be as secure as the ladder was. Stella had insisted he somehow fasten the ladder to the windmill. He had used galvanized stove pipe wire to join the ladder to the cross pieces of the tower. It would have been a nuisance to unfasten and John had left it up. The weather would not damage the aluminum and it might be needed again. Juju knew of it.

And then a Golden Eagle swooped past her in a power dive to get its talons into a rabbit in the tall grass about 60 yards behind the Great Hall. Its shadow went across her face and she noticed. Its return to altitude was slower as its pinions fought gravity lifting itself and its supper. The girl vaguely made out the motion while the settling sun outlined the majestic bird. To her blurry vision it was an angel with a halo.

"Huck, it's my angel." She grabbed the windmill to hoist herself to her feet and rolled her less damaged eye to find the ladder. She remembered her promise not to climb trees or big rocks and to be careful on steps. These were steps. If she was careful she was allowed to climb steps.

Holding the doll against her chest with its head on her left shoulder so he could watch her angel, she began a one-handed climb. When she was just a couple of rungs up Mokey became very uneasy and began whining the way dogs do to plead with their owners. "Quiet, Mokey, this ain't a tree or a rock. You hush up."

Since it was a one-handed climb, she kept her fingers behind the upright where she could squeeze as she moved up a rung and then slide her hand higher, Squeeze. Right foot. Left foot. Slide fingers up. Repeat. Had she been using both hands alternately as climbers should, it would have been okay. Or had she been able to see a hazard it could have turned out well.

But in a sheltered spot where the ladder was in contact with one of the horizontal angle iron cross braces a hornet's nest was being built. Once it was full size it would be visible from the ground. Now it was no bigger than a tennis ball. As her little fingers lifted toward it, her threat to the nest brought on an attack of stingers to drive her away.

She automatically yanked her hand back losing her balance and slowly rocked backwards. She tried to grab for a rung but her minimal vision and lack of depth perception caused her to miss. The motion of reaching pitched her backwards head first. She felt as if she was flying. Her body did a slow somersault and she fell feet first. Still tightly clutching Huck she reached up with her free hand and straightened her legs the way Superman did in movies. She hit the ground feet first and straight-legged, the worst possible way. Mokey saw all this and tried to break free to get under her but he was too late. The windmill rattled as his lunge broke the rope and he ran to her still and twisted form. He licked her cheek and pushed at her hands to get some response. When there was none he threw back his head and howled.

The kitchen had been hot. Stella had been working most of the day canning. The men had been doing grunt labor in the big garden. All four had been glad to sit in the door-yard and talk, enjoying the cool-down of the day. Bernie lived up to his name of Hawkeye and pointed out the Golden Eagle over the river as it sought updrafts and aimed for its craggy nest a couple of miles away. And then the relaxing laborers were galvanized by Mokey's howl.

It was a living nightmare, the worst thing they had encountered so far. Both hip joints were dislocated, the legs twisted out at impossible angles. John said that since they had no anesthetic they had to relocate her joints while she was unconscious. Even so she groaned in her sleep as the joints popped together.

But her right leg was twisted to the extent that days later when she managed to stand her foot was pointing to the side and the pain was too much for her. She still had partial feeling in her toes but she could hardly make her twisted leg move.

When she became coherent she told of seeing her angel with a halo around it and how she had been very careful climbing the steps on the windmill but something began biting her real hard. She insisted she had been flying.

Aunt Stella gently corrected her. "It was an eagle, Darling. We all saw it except Jojo. And it was hornets stung you. Uncle John destroyed the nest. We don't want them so close to the buildings. And we know it felt like flying, but you were falling. God's angel would never make you fall and get hurt. They love you too much."

The girl finally agreed but still insisted, "When I'm big a Mr. Angel will teach me to fly. Jesus knows I want to fly. And I love to climb but I mustn't."

Encyclopedia Bernardica came up with a non-prescription way to help Juju. He recalled having read about a nurse, he thought perhaps Sister Kenny in Australia, who used massage and warm water exercises for Polio victims who were not in life-threatening condition. He thought even FDR had benefited from her technique. They began to use it a few days after the fall.

Each day for an hour one of the adults brought her with Jojo and Mokey to Saturday Park and the pool fed by a hot spring. There did seem to be a gradual increase in motor control and the return of feeling and she said it hurt less. By the 7th of September she was able to get up unaided and use a walker they had found in Dundee to shuffle from her room to the living room before it hurt too much.

There was still laughter and fun in Knox Valley, but not as much. Times of personal devotions continued but the exuberance seemed to be lacking. They all experienced times when the song God had put in their hearts seemed to go into a minor key. But the song was still there.

John at first felt himself to be responsible but Stella helped him realize there was no way they could protect their charges against all eventualities. He confided to her that what he had considered stressful days in college had been a piece of cake compared to all they had been through. Then he had hugged his wife and smiled at her and together they thanked God for their present life together, times of darkness and all.

Before Summer ended an event took place which brought darkness and pain to millions of lives. The United States was forced into an open-ended period of gloom and distress. One way or another, hardly a family was untouched. Those who were not directly affected were acquainted with someone who was.

For on September 11th happened one of the blackest deeds of modern times as deceived terrorists hi-jacked jet-liners and used them as flying doom's day machines. The property damage was staggering and hard to believe. It still is.

But worse than mere property damage, was the cost in lives. When Mayor Rudy Giuliani was asked how many had died as the twin towers of the World Trade Center collapsed, he replied, "We don't know the exact number yet, but whatever the number, it will be more than we can bear." The darkness brought by that deed would take what seemed forever to be lifted and the shadows would reach far into the future.

Yet even moments after, there would be deeds of courage and self-sacrifice which would light the way for countless others. Volunteers appeared almost magically. The Salvation Army and uncounted religious groups came in force to bring physical and spiritual help plus assistance in grief management. The Red Cross came in strength to help. Lionel Knox and the Tribal Council met in emergency session the same evening and committed the resources of the Mikota Territory to underwriting the expenses of volunteers who would go in teams of twelve and each team spend a week for the next several months.

John and his family in the Forbidden Valley knew nothing of the awful happenings of that frightful Tuesday. A terrorist act had been responsible for their isolation, but God had brought them good out of evil. The blast in the valley was microscopic compared to the devastation of the September 11th attacks but both incidences had been directed by Satanic forces.

Out of the awful evil God again brought them great good. Out of the darkness He sent them great light. To those who love him, He works all things for good. He can turn the darkest pitch black thunder cloud inside out and show us a silver lining.

Chapter Twelve

FALL REVELATIONS

At 2:00 A.M. Tuesday, October 1st, Mokey got very nervous. He first loudly whined and then began barking, arousing the whole household. He would not be silent. John finally put him in the Great Hall where his clamor could not be heard in the Lodge. Even after they got up and brought him back he was so upset and noisy he had to be tied out in the breezeway with food and water available. John wondered if a red fox or some coyotes had been too bold. The previous year, after Mokey had time to make his presence known, the wild canines had steered clear of the place.

It was their custom to have breakfast at seven. At ten Juju was dressed in her swim suit, bundled up in blankets, and taken to the warm pool in Saturday Park. It was his turn to take her. Jojo almost always came along. Mokey had been excluded this trip because he refused to quiet down. He normally rode in the back seat but if he went swimming he had to follow the car home. A comfy cushion was in place in the cargo area behind the rear seat so Juju could lie down and ride at ease. Jojo always rode up front with Aunt or Uncle.

It was about 10:30 when the swimmers arrived at Saturday Park. Juju had fussed all the way protesting that she hurt too much. She had not rested well after being awakened by the furry alarm at the foot of her bed and had tossed and turned in her sleep which did her leg no good. She had been in tears and started protesting noisily that she would not go without Mokey. Perhaps his presence might have calmed her but it is too much to expect that a little girl can be stoical when the necessary massage did hurt. Even mature supposedly self-disciplined adults lose control sometimes.

The man and boy had their suits on under their Levis and were ready in a jiffy. The man as gently as possible picked up the girl and stepped over and into the pool with her. The adults would always ease her into the soothing waters and let her float until the therapeutic waters began to make it possible for the girl to move the disordered limb. But today she wanted none of it.

"Don't put me in the water. I don't wanna. You're hurting me. I wanna go home by Mokey." She began feebly hitting John with her little fists but her own motions added to her pain. "Ow. I wanna go home. Please don't."

Jojo got into the water and gently pet her shoulder saying, "Don't cry. It'll be okay, Juju." He was sniffling and on the verge of tears himself when he and John both heard loud metallic clicks such as automatic rifle bolts make.

"Freeze! Don't make any sudden moves. Put the girl down and send the two children over to us."

Two men in camouflage combat uniforms stepped out of cover with automatic rifles aimed high at John's chest. They wore shapeless hats. All exposed skin was covered with varied blotches of greens and blacks. John could not see any insignia but it was obvious they were a part of Special Forces such as Seals. He hoped they were on our side and not part of an invasion force.

He stood stock still holding his precious cargo and responded, "I think he's too scared to come to you and she fell off a ladder and got crippled. She can't walk. The best we can do for her is massage and this warm spring for therapy. Just why are you guys trespassing in Knox Valley? We live here. This is our home."

The second soldier spoke up, "Sarge, this man looks like one of the people in the memorial display in the Tribal Hall where we were briefed." John confirmed his identity as one of the six thought to be deceased. There was an immediate radio conversation between the Sergeant and his Captain who had staked out the Knox Farm with the rest of the covert investigation team. They had arrived as Mokey began sounding the alarm. The men at the farm had just made contact.

"Mr. Knox, my orders are to help you in any way possible. I'm sorry I misread your actions with the girl. A Medi-vac chopper will be here in a few hours but only has room for one passenger besides the patient. Your wife has insisted she be the one to ride along to the Mikota Middlebridge Clinic. We can provide rides for all of you when we leave."

"When are you scheduled to leave?"

"After we've checked out the whole valley. We're making sure there isn't a secret training camp or supply dump for terrorists. If there were any they would have scrupulously avoided you or killed you."

John was puzzled why that had to be done but switched his focus back to Juju's exercise. Jojo went from scared to amused as he watched the soldiers remove their hand and facial makeup. He begged them to paint his face and with John's permission they doctored his appearance and told him how brave he looked. When her hour in the water was over she begged for the same treatment.

It would almost take a second book to fill in all the pertinent details from September 11th to October 11th. Much will be compressed or just mentioned in passing. As much as possible the narration will be in chronological order.

Immediately after the attack on the Pentagon and the collapse of the World Trade Center, the President was demanding answers from the heads of military and civilian intelligence agencies. A high priority was given to determining where the terrorists had come from and where their bases of operation and training were. Considering the Hidden Valley incident, a big question was whether there were any covert camps in North America. While there were many isolated possibilities, only one had been exempt from direct observation.

The Forbidden Valley had been the only place where peacetime military or other flights were off limits. Spy satellites, however, had been periodically sending back routine electromagnetic images but these pictures covered vast land areas and small details could not be clearly seen. Had the need arisen very small areas could have been zoomed in on and even people detected.

After September 11th the file of satellite pictures of the valley was carefully scrutinized and some anomalies were found. In the river or either lake, in different places each time, was found the image of a tiny object which could have been a boat. In some pictures there seemed to be blurred areas in various spots along one or the other of the dirt roads which followed the river. It was assumed the blurring was from dust raised by a vehicle.

The only conclusion possible was that there had to be people in the valley. It had been conjectured that they may have been brought in by night from the west in low flying choppers hugging the contours of the mountains to avoid radar detection. When this information was brought to Lionel and the Council they secretly gave immediate agreement to suspend the military fly-over ban and to allow whatever kind of incursion was necessary. With the Nation near hysteria over terrorism, it was not imagined there was likely to be any other explanation.

The order of events which led to a troop entry was this:

1. High altitude "spy" planes orbited the valley doing broad band electronic surveillance but did not pass directly over it. No signs of electromagnetic emanations were discovered.

2. A stealth bomber silently passed over at night taking pictures and monitoring any possible low level emissions.

3. Analysis of the information garnered pinpointed a great deal of human activity at the farm and additional satellite pictures indicated daily trips to Ribbon Lake.

4. Shortly after midnight on October 1st, a dozen Special Forces men parachuted in on a high altitude drop to make a methodical sweep of the valley. Two had been assigned to find out what was going on at the lake. When the other ten approached the farm, Mokey had known.

Sergeant Simpson and Corporal Tomko, the two who first met John, were assigned to secure the farm and set up a communication center while the rest did their sweep. The Medi-vac chopper would be bringing in the necessary equipment when it came to shuttle out Juju and Stella. Simpson had to stay behind when the other eleven left until a second team could bring in a more permanent setup with an automatic generator.

That Tuesday night was the first time John and Stella slept alone since the wedding. They had been totally celibate before their vows, now it seemed totally strange and unnatural. Late that evening they conversed at length over the military radio. They were facing a crisis in event information overload. The events of the outside world were affecting them much like a sensory overload. But at least there was good news.

Juju was to undergo corrective surgery Wednesday afternoon. The surgeon had informed Stella that under the circumstances what they had done with massage and hot water had been the best possible course. Bernie was highly commended for thinking of it. The girl would have a cast for a while and then need a metal brace for a number of months but after a couple of weeks she would be able to get around on crutches until full recovery which would have been unlikely had she gone through the Winter without surgery.

As for her eyes a specialist would be coming in. The Clinic Chief Surgeon was certain Laser Surgery could greatly improve her left eye, possible bringing it nearly to its pre accident capability. The right eye would probably need a corneal transplant. Once these things were done, with proper corrective lenses she would see better than ever before.

Stella told of her excitement at seeing her Aunt Bonnie, Uncle Ray, and cousins again. Isabella and Miguel Juarez, her parents, who with his retirement bonus had purchased a low-mileage used truck with attached camper and headed out on their first vacation without kids along since their honeymoon. Their itinerary was unknown. They intended to wander and enjoy. It was hoped they'd see one of the happy CNN or other updates about the survivors. Authorities were seeking to track them down with the joyful news.

September 11th was almost impossible for our young couple to comprehend. They praised God for the bravery and unselfish response of millions of people. They were pleased by the help the Mikotans were giving; it was no less than they would have expected. They were saddened by Esther's accident but glad that Uncle Lionel could step in to help. He had gone to New York so he could personally report back on progress. He had received word of the six survivors and was struggling to book air passage. In the barrage of details somehow neither John nor his uncle found out the other was married.

Stella and John agreed one of the other of them would have to be staying in Glasgow so Juju would always have a familiar voice by her when she was awake. Huck of course was with her but she was the only one who ever heard him speak. And despite her fervent plea, Mokey could not sleep at the foot of her bed.

The need for valley folks to stay by Juliet's side became unnecessary for a six passenger Cessna Stationair arrived at the Mikota air strip escorted by a Tomcat which had led it there. A Public Safety Jeep was waiting to deliver the pilot and passenger while the girl was still in the recovery room at the Middlebridge Clinic.

Bernice Eberhard and "Alf" Considine, the pilot and very close friend of his passenger arrived before the little blondie regained consciousness. Her mother's voice was the first she heard. The gentleman with her owned and operated Considine's Cruisers Inc., a small diversified aeronautic business which did crop-dusting, freight and passenger hauling, charter work, and ran a small craft pilot's instruction school. The private Considine air strip used was located on his father's 600 acre farm in the heart of Kansas.

Bernice had been embroiled in divorce proceedings on the fateful day Humphrey Bogardus had set off the blast. She was vacationing with Juliet on what she feared might be the last time she would be able to spend with her daughter. Her philandering husband and his wealthy family with their high- priced lawyers would certainly have gained full custody without visitation rights. Once Juliet was believed dead, the biased court swung its sympathy to the mother and she received a cash settlement but no alimony, and they had signed off on any possibility of going after the mother for any reason.

She had purchased a new compact car, a Neon, and had fled Connecticut with the rest of her money. She had found employment with the Considines multi-tasking at a little light housekeeping, bookkeeping, secretarial tasks, and as a receptionist. Her salary was low but she had the fringe benefit of room and board at the peaceful farm.

Bachelor Alf was forty, ten years older than Bernice and had devoted 22 years to his business. He had six planes for various purposes and six employees including Bernice. After her divorce she had tightly tied her heart strings. But the gentle and gracious Mennonite family had by kindness gradually unraveled the knots and their solid but unobtrusive faith was beginning to awaken her sleeping childhood faith. She had confided to Mama Considine that she was beginning to feel as if she had been reborn.

As this was happening, Alf had been pumping up his courage to propose to this very attractive blonde, such a refined lady. Tragedy had steered her to him as if it was meant to be. But before he could act, the late news told of the survivors. They had spent several hours on the phone to get confirmation and details.

The Cessna Stationair was his best choice to take her to her daughter but it required maintenance and was not ready until noon. During the flight her entire attention was centered on thoughts of her baby and being rejoined with her. His attention was on the business of flying. As soon as they could give full attention to one another, he would pop the question, that is, if the daughter could accept him as a step-dad.

Once the girl was past the disorientation of anesthesia, she introduced her mother to Auntie Stella and babbled on about all she and Uncle John had done for her and the other kids. The mother embraced Stella and wept on her shoulder thanking her over and over. John would get the same treatment later.

Juju soon introduced her mother to Huck and told her about Mokey. She then asked, "Did you take Ginger out of the canal and bring her along?"

"Not a canal, a kennel. Ginger was so sad when we thought you were gone to Heaven that I gave her to your

260

little friend Caroline. She loves her and takes good care of her."

The girl considered this and then asked, "Mommy, when I go home with you can I take Mokey with?"

Alf answered, "Sweetheart, your Mama lives in a big house on a big farm. There's lots of room for a big dog and he could play with the puppies, Prince and Brownie." With that settled, the girl yawned and went back to sleep.

Lionel and Margaret arrived just before Stella was due to be transported home in a military chopper. The Council was in the process of leasing a helicopter which could be flown by a licensed citizen of the Territory who had flown in service. He would be able to make "bus" runs to carry people and supplies as needed and respond to emergency situations.

There had been a long delay to get tickets from New York and Len and Meg had accepted the first possible westward flight which was to Denver International Airport. They had chartered a private plane to get to the Glasgow air strip. Their paths crossed with Stella just as she was leaving. A chopper was ready to depart from the lawn behind the Clinic.

"Uncle Lionel?"

"That's you, Stella Juarez?"

"No. Stella Knox now. I'm so glad to see you. John talked about you all the time, Uncle Lionel."

The man did not know how it could have happened, but if this woman had become his nephew's wife, she was family now. He opened his arms to her, congratulated her, and welcomed her into the family with a strong hug and a kiss. Stella clung to him a moment rejoicing that he had accepted and not rejected her. Not really knowing him, she had been a bit apprehensive.

He then directed Stella's attention to his wife who was waiting a few yards away. "Dear Stella, my new niece, this is your Aunt Meg. We got married in Scotland. Don't tell John. Let us surprise him. We'll be there tomorrow."

That evening there was limited availability of the military radio so John and Lionel only had time for a short chat. However word was passed along that the Krauses would be arriving at Glasgow on Thursday in their Chrysler van. Lionel kept mum about his wife.

Thursday morning eleven soldiers were transported out leaving one behind to handle communications until the Mikotans could set up their own system. But the chopper that air-lifted the GI's brought in the Scotland Knoxes. Lionel and his uncle had been too emotional too speak for several minutes as they had bear-hugged each other and finally the older man spoke.

"Son, I'd been told you were dead, drowned in the Sentinel. I was never ready to believe it. You will have to tell me the whole story, all the details, but not just now. Now's the time to get acquainted all around. I met that dear unfortunate, Juliet, and her mother. She's gonna be fine. And you know I met your beautiful wife, my new niece, Stella. Hi, Dear. And these alert youngsters must be Marian and Bernard and Joseph and of course, Mokey. Wow, what a great dog."

Jojo blurted out, "Who's that lady?"

"Oh. That's just a hitch-hiker I picked up in Scotland. You may all call her Aunt Meg."

John asked, "Aunt?"

"Yeah. She used to be Margaret Holmes. Now she is Mrs. Lionel Knox."

John was taken aback but quickly recovered and graciously welcomed his new relative in Lionel's fashion including the kiss. "Aunt Margaret, uh, Aunt Meg, you've already met Stella. She's a hitch-hiker I picked up in Dundee."

The older woman forced a stern expression onto her face and asked, "Stella, are all Knox men so exasperating?"

Stella donned a matching frown and replied, "Every last one of them without exception. I find a cup of tea can help soothe my jangled nerves. Let's have one. C'mon Marian, us women to the kitchen."

The two wives went arm in arm out of the living room followed by the redhead and their laughter burst forth once out of sight of the male segment of the family. The two women were totally dissimilar in appearance, but in personality and humor they were kindred spirits. The rest of the hours of the day, even during chores, were full of jokes and laughter, almost to the point of giddiness,

Late Thursday the Bell Helicopter being leased was flown in to the Mikota air strip by Nick Sloane. Sidney Crowe had air-taxied the veteran to the delivery place in M.A.F. #1, the Tribe's Piper Cub. Nick spent the bulk of the afternoon being instructed and oriented. The flight characteristics of the Bell were quite different from the military gun ships or Evac units he'd flown.

Apple pie and an almost ready chicken dinner were promised to the Krauses when they were delivered to the Knox Farm. Nicholas shut down the machine for there was quite a bit of unloading to do. A rather large fresh food grocery order was being delivered with the Krause couple, Jolene, and their luggage. Not least among the groceries were fresh beef, oranges, and bananas. The pilot was invited to stay for supper but declined, not wanting to intrude on the reunions.

Jojo had raced across the lawn to his mother, beating Bernie's dash to his parents. Jolene's first words to her son were, "I was so sad. I thought angels carried you to Heaven. I wanted to give you chocolate cake. I cried and cried. I love my Jojo. Now I'm happy again."

Maxine looked ten years older. She had ceased trying to cosmetically look less than she was. She had stopped tinting away the gray. She had gone through long periods of depression and with it virtually no activity. She had been stout before but snack-consolation had added over twenty pounds.

After a few minutes of squeezes and kisses and murmurs of loving each other, she had looked toward the sky and raised her arms straight up. Herman saw what she was doing, as did her son, and all three stood in a circle with hands and eyes lifted to Heaven. In unison they recited a Psalm in Hebrew and then a prayer of praise and thanks. This was followed by surrounding Jolene and Joseph in a circle of embraces.

John, addressed as "Mr. Mayor" was the next recipient of the same treatment by the two Jewish mothers and it was repeated for Stella. Herman just shook hands and verbally gave his thanks.

At the table John asked both Uncle Lionel and Herman to return thanks. During the eating the three valley children told of various activities, adventures, about Lady Regina and their schooling, and a bit about the events immediately after the blast.

Stella informed the Krauses that the Honeymoon cottage was waiting for the five of them. The couple would use Lionel's front bedroom, Jolene and Jojo John's and Hawkeye the couch. When they all moved in for the night, they were convinced of the total sincerity of the Knox invitation to stay as long as they wished and come back as often as they could.

Bernie sat up late with his folks after Jolene and Jojo had their pre-bedtime cocoa. The little one had sung his alphabet song, pointed out many letters on a plaque, recited numbers up to 25, and then read the time off Cousin Bernie's watch to make sure it really was bedtime. He and his Mama giggled in bed for quite a while telling little kid's jokes. Uncle Lionel had said he'd do the lad's chores, indeed forbad him doing chores both that evening and in the morning while his parents were there.

"So we were so busy with everything, we never did get around to our Spanish lessons. But Marian and I did learn a lot and completed our Algebra. I'd really be sad if I never saw her again. She's like real family, like a real sister. And Uncle John and Aunt Stella seem like real family, too."

Maxine answered, "I'm sure your father and I agree that any or all of them are welcome in our house any time and we want to come back here when we can. And as far as we're concerned John and Stella are indeed real kin to you and that no good Harold and his wife are strangers we'll be polite to if we can't avoid them."

Herman added, "I can't tell you how proud I am of you. You've been a good boy and learned a lot of practical stuff. I could never repay the Knox family for all they did for you although I have been getting some ideas about that. You and Jojo could not have been better off under the circumstances."

"Papa, they're all Gentiles and Christians."

"I know that and I don't think I know any finer people. They are reverent to God and they try to keep His holy law."

"They believe Jesus is God, God's Son, and the perfect Lamb who died for their sins."

"I know. And this is a land with freedom of religion. They have that right. I have great respect for them."

"Papa. Mama. I have to tell you something. Even if you disown me for it, I have to declare I'm a Jewish Christian now. I'm sure Jesus is our Messiah. I believe in Him."

His father's face hardened and he looked very angry. He got up abruptly from the table and went out on the front porch. He was dimly illumined by light through the window from a lamp on the mantel. The voluble mother was stricken speechless for several minutes. The boy confirmed his deep love for his parents and siblings.

He declared, "If I told you I had not received Jesus Christ as my Savior and Lord, I would be liar. I can't recant what I know is the truth. Please Mama, Help me with Papa. Tell him how much I love him."

She stared at her son intently before standing. She motioned to him to do the same and to stand in front of her. She said, "Bernard, no matter what your father thinks or does, you are my son. I can't understand how or why you would do this, but you are not stupid. Your mind is keen and you must have good reasons why you would do this. I still love you. I always will. I thought I had lost you and God gave you back to me. I will never deny you no matter what you are or do." She gave him a firm hug and a kiss and ordered him to make another pot of coffee because it looked like it might be a long night.

After a long porch conversation many would have called a lecture for its one-sidedness, the man somewhat sheepishly came back in to talk to his son. His reaction had been more shock and a denial of what his son had said than a rejection of the speaker. We must not overlook the impact of his wife's forceful persuasion. It is commonly held that the closest thing in nature to an irresistible force is the power of an aroused Jewish Mother.

"My son, you shocked me. Bar Mitzvah. Spiritual manhood in the congregation. I kept asking myself how my son, carefully raised in our ancient faith, could do such a thing. But Mama and I know you have never made rash decisions nor can anyone force you to change your mind once you make it up. So tell me the whole story about you and this fellow Jesus."

The lad told of how the gentle Gentile had worked to gain their deliverance from the Sentinel and then brought them safely to Knox Farm. He told of how the man let him take as much time as he wished for Sabbath meditation and prayers. He told how he had voluntarily played the piano at their church service and how Uncle John had let him read from the Old Testament and comment on it with no arguments. He related his 14th birthday party and the driving lessons and Christian Apologetic books which presented evidence and left the conclusion up to the reader.

Bernie told of Marian's conversion and how guilty and unclean he'd felt because he could not then love or trust Jesus. He explained how he'd pored over writings of prophets such as Isaiah and everywhere he'd looked he'd seen the Nazarene. He confided he had also seen the Christ in the lives and attitudes of the others. He mentioned his anger with John for delaying the wedding but how quickly John had made it right.

"Mother, Father, no one ever pushed me. No one ever tried to argue with me. Christianity was never crammed down my throat. On Good Friday when all Christendom commemorates how the perfect Lamb of God, Jesus, died on the cross for the sins of the world, I invited Him into my heart, my life. Then I was baptized by immersion as an outward sign I had repented of my sins and trusted Jesus' death, burial, and resurrection for my salvation."

Bernie quoted Revelation 3:20 and added, "He's a perfect gentleman. Each person has to say either yes come in or no don't come in. I said yes and He came in. Papa I didn't stop being a Jew. I have Jewish genes and DNA. If you let me I'll be glad to go to temple with your every Sabbath or holy day. I'll eat only Kosher if you say so, whatever Mama puts on my plate. I will honor and obey both of you. But I do request you let me keep my Christian books and stuff in my room and that you'll let me go to Christian Sunday worship. I could walk to that Wesleyan Church a few blocks away."

The father stared into his son's guileless eyes and then held out his hand to shake with his boy. "I agree, Bernard. I can not see any shame coming on the family name from your behavior. I do think some of your ideas are very strange but they are making me very curious. From time to time we'll discuss these matters. And perhaps you'll let me glance at those books you mentioned when we get home. "

Friday at first light Alf flew away. There were matters demanding his attention at home but he promised to be back the following Wednesday, October 9th, to bring the mother and daughter to Kansas. Doctors in Wichita, which was a commuter flight from the Considine air field, were already well informed about Juliet and ready to bring about full eye and limb recovery.

In the late afternoon the Eberhards were flown to the Knox Farm with the girl's wheelchair aboard. The vacant Krause boys' room in the Lodge was ready for them. There was a glow to Bernice's face which had been missing for years. At the Kosher supper Maxine had prepared to precede a Sabbath service which all attended later, the radiant blonde shared her happy news with all.

"Alf insisted on a mysterious private conversation with Juliet. He calls her Juju like you all do and I thing I'd better, too. I'm not sure what all they talked about but after my darling was sound asleep we dined at the Glasgow Inn where we had been put up. He said he had asked my daughter's permission to ask me something. He told me he loved me and it had all started the day I walked in looking for a job. I admitted I had come to completely trust him and had started to love him too. He asked me to marry him. He made a joke about it was really because he had fallen in love with my daughter Juliet, uh, Juju and wanted to be her daddy and take care of both of us the rest of his life. She had already accepted the proposal."

Bernice choked up half crying and half laughing. Marian asked, "So tell us. What did you say?"

Juju chimed in, "Mama said yes. I'm gonna have a new daddy. He promised to be real good to us and Mokey too. And I'm gonna have a new granny and grandpa. Show your pretty ring, Mama." Until this ideal moment to show it off, she had kept her hand hidden in her apron pocket.

Marian's father and mother had been high school sweethearts. Martin Conrad, now President of Conrad

Concrete Inc., a business his grandfather started and his father expanded, had been a close friend of the couple before they had been a couple. Martin had married a gorgeous cheer leader, Queen of the Prom, who had shallow morals. One man could never hold her interest and pregnancy was out of the question. Six months later there had been an out of court settlement and she had begun making a career out of short lucrative marriages and profitable illicit dalliances. After her, Martin had thrown himself body and soul, into the family business.

Conrad Concrete and O'Connor Construction had frequently sub-contracted back and forth and Marian had grown up considering jovial Martin as an honorary Uncle like John. When the widow thought her daughter was dead, the constant friend Martin had consoled her. In September of 2001 they wed and went on a secret 30 day honeymoon. After the shock of 9 11 they avoided the news. The capstone of their trip was a coastal cruise from Victoria, B.C. to Anchorage and back. Via satellite while asea on October 3rd they saw a CNN report of the survivors. They sent word to the Mikota Territory but had to wait until Anchorage to "jump ship" on Friday A.M. and charter a private plane.

Marian had known since Thursday night her mother was coming. She had bubbled over about it to every person she came in contact with and included the cows, pigs, and Mokey. At noon Saturday the chopper arrived. After the initial impact of the two redheads, Marian had noticed Martin standing by.

"Uncle Martin!" She dove at him and gave him an almost violent hug and kiss. She said, "We didn't know who Mother's companion or escort was on her trip but there's a cot for you in the library and we'll be sharing the room the Krause boys used."

Glances flashed between the newly weds. She looked puzzled. Martin smiled and said, "That will be fine. You two need quality time alone together to catch up. It'll give me a chance to get acquainted with John and the rest of the Knoxes. And is that Herman Krause over there? His firm does our tax work."

As soon as possible in private, before telling others, Corinne told Marian of her new husband. "I was alone. Doubly lost without you. Martin was always there for me. I always had a shoulder to cry on. And I know your father must approve. No one can ever replace him, but Martin will always care for both of us in a special way. He and I both loved your father. Now we love each other. He's become my very best friend. I hope you can accept him as your second dad."

Marian promised she'd try hard. She'd always liked and trusted him. But she asked if she could call him Uncle Martin for awhile until she got used to the change.

In a three way conversation he'd agreed and Marian shyly gave him a demure kiss and hug. He assured her he and Corinne were not only married but the best of friends. "And in this big valley, who is your best friend, Marian? Who do you like best?"

Her happy face beamed even more as she shot back, "Jesus is my very best friend and I love him more than anyone else including you Mama. After that it must be Bernie. He's a pain sometimes when he spouts off from his books, but he's always kind and he helped me get through Algebra. I will be able to see him once in a while, won't I?....Uh....One other thing please. John has a church service every Sunday morning and I was hoping you'd both be there tomorrow. And I'd like to go to church with both of you back home too."

The offshoot was that Marian did end up going to a Baptist Sunday School that ran a bus near the new Conrad home. Frequently Martin and Corinne would attend the worship service after S.S. and then they'd go out for dinner together. They also looked into the possibility of enrolling the girl in the church's Christian Day School.

That Saturday night the men had a long gathering skeptical people call bull sessions. Martin had quoted his company motto. "No job too big. No job too small. If you want it done right, give Conrad a call." He had boasted, "I am 110% proud of the work we do and this situation has set my brain tingling with possibilities. Lionel has told me how the radiation has nearly vanished except on the Blast Lake bottom. So there's no reason to fear in the Forbidden Valley becoming the beckoning valley, as long as radiation is monitored.

"I think big and I think in terms of concrete. I love that stuff. It's one of Man's greatest discoveries. Ancient Romans used it to build things that still stand and are strong. It endures. What if we could build a power plant at the foot of the cliffs by the river? There'd be a 90 foot head of water to turn turbines and generate current. Probably enough for all the needs of the valley and much of the Mikota Territory.

"But the dam formed by the earth slides would not be adequate. What if the rock, and iron, and earth were veneered with thick concrete the way many massive earth dams are? That could make a formidable structure. Then further suppose the existing ramp was enlarged to carry a new road over the dam and an elevated causeway built over the submerged road? Voila! Access!"

"Then that beautiful hotel could be opened for business. Let's say in a couple of years in time for the Autumn colors. It could happen. All these projects could be done simultaneously."

The man had an evangelistic fervor and once on a theme became charismatically compelling. He could become a real spell binder and cause his listeners to picture what he saw so clearly as possibilities. He called for input all around and there was unanimity about the possibility of his new dream becoming a reality and bringing about great good. After their input he concluded by saying, "I'd love to present these ideas to the top man for his consideration. I believe a feasibility study should be started immediately. Is there a chance I could see the Tribe's Chief or Governor or whoever is in charge?"

Lionel and John both smiled as John said, "You just did. My Uncle is General Manager Pro Tem."

Lionel said, "You make a case worth looking into. Could you be at our Tribal Council meeting Monday afternoon?"

The question of financing such huge undertakings came up and Herman revealed that through his business he had contacts with a goodly number of philanthropists, financiers, and venture capitalists. He was sure viable financial arrangements could be made which would in no way compromise the Mikotan philosophy as to ownership and leasing.

He extended the conversation on a subject close to his heart, more so now that he had seen the good health, strength, and new skills of his son. He said, "There are inner city kids on the road to hell. Their poverty, sordid environment, and lack of opportunity frustrates them. They become addicts and criminals, almost without hope.

"A few months in a place like this might turn their lives around. With hard work, good wholesome food, and strong moral teaching, they could get a sense of accomplishment and some self respect. They would see that they could do something to make their lives better. John would surely teach them that Lord God Almighty can and will bless those who keep His Commandments.

"My thinking is not yet clear as to exactly what should be done. An Orphanage? A Summer Camp? A Tough Love Penal Camp? A place for year-around retreats? I'm not sure what would be best but I'm willing to put my money where my mouth is and see what can be done and how I can help. I believe John and Stella are the perfect people to lead such an endeavor. I hope they will at least give it serious thought."

At Sunday Worship Lionel preached. His theme was the Grace of God revealed as He worked behind the scenes to bless people and bring Himself praise. It was a joyful service. Marian sang The Love of God and The God of Abraham Praise. She had never done better in a service.

After dinner the Knox Valley Percussion, String, and Reed Band had a jam session of old folk songs to which the guests were glad to join in. Juju in her wheelchair vigorously used her tambourine. It would be the last performance for the foreseeable future.

Meg and Len had to leave afterwards. She had a secret mission to perform relating to the young married couple. He had to prepare the agenda for the Council meeting. His personal office and study was in the bungalow they were presently occupying in Glasgow.

After Nick Sloane flew away with the older Knox couple, Hawkeye had permission to give his parents a grand tour of the valley with Marian along as tour director. Jolene preferred to stay at the Lodge and play with the Jays and Mokey. Bernie and Marian were becoming poignantly aware of the extent to which the other had become an integral part of their individual lives. It took the reality of soon parting to make them each realize how deeply imbedded the other was in their hearts.

The Council met at one Monday. They efficiently dispensed with minutes, reports, and old business. Under new business was the matter of issuing a retroactive marriage license and recording the name change for Estellita Juarez. All at the hearing were of the opinion that a legal and proper Christian wedding had taken place. It was time for paperwork to catch up to the accomplished fact.

Martin Conrad was given ample opportunity to present his ideas. He was rather surprised to learn that even many years before the blast there had been discussion in many circles by prominent citizens about the possibility of a small hydro-electric plant. Esther, spectating from her motorized wheelchair, spoke up as a concerned citizen.

She said, "I don't expect to be around for a long time. I want to see this body get a move on and not drag its moccasins. Chairman Knox, don't you let them stall around. I'm gonna give you my lance. It's sharp. You can prod them into action like I used to." This brought laughter from both officials and observers for it had been a threat the gentle woman had often used but would not have dreamed of trying to do.

Tuesday the 8th was the final day in the no longer Forbidden Valley for the Krauses, Marian, and the Conrads. A farewell picnic was held at Saturday Park. Featured from the Monday grocery delivery were grilled all-beef hot dogs on bakery buns and a variety of junk foods which had been absent in the Knox diet for over a year. But what kids don't like chips and cheese puffs and the like? For that matter even adults like them.

Then back to the Lodge for a bittersweet parting. The Krauses stayed at the Glasgow Inn that night and their Chrysler van was on the road home early the next morning. Martin had arranged for a charter flight to Denver International and from thence a commercial airline ride to O'Hare.

Early Wednesday morning the drone of a Cessna was heard. Alf had installed floats and landed on Ribbon Lake where John and Bernice met him at the boat launch. Once back to the Lodge the pilot had quickly commandeered the wheelchair with its content and Mokey as chaperone to take a walk. They ended up on the middle of the bridge where she told of her encounter with Lady Regina and how brave Mokey had been.

She also confided that she was sure an angel was going to teach her to fly. He had solemnly promised that he would give her free flying lessons as soon as she was old enough. She could hardly wait to tell the others.

Before Mokey, his mistress, her mother, and dad-to-be departed, after persuasion from Bernice, Alf explained his nick name. "Back in Kindergarten we learned the A B C song Juju and Jojo learned. When the kids found out my initials were A.B.C. they dubbed me Alphabet but soon shortened it to Alf. Alf has stuck with me all my life."

Stella asked what the initials stood for. "My whole name is Angelus Bertram Considine. Some of my associates sometimes tease me by calling me Angel, particularly if I flub up. They point out that Angels shouldn't make mistakes. Please just call me Alf."

As the Cessna took off, John and Stella waved and could hear the big Saint Bernard barking a farewell. When sound and sight of the plane were gone, the young couple was totally alone in the valley. She looked puzzled and murmured, "Angel? Juju always said she was sure an angel would teach her to fly."

John hugged her and answered, "Unless your faith is like that of a little child you will in no wise enter in. Never be surprised at how wonderfully God will act even if your faith is less than a child's and more like a mustard seed,"

Stella called John to the radio-phone Thursday morning just as he was coming in for breakfast after first chores. Uncle spoke allowing no interruption. "Aunt Meg and I want you to spend a couple of days with us. Stella's folks will be here tomorrow and a gang of your friends are chomping at the bit to see the two of you. The Great Hall would work if we could drive in with folks and food but it would be impractical with our chopper. We've reserved the school gymnasium. It's all settled.

"I also scheduled complete physicals and dental checkups for both of you. That will still leave plenty of time for shopping. Aunt Meg and I have gift certificates for you as belated wedding gifts. Oh! One more thing. I'm sure you remember your high school soccer team buddies. The Sierra twins and their wives are on the way right now to take care of all your chores while you're gone. It's their gift to you."

That evening after all the above was attended to plus a few random happenstance meetings with old acquaintances, the couple was finally alone again. They had use of an attic bedroom with a fine view of the Mikota River. She smiled and said, "About my physical. I learned something interesting but I don't know if you're interested too,"

"Nothing serious, was it? Nothing wrong?"

"Serious, yes. Wrong, no. Well, good night Dear." She closed her eyes and prepared to sleep, or so it seemed.

"Whoa! What else have you to tell me?"

She led him on for a while rambling about the darling blouse she'd bought and some recipes she had to try out from her new recipe book and on ways to improve the Lodge kitchen etc. He finally sat up in bed, turned the bed lamp on, grabbed her shoulders, sat her up, stared into her eyes, and demanded an explanation.

"It's nothing out of the ordinary. Nothing to be concerned about. It's as natural as the budding of trees or the blossoming of flowers. The doctor ran a couple of simple tests and they indicate I'm pregnant. I'm probably due next June near your birthday. How would that be for a birthday present?"

We will omit their embraces and conversation for the next fifteen minutes. A moment of silence did come when they just peered into each other's eyes. She said, "Don't look smug as if you're solely responsible. How quickly men think they should get all the praise. But Honey, you know it's fifty fifty. It takes two to make a baby. But later on it's the woman who does all the work."

Stella was reunited with her family at the Town Hall. The Santa Fe Café #2 provided lunch. John was sized up by the family and found not wanting. But he wondered if he'd ever get all their names straight.

There was not a single glitch in Aunt Meg's planning. The supposed gathering of friends and relatives was a surprise wedding reception at four Friday afternoon. The Polaroid wedding pictures were on display. There was a fantastic buffet which included many ethnic dishes for the over 200 guests.

Gifts were allowed only in cash or checks designated for relief of suffering terrorist victims in New York. This was sent in the couple's name. They totally agreed for they felt they had everything they needed. Almost twenty grand was raised.

The reception line took an hour and a half. Stella and John were amazed at how many friends they had. When they tried to enjoy their food, the rapping of silverware handles on the table demanded the couple stop to kiss so often they could hardly eat. Esther was the emcee and she commented into her mike, "It sure looks like they had plenty of practice." When they cut the cake and fed each other pieces, dozens of camera recorded their smeared faces.

And then there were many congratulatory speeches but John was ordered by Esther and his Uncle to make the concluding speech of the day. He told first of his conversion many years earlier and how he trusted Jesus as his Lord and Savior. He told of how God had kept him through the years. He gave God the glory for their deliverance from the Sentinel and their shelter and sustenance ever since.

"My Lord loves to give and gives to love. And He gave me a beautiful woman I could love and who amazingly loves me too. He has given all of us from the valley a present time that is very good. His goodness overshadows all of us.

"But there is no guarantee to any of us that evil days and deeds will never overtake us. Bad things do happen to good people. We are only sure of right now and God's eternal love and we rejoice in it and praise Him.

"We can't know the future for sure; it is just speculation on our part. Will there be a power plant and a new road into the valley? Will there be some kind of haven for youth in the valley, a place where twisted lives can be straightened out. Will there be more acts of terror? We cannot know.

"We have to be satisfied that God who loves us so much He sent His Son to die for our sins has plans for our futures that will prosper our souls. My friends and relatives, love Jesus. Trust Jesus. Obey him. Tell others about him. Try to win them to him. Nothing more is required of us than this."

The End

About the Author

The author is a retired sheet metal journeyman. He loves carpentry projects and in the Seventies built a new home for his family. All of his adult life he has served in volunteer ministries in major denominations, and is now Sergeant Major of the Grand Haven , Michigan Salvation Army. All his life he has used his imagination to create stories and skits for church use. His current major interests are working with people, travel, and camping. He draws on his vast background to create scenes, events, and characters both good and evil. His purpose is to entertain and also to provoke thoughts about moral and spiritual principles.

Printed in the United States
32875LVS00001B/13-30